The
Wheaton.

The
Wheaton.

A novel

by

Joanne Jackson

Stonehouse Publishing
www.stonehousepublishing.ca
Alberta, Canada

Stonehouse Publishing Inc. is an independent
publishing house, incorporated in 2014.

Cover design and layout by Anne Brown.
Printed in Canada

Stonehouse Publishing would like to thank and acknowledge
the support of the Alberta Government funding for the arts,
through the Alberta Media Fund.

Alberta
Government

National Library of Canada Cataloguing in Publication Data
Joanne Jackson
The Wheaton
Novel
ISBN 978-1-988754-17-8

This book is dedicated to Ann Ireland.
Author - Teacher - Editor - Mentor - Friend.
1953 - 2018.

Prologue

Late winter 2014

The motor makes a slight whirring as it lowers the coffin and I find my thoughts drifting to the men who lost their jobs because of this mechanization. When there's nothing left to watch, everyone seems to shrug as if to say, 'Is that all there is?' and I want to shout, *no*, that can't be all there is! I never imagined this, not so soon. We deserve more.

The mourners begin to disperse, picking their way across the mounds of earth, the loose dirt covering their dress shoes and pant cuffs in a layer of dust. This is what I focus on as they walk towards me, avoiding the sight of the ragged hole.

The wives poke my cheeks with dry lips and whisper condolences. "You still have your family," they say as they pull their children back, threatening them into good behaviour. The husbands pump my arm with double handshakes and growl stories about so-and-so whose wife died and he's doing fine. *Just takes some adjustment, that's all*. I'm quiet as I listen, too numb to argue. I turn from the grave as they walk to their cars, shadows outlined against the backdrop of grey this late-winter sky has offered. When the children are far enough away, they pull free of their mothers' hands and run, the young parents unaware that the separation that began at birth is already getting larger.

My son takes me home. He tries his best to say something to comfort me, but in the end, we sit quietly most of the twenty-minute drive. With an awkward hug, he leaves me alone in my empty house to go to his own home bustling with life, his sisters joining him. To be fair, my son did ask if I wanted to go with him, but I saw the look of relief cross his face when I declined. We both knew I wouldn't be comfortable with grandchildren showing me their latest piece of artwork or hounding me to play a new video game or with their Barbie dolls. Becoming involved in the kids' lives is not something I am inclined to do; that was Elaine's domain. She was the nurturer; she was the caregiver. The children always went to their mother first. We're strangers, my kids and I.

I sit in front of the television with the sound turned down and my eyes dry. My grief has been overshadowed by my fear of the remainder of my life, now unmapped. The thought of having to be a parent and a grandparent, giving career advice, financial advice, or even relationship advice to my children, makes my stomach cramp. I finish my beer and call Clementine. She trots towards me the way golden labs do; head low, body submissive, eyes soulful, hopeful for a pet, then slumps to the floor when I don't oblige. I lie on the couch, shrugging my shoulder and hip into the indents that now never seem to reconfigure themselves, and sleep the next year and a half away.

Chapter one

Late summer – 2015

Pine trees line the property from the front sidewalk to the alley in back, hiding the building from view. For years I've driven past this place with a blind eye, too involved with my own life to consider what might be here. Today, for the second time in as many days, I turn down a driveway concealed between trees that have probably guarded this land for over one hundred years. The air heavy with the pungent smell of pine needles, I follow the twisting road to its destination, a staff parking lot. Reluctant to get out of my car, I sit looking at the massive structure in the distance, afraid of the changes that venturing inside may make in my life.

Years ago, my wife, Elaine, suggested I make a plan. She warned me that without some forethought, the transition from working life to retirement wouldn't be easy. With a wave of my hand I brushed off her advice as casually as dust off my knees. "Don't worry about me," I said. "I'll find something to do." I convinced myself nothing would change except I wouldn't have to go to work every day. But things change when you least expect them. Hindsight gives you perfect vision.

Elaine had a plan of her own. She was always one step ahead of me. After our youngest moved out, I marvelled as my wife, who hadn't worked outside the house in over twenty-five years, got herself a job. Just a couple of days a week at the library, but she would come home glowing as if she was saving the world, not working a tedious job re-stocking shelves at minimum wage. I blush when I remember my arrogance in reminding her my pension was our retirement income and once I'd put in my maximum years, there's no way I'd consider getting a part-time job. So now here I am, stuck between relief at having nothing to do, and frustration at the same thing. Elaine could make a decision to do something before the coffee finished perking in the morning and have it completed by supper. Me, I've always been the fence-sitter.

I force myself out of my car; my resumé, such as it is, in hand. It's a long hike from the parking lot to the front door and by the time the entrance comes into view, I'm out of breath. Walking the dog for an hour a day is not enough to keep me in the shape I was in when I delivered mail. Two years into my retirement and I'm getting fat, with no motivation for meeting friends, joining a gym or even volunteering. Working at a job for thirty-five years, where each day is filled with the same mindless chores, then shoved into a life where you have all these hours on your hands and no one to tell you what to do with them, will do that to a person. As I puff my way towards the building I make a silent vow to do more to get back into shape. Perhaps instead of walking Clementine, I'll begin a running regime with her, like Elaine did when she was a pup. She'd like that; get both of us out of this slump.

I'm pulled out of my ponderings when the words, "What the hell are you doing, you stupid man?" ring across the parking lot. I stop walking and look for the source of the voice.

At the entrance of the building, which looks more like a castle than a seniors' residence, the back doors of a disability bus stand wide open and a woman in a wheelchair is being manipulated up a ramp. The man doing this wrestling of metal and flesh is perspiring heavily, the shirt between his shoulder blades darkened with sweat. Swinging from the handle at the back of the wheelchair is a large purse which keeps knocking him in the knees, but he does nothing to move it out of his way. By the sounds of things, the woman being muscled into the bus is not happy with how it's going.

"Don't put me here. I always sit on the other side. And closer to the front. I get car sick at the back. What the hell am I paying fees for if you can't remember from one week to the next? It said in the brochure, *expert bus driver*. Well if this is expert, I don't know...."

Her voice becomes muffled when the man, bearing her complaints in silence, pushes her to the front. A hand gesture, something I would never imagine this woman would know, flashes from the shadows at the poor man's back as he exits the bus to begin the task of labouring the next person up the ramp. I tell myself, *if that's the job I'm applying for, then I'm declining.*

Yesterday, all that greeted me were a few ancient residents sitting in the lobby listening to the music of Artie Shaw. One of them informed me, in her piercing old lady voice, that Mrs. Crockett, the woman I had the appointment with, wasn't in and she left instructions for me to come back the next morning, bright and early. I went home, relieved I didn't have to be interviewed, but disappointed I would have to talk myself into doing this all over the next day.

Today the lobby is far from empty. A long line of wheelchairs, walkers and scooters, all occupied by people in various states of decrepitude, snakes out the propped open door. I squeeze past, keeping my face averted from the twisted and misshapen bodies, but feeling my eyes pulled in their direction.

A man, his back so rounded his chin touches his chest, reaches for my hand. In alarm, I jerk away and come face to face with a woman in a wheelchair who wears a bib tied around her neck. A glistening string of drool is dribbling out the corner of her mouth, covering the bib in a wet sheen. I feel the bile collect at the back of my throat and turn away, swallowing hard.

I'm not an empathetic man; one of the many faults Elaine always pointed out to me. I also lack understanding, am far from enlightened, and have absolutely no imagination. But being un-empathetic seems to make the top of my deficiency list. I told Elaine years ago that she's never to move me to a nursing home where everyone is on oxygen, or in a wheelchair, stinking of their own piss and feces. Where the food is nothing but strained peas and Jell-O and everyone sits and stares at the same spot on the wall all day long. I said if

I get to the point where I can't look after myself, where I'm nothing but a drooling, diaper-wearing old man who can't string a legible sentence together to save my soul, just push me down the stairs, feed me poison, anything to put me out of my misery. So, when I saw the help-wanted ad, I don't know what possessed me to apply, but I felt compelled. Perhaps next time I shouldn't listen to that inner voice.

I approach a man with a weathered face older than God. He looks at me through watery blue eyes. "Can you point me in the direction of the office?" I ask.

"Hey?" He cups his age spotted hand around an ear sprouting a tuft of grey hair.

I shout, "The office, where's the office?"

He lifts his arm — the skin hangs down like bread-dough — and points towards the far side of the lobby. "Coffee's in the kitchen."

"No, not coffee, the office." By this time, I'm so close I can see pits carved into the bulb of his nose. I shout into his face as I slowly enunciate each word. "I'm looking for Mrs. Crockett. I need to find the office." I glance around in embarrassment, but not one person seems interested in our exchange. Either they're all as deaf as this man, or simply used to people shouting at one another.

"Crockett? Mrs. Crockett? That who you're looking for?" he squeaks at me. "Why didn't you say so? Dining room, settling a squabble." Again, he points a crooked finger. "Short woman, long dress. Can't miss her."

I turn this way and that as I maneuver between people wearing sunglasses big enough to block out a nuclear explosion, and others carrying purses larger than my suitcase, held on blue veined forearms that could snap in a breeze. Some use canes, a few ride scooters, but most appear to be moving under their own steam and I wonder what would possess them to live here.

In the dining room, a knot of people stands near the end of a table. I hear snippets of, "She did this," and, "He said that," and, "You're wrong," and, "Quit taking sides," before a hand raised by someone I can't see standing in the centre of this melee, quells the throng like the pope before a congregation of Catholics.

The crowd parts and a small woman speaks. "Arnold, I doubt Rachel would want your teeth. She has a full set of her own. You must have done something with them."

"She —" the old man points at a woman clutching a walker, "stole my dentures. Damn poppy seed muffins." His lips bulge as he slides his tongue around his gums. "I tucked them under my plate. When I wasn't lookin', she took them." A string of saliva spreads between his gums as he talks. He slurps it back in.

"Rachel," the woman I assume to be Mrs. Crockett, asks, "Did you take Arnold's dentures?"

"I certainly did not." She screws her face up. "Disgusting things, I wouldn't be caught dead touching them." Her thin fingers push glasses back up her equally thin nose.

"Yes, you would!" another man, presumably a friend of Arnold's, says. "Yes, you would. I've heard you say that if Arnie here takes out his dentures one more time at the table, you're going to steal them and throw them away." He looks accusingly at Rachel.

The crowd stirs and murmurs.

"I may have said that, Mr. Granger, but I certainly didn't do it." Rachel shivers so hard her walker rattles on the floor. "Don't know how he can even touch them."

"Arnold," Mrs. Crockett says. "Perhaps you misplaced them. If Rachel says she didn't take them, then we have no choice but to believe her. We do not call people liars."

"Quite the fight, hey?" A man with a head of hair thicker than my own is standing by my side. "And this isn't the first time those two have had at it. Mix like oil and water." He points his chin towards the resumé in my hand. "You here to apply for a job?"

I nod and take a step forward.

He steps up as well. "This place always seems to be hiring people. Can't seem to keep employees. I suppose us seniors are hard to get along with." He holds out a hand ravaged by arthritis. "Name's Ezra Adelman. Wife and I moved in five years ago." He looks at the wedding ring I've been disinclined to remove. "You married?" he asks.

"I am."

"Let me guess, your wife wanted you out of the house? Pensioned off after thirty years at the same job."

"Thirty-five, actually."

"Good for you, good for you. Nothing like double-dipping. It's what everyone does nowadays, or so I've heard."

We look towards the mob. Rachel is trying to walk away but Arnold has hold of her walker.

Ezra shakes his head. "Personally, I've always liked dogs better'n people. I was a vet before all this." He holds up his misshapen hands. "Most times I loved the animals more'n their owners. Had a fire long time ago, burned our house to the ground. Saved the dog first, then the wife. Lived to be seventeen; dog, not the wife. She died a year after we moved in here. Skin cancer. Never thought something so small would kill her." He lifts a gnarled finger to wipe away a tear that's sliding down his cheek, soft with wrinkles. "After the dog died, the wife said I'd spent the last seventeen years with him, wanted me to start doing things with her. Joined a bowling team. Said if you try you can usually find something to talk about with most everyone. Compromise, that's what Cynthia called it. A few complainers," he nods at Rachel and Arnold, "but most are easy to get along with. Some days go slow. The years go by too fast."

Mrs. Crockett is patting down Arnold. She pulls a set of dentures out of his jacket pocket. "Arnold, what's this?"

"Hey?" Arnold says. "How did those get there?" He points, "That witch put them there! Brushed up against me and dropped them in my pocket after she nipped them. Didn't want to get caught. Thought she was getting friendly with me!"

"First you call me a thief, now you're calling me a groper? I'd no more brush up against you, Mr. Arnold Switzer, than I'd touch your teeth."

"Okay," Mrs. Crockett claps her hands. "Everyone go back to what they were doing. Mr. Granger, didn't I see your name on the list for shuffle-board at nine-thirty? And Rachel, your daughter must be waiting in the lobby to take you to your hair appointment by now."

They start to move and soon I'm a stick bobbing in a stream of scooters and walkers.

"John Davies, I assume. Sorry I wasn't here yesterday. Had to accompany someone to the hospital."

I've always been tall and I look down. A child-sized woman is standing at my chest. She looks up at me, miniature eyebrows raised over large dark eyes. A pug nose hides between chubby cheeks and a cupid mouth leads to a chin that is practically non-existent.

"I lose more potential employees that way. Once they've seen the place, they don't seem to come back for the interview. Don't know what they expect if not people in the autumn years of their lives."

I did pick up the phone this morning to cancel my appointment but I could hear Elaine's voice in the kitchen, where she stood every morning for forty years rinsing out the coffee pot, telling me to smarten up and quit avoiding life.

I hold out my resumé. "No problem."

She takes the paper and, without looking at it, stuffs it into a pocket in her voluminous skirt. "Hope you don't mind but I sure could use your help before we talk. I need to get those people cleared out of the lobby and onto the bus for the tour today."

"Tour?" I say.

"Local winery. Popular excursion, lobby's crowded." She presses a pencil and paper at me. "Find out if they're on the list then check them off. Once that's done, take the list to Julio so he can load them into the bus."

I take the paper from her.

"Don't worry about the ones in wheelchairs, I'll look after them. They're going back to their nursing homes. They've been here for breakfast and a sing-a-long."

"They don't live here?"

"We offer events for the infirm, but if potential residents aren't able to look after themselves, we suggest alternatives. We're what's called an Independent Living Facility, for people not saddled with too many health problems. Our residents are all quite independent. They chose to live here, at The Wheaton, to eliminate the responsibility of home ownership." She taps the paper in my hand. "The ones on the list are our residents."

We're back in the pandemonium of the lobby. "Does this happen often?" I ask.

She shouts up at me, "Once or twice a week. We have lots of activities for those who want to participate. Tonight we're having a concert. Groups coming soon to set up, have to move these people out of the way."

"But yesterday — it was so quiet."

"You arrived mid-afternoon. Doctor Phil is on." She turns to say something to a woman helping her, then stops at the old lady with the bib around her neck. She gives her a kiss on the cheek before wheeling her towards the bus.

I'll help her with this, I think, then go home and pretend it never happened. No harm done. I wade into the crowd. "Are you going on the tour?" I ask a woman whose white hair is dyed a cotton candy pink.

"I most certainly am, young man."

"And your name?"

She points at the paper. "That's me, Mrs. Fielding. Do you dance?"

I check off her name. "No, Ma'am, I don't."

"Too bad. There's a band playing here tonight and I like having a good-looking man on my arm. Not easy to find our kind of music anymore. So, whenever we can, we dance, even if it's a concert." She twirls her hand over her head with a flourish, like a flamenco dancer.

The man beside Mrs. Fielding turns to me as he's finishing a sentence directed to the man behind him. "The cat's meow, that Glenn Miller music."

"Pardon me?" I say.

"Glenn Miller. Big band leader. Died in a plane crash. *In the Mood, String of Pearls, Moonlight Serenade*, best music there ever was. Wife and I loved to dance on that horse-hair floor." He winks at Mrs. Fielding.

"How long have you two been married?" I ask, hoping this old guy doesn't take a swing at me.

"Heavens, we aren't married. Lost our spouses a few years back. Found out all four of us danced at the same place every Saturday night for years, but didn't meet until we moved here."

Mrs. Fielding pats him on the shoulder. "She was a good woman, Allan, a good woman."

"And a damn fine dancer," Allan says. He grabs Mrs. Fielding's hand. "But she didn't hold a candle to you, Beatrice."

As I go through the lobby ticking off names, I hear stories about kids spending too much money and others too cheap to spend a dime. I hear of grandchildren who are smart, and grandchildren who must take after the other side of the family. I learn who's dating whom within the seniors' home, and who's broken up. Who's doctoring, as they apparently call anyone visiting a doctor more than once about the same malady, and who enjoys titillating books, are whispered behind wrinkled hands. By the time I'm done checking all the names off my list, I've heard more stories about more people than I've known in my entire life. As Julio loads the last of the residents onto the bus, I find an empty chair and sit, my head aching from all the listening and nodding I've had to do.

"Sorry to throw you into the fire like that," Mrs. Crockett introduces the woman who's been helping. "This is Melanie, the other shift manager."

I hold out my hand. Without making eye contact, Melanie presses her limp palm against mine. The polish on her nails is blue, matching the streaks in her hair. She's wearing a vest with the facility's logo on the shoulder but has not zipped it up, and the words, *Arrested Development* peek out from behind the zipper. For a moment I'm confused until I realize it's the name of a music group. She can't be more than twenty years old, making me again wonder what the hell I'm doing.

"Melanie's going to show you a few of the things you need to know. I have errands to run before the concert tonight." She says to Melanie, "Send the orchestra to the community room when they arrive. I should be back before the bus returns." She turns to me, "We'll talk then," and she whisks out the door in her long skirt, leaving me alone with Melanie before I get a chance to tell her I've decided not to take the job.

Melanie waggles a blue fingernail, motioning for me to come behind the reception desk. We stand facing each other, her eyes on the wall behind my head. She dangles a key that's hanging around her neck in front of my face. "This is the master key. Never, under any circumstances, give it out. It's for emergencies only. It opens every suite in the place." She tucks it back inside her shirt. "This one is mine. Where did you put yours?"

"I didn't get one."

She makes a noise somewhere between a grunt and a snort. "Damn it, Crockett. Do I have to do everything around here?" She begins pulling paper and books out of the various drawers and cubbyholes in the desk, eventually finding an envelope scrawled with the words, *Mr. Fletcher's toilet is plugged*. She tears open the flap and shakes out a key. There's a name tag attached which she tugs off and tosses in the waste basket. "This was Gloria's. Left so fast I had to yank it from her neck on her way out the door. Told me night and day how she hated this job. Only lasted a month." This time she meets my eyes. "Don't know why they keep hiring old people." She holds the key out to me then pulls it back and presses it into her own palm. "Do you have someplace to put it where it won't get lost?" she says, her eyes once again to the side of my face.

"I suppose I do."

"Don't suppose, John. It needs to be put someplace where you'll always have it on your person. And never set it down or for sure you'll lose it. Things go missing around here like it's some sorta black hole."

For thirty-five years I carried multiple keys to multiple mail boxes, every day, all day long. Never lost one. I don't need to be told how to do my job by someone who was a teenager just last week.

"I'll put it in my pocket," I say.

She unclenches her fist and gives me the key. It's damp. I put it in my pocket then wipe my palm on my pant leg.

When I look up, she's tapping her toes and holding a smart phone. "Gotta move quicker than that in this place."

I stare at her, challenging her to look me in the eye, but she doesn't.

"All the old people wear a pendant around their necks. You know, 'I've fallen and I can't get up' kind of thing? When they push the button, this phone will ring." She waves the phone at me. "It only rings when a pendant is pushed. Their name and room number will appear in the display screen. You can't call them because if they really have fallen and can't get up they can't answer anyhow. You have to go up to see what's wrong. That's the time to take this," she pulls the key out of her shirt.

"Shouldn't I call an ambulance before I go up?"

"Don't do that." The look on her face one of horror. "Mostly it's things like 'My toilet's plugged,' or 'Someone's stolen the sheets from my bed.' Some of these people are off their rockers. There's one old lady who's begun telling everyone the grim reaper is coming into her room." She circles the hand holding the phone, around her ear and rolls her eyes. "We'd have the ambulance here twenty times a day if we called one every time this phone rang. Wait until you know for sure you need one before you call. But don't assume it's not important because if it is, you could get into a lot of trouble if you didn't go and find out what was wrong."

And if there's a person who needs help, they'd be in trouble too, I think to myself.

"The front door is one of those automatic doors, you know, like in the grocery store?" She pauses as if expecting me to answer.

"Of course," I say.

"Lock that door at nine sharp every night. There's an app on this phone." Her smile is condescending. "Are you familiar with apps, John?"

"I am."

"Good for you. Most of the old people here don't have smart phones." She touches the screen to show me. "Just open the app and press lock. Download the app to your phone as well." She talks to herself. "I hope Crockett remembered to change the code when Gloria quit, but I guess if she didn't, it's not my fault." She looks behind me. "Only three of us, and now you, have the app. The rest don't need one because they only work during the day. That'll be your key for coming and going when the door's locked. Once you lock it with the app, it can still be opened from the inside, but not the outside. If a resident arrives back here after nine, there's a buzzer outside the door that they have to press to be let in. We used to have key cards, like in hotels?" Again, she pauses, waiting for me to tell her I understand what she's referring to. When I say nothing, she continues. "But these people kept losing them, so we went to the buzzer system." She takes a slurp from her Coke. As she pulls the can away, a trail of brown liquid cascades from her mouth and splashes on the desk.

"At night, you're the only one here so if you're called upstairs, even if it's before nine, manually lock the inside of the door with your master key," she points at front door. "Don't want to leave the front desk unmanned so a resident can leave in the middle of the night without you knowing. You're usually gone only a minute or two so it won't be a problem." She pinches the bridge of her nose. "Oh, I just about forgot. Lock the kitchen and basement doors at nine too. They're keyed latches matching your master key. Can't have a resident sleep walking and fall down the basement stairs. Not that they'd think to sue you if that ever happened; most are one brick short of a load, but it's better to be safe than sorry."

I raise my eyebrows. She doesn't notice.

She pulls another phone out of her pocket. A used Kleenex slips out and drops to the floor. "Anytime you're called upstairs, take this phone with you in case you have to call the ambulance. They're labelled which one is which, see?" She shoves the phones in my face. "This phone," she jiggles the second phone, "is the real phone. You know, like your landline at home?"

I push her hands away. "I carry two phones with me? Why can't I just use their phone when I get up to their suite?"

"Because they're forgetful, John. You never know where they've put the damned thing. Once I found a phone in the fridge, for God's sake. Crockett catches you without one of them, she'll have your you-know-what's in a sling."

She hands me the phones. I gingerly take them, sliding one in each of my pants pockets. The right one clangs when it hits the key.

When I look up she has a book pulled out from under the counter and is already beginning to talk. "Here's the guest registry as well as the rental book for the community room. People can stay in the guest suite overnight, but they have to sign in."

"Who stays overnight?"

"Mostly people wanting to try out the place before they decide to move here. The occasional relative. Just sign them in and make sure to sign them out. They've probably already had a tour so know where everything is. Three-night max. Don't want some niece camping here for a month while her apartment is being renovated." She flips the pages to the end of the book. "This book is also used for anyone wanting to rent the community room. We get residents booking it for birthdays, anniversaries, family reunions, Christmas; even had a wake here. That was something to see. Coffin and everything. Went all night."

She pushes that book into its cubbyhole and pulls out another. "This is the appointment book. Any workmen, home-care workers, people claiming to have business in one of the suites, has to have their name written in here in order for them to go upstairs." She pats the book with her chipped nail polish to emphasize her words. "Can't have anyone coming in saying they're going up to so-and-so's place to fix the cable. They have to have an appointment." She flaps the two books in front of my face. "Blue for booking the guest and community rooms, red for appointments. Got it?" she says to the wall.

"I do," I say.

"You sure? That's a lot to remember."

"I'm sure." I'm beginning to feel panicked — there's more to remember than I thought there'd be, but there's no way in hell I'm letting this smart-ass kid know.

"Ok, don't say I didn't ask." She holds up a small brown book. "This is the list of residents and the rooms they live in. Important to use when people expect you to know who they are and what room is theirs. And believe me, these codgers expect a lot. You'd think they never worked a day in their lives." She looks to the side of my head. "Well, John, since you say you understand everything, then you're good to go." She pushes some chocolate bar wrappers out of the way and grabs her purse from underneath. "And I'm outta here."

"You're leaving?"

"My shift is done. Did Crockett a favour just staying behind to train you."

"What do I do?"

"When there's nothing to do, enjoy the quiet. I usually bring a mag or answer my texts. I guarantee it won't last long."

She rushes out the door and gets into a car, then leans over and whispers something in the driver's ear. They both look through the window at me and laugh. I search through the desk and find a spool of string then hang the key around my neck. Immediately, one of the phones in my pocket, rings. It's the land line.

"Hello," I say. "Wheaton Senior's Residence."

"My granddaughter there yet?" a man asks.

"Your granddaughter?"

"Tall, skinny, pierced lip."

"You live here, at The Wheaton?"

"Room 310."

I look around the lobby. The only ones here are two old ladies and Ezra Adelman, occupying the couch across from the desk. "There's no one here fitting that description, Sir."

"When she shows up, send her to my room. Supposed to be taking me to the doctor for my eye appointment. Can't drive with those darn drops in."

"I will," I say as I start flipping through the pages of the brown book looking for the name of the resident of room 310.

"Metal stickin out of her everywhere. Lip, ears, nose, probably even in places I can't see. Walking pin cushion. Why do they do that?"

"I don't know..." I slide my finger down the row of numbers, "Mr. Gibson."

"And not just the girls, the boys too. I've seen grown men with pierced ears. Can you imagine? Grown men. What's this world coming to? You don't have pierced ears, do you?"

"No, Sir. I don't."

"Thank Christ for that. Can't abide looking at a man with earrings. But I'm lucky. At least I have some family. More'n some people in here."

"I'll send your granddaughter to your room the moment I see her, Sir."

"What's your name?"

"Davies. John Davies."

"It's been a pleasure talking to you."

The second I press off, the phone rings again.

"Hello, Wheaton Senior's Residence. John Davies speaking."

"I need my supper plate brought up to me tomorrow."

"Yes Ma'am. And your name and room number?"

"Christine Pearce. Room 315. Tomorrow, not today. You got it?"

"I've got it," I say as I jot down the message

"I call a day in advance because you guys always screw it up. And don't be late. Blood sugar acts up when I don't eat on time."

"Yes, Ma'am." She hangs up in my ear.

I'm checking out things behind the desk, glad the phone has stopped ringing for a few moments, when the elevator opens and a large group of people step out. They're silent as they squeak past on their rubber-footed walkers, eyes looking neither right nor left. Like a school of fish, they turn towards the dining room then stop in front of a closed door. A shaky hand reaches out and rattles the knob; the door doesn't open. They melt back a few paces and wait in a huddle, every one of them looking towards the sun-dappled driveway just outside the front door. I frown at this peculiar scene until it dawns on me what it's about; the letter-carrier's due to arrive.

When I was delivering mail, we had a name for routes like this — rookie routes. No self-respecting veteran would bid on a walk that took him inside a seniors' residence. My first year on the job I delivered to Bethlehem Seniors Home. There was always a crowd in the lobby waiting on my arrival, parting the way like I was Noah himself. They'd smile pleasantly, pat me on the back, say good morning and ask how I was; pretending to be interested in me. But it was all a ploy. The moment I turned that key and entered the mail room, they would crowd in behind me like kids at a rock concert heading to the mosh pit, bony hands and frail arms half carrying, half pushing me across the floor. There were times I was afraid I was going to gasp my last breath smothered by soft breasts and bald heads. But they always managed to deposit me right beside the mailboxes, then stand in a pulsing group of flesh — peppermint breath and Old Spice mixing together in an odour that made me retch — as they waited for me to pull the master key out of my pocket. Every day I would slide that panel up, exposing all of the boxes at once, to the same smattering of applause, as they commented on how marvellous it was I didn't have to open each one individually and 'wasn't technology wonderful?' The moment I reached into my mail bag, like marionette dolls on one set of strings, the group would lean closer and squint cataract-clouded eyes at what I was holding. Then as surely as winter always arrives, someone's arthritic fingers would pinch a piece of mail from my hands with the words, "I've got one," shouted for all her peers to hear. I'd have to threaten that if every single one of them didn't stand back and wait until I had the boxes filled and locked, I'd leave, taking the mail with me. I'd go to bed and pray there'd be no mail for them the next day, even though I knew it was a pipe dream; they always got mail. Catalogues, magazines, junk. Bills, letters, postcards. It didn't matter if it was a flyer from 7-11 or an income tax cheque, they'd press it to their chests, cherishing it like the Magna Carta, proclaiming for everyone to hear how important that piece of mail was and accusing the post office, meaning me, of purposely taking too long to deliver it. The moment I was able to sluff that puppy off onto another unsuspecting rookie, I did.

This morning the front door opens and the letter-carrier enters. It's a rookie — she has her Tilley hat on backwards; the Canada Post insignia is at the back of her head. The crowd murmurs with anticipation. I just about wave — I remember Elaine asking me if we had a secret handshake — and acknowledge to her that I'm a retired postie, but think better of it. Don't want to get involved.

She pushes the brim of her hat up and a look of terror crosses her young face. Then using her bag like a shield, she rushes towards the mail room. The group stays back until she gets to the door then they move in for the kill, herding her towards the knob. I hear keys clang as they hit the floor. She bends to retrieve them and for a moment I lose her as she's swarmed by grey heads and crooked backs, all attempting to pull her up by her armpits. At last she stands and holds the keys high in the air, triumphant in her victory. With shaking hands, she unlocks the door and the group crowds her inside. The last thing I see is an age-spotted hand gently tugging the door closed behind them and I say a little prayer before turning back to the empty lobby.

Just as Melanie predicted, my quiet doesn't last long. A plumber, a person delivering flowers, and a home-care worker arrive wanting to know where they're supposed to be. I pencil in tours and book birthday parties. I order a bottle of vodka for one resident and a pizza for another. I take calls from residents asking about the concert tonight as well as writing down names of those wanting their lunch sent to their rooms. At one point the police enter in response to a 911 call. We all rush upstairs with my master key only to find Mrs. MacIntosh, who can't get her television working. The police leave me to explain what 911 is used for and to plug her television back in.

I'm showing the big band to the community room when Mrs. Crockett returns. She has a large bag in her arms with streamers, paper hats, and some sort of a silver ball sticking out the top.

She steps behind the reception desk and shoos me out. "Go, in the dining room, help yourself to a cup of coffee. We'll talk after that."

The dining room is empty and I sit next to the windows wondering what I've gotten myself into. I could have stayed on the couch, walked the dog, gone out for the occasional coffee with an old friend and lived out my life in peace. I've paid my dues, more than my dues: slipping on ice, my mail bag skittering out in front of me, cheques and Christmas cards tumbling into the snow. Tripping over extension cords, climbing stairs no one has bothered to shovel, or dodging sprinklers as I tried to make my way to the mail box. Getting chased out of yards by dogs, or harassed by people whose welfare cheques hadn't arrived yet, as if it was my fault! Frozen fingers, sore shoulders, varicose veins; thirty-five years of pounding the pavement should be enough work for anyone's lifetime.

A woman enters interrupting my thoughts. Her spine is crooked, but she seems more than capable of looking after herself. She pours a cup then sits across the table from me and holds out her hand. "Marigold," she says.

I stare at her with a blank face.

"My name. Marigold Blossom-Rutherford. Parents liked to garden."

We shake hands as she continues to talk.

"Hyphenated my maiden name after I married. Not common back then like it is now, but I've always been a generation or two ahead of myself."

She keeps pumping my arm until I realize she's waiting for me to introduce myself.

"John Davies."

"Good name," she says as she releases her grip. "Lovely morning. Thinking of going for a walk, wear off the calories from breakfast. Don't get the exercise I used to when I lived in my own place. Creeping obesity, or some such thing. Sneaks up on you when you're not looking. Just because I'm old doesn't mean I don't want to keep my figure." She pats her round hips, "Such as it is. Sixty years ago, you should have seen me! Eighteen years old and fit as a fiddle. Liked to run. Ran everywhere. To school, to work, to church. Once a policeman stopped me and said I shouldn't run unless I was being chased. Told him I liked to run and was I breaking the law? Surprised him, I think, talking back."

I attempt to excuse myself but she keeps talking.

"I enjoy a brisk walk in the morning. Not too far anymore, mind you. Three or four blocks seems to be enough these days. The lungs are still good, no troubles there, never smoked a day in my life. Just the old bones get tired. Who are you visiting?" she says without taking a breath.

"I'm not visiting anyone." I offer no further information.

She scrutinizes my face. "So, you're either helping someone move in or you've got yourself a job. You're too young to move in yourself."

"Applying for a job. Don't know if I'll take it."

"When did your wife pass?"

"Pardon me?"

"Had that same lost look myself twenty-five years ago. Died in his sleep. Never gave me any warning. Just wham bam and I was alone. Moped around for a year before I pulled up my socks and started to work again. Best decision I could have made. Then the old arthritis kicked in so I moved here. It's the circle of life, isn't it? We live, we die. As long as I have breath in me, I've no intention of sitting still. Speaking of which," she stands. "Better get going. Walk won't happen by itself." She pats my hand, "Hope you decide to join us, John." On her way past the door she raises her arms in the air and presses her body against the frame — I can practically hear her vertebrae crack — straightening out the S in her spine, then walks out, head high, shoulders back, and a spring in her step.

I sit with my face in my hands. As much as I liked to fool myself when Elaine was alive, as much as I liked to pretend I was in charge, she was the one who always took the lead. Without her I am lost, just as Marigold said.

"I need a sign," I mumble into my hands. "Just tell me I'm doing the right thing."

The giant clock above the door ticks down the time. No magical voice from the beyond gives me direction. No lightning strikes or thunder claps, to tell me I'm making the right decision.

I shake my head. "What am I doing?" But the feeling that this is a crossroads is overwhelming. "Well, Elaine, here I am, sixty-one years old and still trying to find my way in the world." I finish my coffee and walk back into the lobby just as Julio pulls the bus up outside the doors.

Chapter two

"Thanks for pitching in this morning, Mr. Davies," Mrs. Crockett says. "Glad for the extra pair of hands. Ever since the last shift manager quit, I've been trying to juggle everything with a very small staff. Come, we can talk in my office."

I follow her down a gloomy corridor stretching out behind the reception desk. Wooden panelling extends half-way up each wall, the top half painted a colour I can only assume was on sale. Near the ceiling, dim lights are spaced unevenly with electrical wiring connecting them, as if added as an afterthought. The occasional window, placed high on the opposite wall, shed little light along the way.

Just as I'm thinking I'm going to turn around and forget the whole thing, we arrive in front of a door displaying a name-plate with *Mrs. A. Crockett,* carved in the gold metal. It stands out sharply against the wood, crackled with decade's old veneer. Around the knob, any paint, or stain that was once there is worn away from years of hands having pushed the door closed. She yanks the door open.

There are no windows in this claustrophobic office, with an oak desk taking up most of the space. A chair sits on either side of the desk, and an ancient wooden filing cabinet completely fills one corner. A plant, struggling to stay alive in this windowless office, sits on top of this cabinet. A newer, metal filing cabinet stands against the other wall with bulging files stacked on top. I attempt to pull the door closed: it won't latch.

"This corner of the building seems to be settling to the north," she says as she takes the knob from my hand. "Soon we'll be walking uphill to get to the kitchen." She pulls on the door three or four times, the door itself making a stuttering sound as the wood shakes, before it finally latches. "All of the common areas and the suites were renovated years ago." She takes my resume out of her skirt pocket, and points at a chair. "Haven't got around to finishing the office space yet. Privately owned. Don't spend much time in here anyhow." She sits opposite me. "I'd like to ask some questions, if that's okay with you? Something I do with all the applicants."

"Sure."

She folds her doll-like hands across her lap and clears her throat. "If one of the residents were to tell you a joke you deem vulgar, would you be upset?"

I think back to my days at the post office and the jokes some of the more unenlightened men would tell, especially in the later years when women were carrying mail. And while they weren't the kind of thing I'd ever participate in, I didn't tell them to stop either. "I'll be fine," I say.

She nods her small head. "Do you understand the aging process? And by that I mean, are you sympathetic to it? Sometimes the elderly say and do things we younger people would never consider saying or doing. They can be abrupt."

"My grandmother lived to be ninety-five, so I've been around old people." I make no mention of Elaine telling me my biggest fault is being un-empathetic. Or that Mom, my sister and I, stopped visiting Grandmother when I was a boy.

"That's good, that's good," she says. "And if you have to help someone off a toilet or out of a bathtub, would that disgust you?"

In the last ten years of Mom's life, she was an invalid. Neither my sister nor I could afford nursing care so looking after Mom fell onto our shoulders. "I've seen what age does to bodies."

"Ok then." She reaches out to shake my hand and the phone in her skirt pocket rings. She answers, leaving my hand dangling in mid-air. "Be right there," she stands up. "Sorry, an emergency. It shouldn't take too long. Wait here, please."

She swishes out the door and I begin debating the pros and the cons of starting work again. Making more money but having to get up early. Having something else to do besides babysit my grand-kids, but not having as much free time. Not being at home with my dog. That's a big one to the con side of the list. Ever since Elaine died, even though Clem belonged to her, that dog seems to need me more and more, as I need her. Just as I'm placing my hands on the arms of the chair, ready to leave, Mrs. Crockett returns.

"Needed to wait on an ambulance," she says.

"Oh." I sit back down, hoping that's a job out of my scope.

She begins to read my resumé. "Good name," she says as she taps the page.

That's the same thing the woman, Marigold Blossom, said and I can't help but wonder why everyone's so worried about names.

"Sometimes we get people here with odd names. Seniors pick up on things like that. You'd think with their advancing years they'd be more enlightened, but some seem to revert to a high-school men-tality. Had someone work for me once named George Pissonya. Well, you can imagine…." She keeps her gaze on me as if expecting an answer.

"Sure," I say.

She looks back down and reads my name again, "Yes, Mr. John Davies. A name that will demand respect."

"Does this mean I'm hired?"

"My questionnaire usually brings to light any reservations I might have about potential employees. Compassion and physical capabilities are the most important attributes and you appear to be a strong young man."

Sixty-one must be considered young in this place.

"Our staff turnover is very high. The elderly, as you'll discover, can be challenging to look after. But some people are fine, actually thrive. There's always something to learn, even from the old." She slides my resumé on top of the slanting pile of file folders behind her — it teeters but doesn't fall — and stands. "Well, Mister Davies, or is it all right if I call you John?"

"John is fine." I do not ask her first name.

"Ready to go to work?"

"Now?"

She pulls a vest with *The Wheaton Seniors Residence* logo on the shoulder off the coat rack behind the door, and hands it to me. "There's no time to waste when you get to be eighty. These people need you now." Her hand is stronger on my back than it appears and I'm ushered out of her office and back into the lobby. "Come, I'll show you the garden, then tour you through the building."

By the time I've seen the garden, walked down endless miles of hallway, toured the community room, chapel, and media room, been introduced to countless residents and three staff members, I wouldn't be able to find the front door if the building were on fire, let alone help an eighty-year-old to safety. I've always been bad at finding my way. I can get lost in a department store, and hospitals are impossible for me to navigate. Even at the end, Elaine took the lead.

I catch a whiff of cooking coming from the kitchen, the only room we didn't tour because Mrs. Crockett said Dave, the cook, doesn't like people in his kitchen while he's preparing a meal and most times even when he's not. He's been at this job for just over a month and is a loner, she tells me, but is an excellent cook and that's what matters. I'm glad; someone I won't have to make friends with. My stomach grumbles and I remember, in my rush this morning, I forgot to eat. Nor did I feed Clem. I guess both of us are on a diet today. I assumed I would simply get an interview and return another day if I was hired.

We're standing in the lobby when a gaggle of women emerge from the elevator. They're all talking at once as they squeak past in their crepe-soled shoes, hands fluttering like the wings of baby birds as if they won't be understood without the mime. When they see Mrs. Crockett, they wave without breaking this verbal blitz, then continue their noisy migration towards the dining room.

"Come, John. Time to put you to work."

In the dining room a queue of walkers and scooters, like bicycles lined up in an elementary school bike rack, are parked against the walls; the chairs around the tables, filled with their owners. Baskets have been placed in the middle of each of the tables, and knives, held by shaky hands, glint as they spread butter onto buns. Bent fingers then pop the buns into ancient mouths that gum the bread into dough. Talking and laughter fills the room. It seems every thought these people have has to be vocalized; the noise is deafening.

Mrs. Crockett shouts over the din, "John, you're to pour beverages. Other than serving the food which is done solely by the kitchen staff, we rotate tasks. Pouring the beverages, fetching special requests, refilling the bun baskets, leading the prayer; that kind of thing is done by the shift manager and me. But don't think pouring coffee and tea to be one of the easier jobs. Everything around here takes a light touch, a bit of finesse. You're dealing with people in their home, just remember that. Make sure to ask if they want regular, decaf, or tea. Once you've done it a few times you'll remember who gets what but today, hopefully they realize you're new and are willing to tell you."

"They expect me to know?" I say.

"The elderly look at the world in terms of how it affects them. There's a few who would complain about the noise if someone was choking on a piece of food, let alone be compassionate if you're new to the staff and need a bit of help. But don't take it personally. Just understand it for what it is; their worlds have shrunk from what they were on the outside. Empathy, John. That's what works in this job. Empathy for the fact that, God willing, we will be in the same boat one day."

She points to a wall of tables where coffee urns stand polished and steaming in the overhead lights. Each is surrounded by an array of carafes waiting to be filled. As I follow Mrs. Crockett to the table, I keep repeating: *this is not beneath me.*

"Fill the carafes and place them on the serving cart. Then wheel the cart to the back of the room and work your way forward. We al-

ternate where we begin from meal to meal so no one can complain
someone is getting preferential treatment. The food servers follow
the same protocol."

She leaves me to my job. I watch as she mingles with the residents like they're old friends, shaking hands and giving kisses. I can
almost hear the papery sound as her lips rub against those withered
cheeks. I make a silent vow to never kiss one of them, then grab a
carafe and start filling.

"That's wrong," a voice says behind me. I jump and spill tea on
the floor. "Now you've done it. You're gonna have to wipe that up.
Mop's in that closet over there."

I look at the person who made me spill. He's got to be at least
ninety years old, though estimating things is something that has
always eluded me. Elaine used to laugh that I couldn't guess myself out of a paper bag. At one of the kid's carnival nights many
years ago, there was a jelly bean guessing jar. I guessed fifty. Elaine
laughed so hard I thought she was going to pee her pants. She
guessed two-hundred and fifty and came home with the jar. This
old man could be anywhere from seventy-five to one hundred and
ten. His head is completely bald and the teeth large, with thin lips
stretched tight over the yellowing enamel. His cheeks are sallow,
and his eyes have sunk into their sockets. He looks like a jack-o-
lantern a month after Halloween is over.

I'm ready to ream him out, then remember Mrs. Crockett's
words; empathy. I take a breath. "What do you mean, *that's wrong*?"

"Wrong pot," he says. "That there's a coffee pot. This here's the
tea pot." He picks up a pot identical to the one I'm holding.

"They look the same to me."

"Quit arguing. If I say it's the wrong pot then it's the wrong pot,
he says in a voice that defies his age.

Mrs. Crockett lifts her head from the person she's talking to,
then turns back to refilling a bun basket.

The old man shoves the pot in my face. "Now get a mop and
wipe up this spill before I fall and break a goddamn hip!"

My anger surfaces and I'm ready to quit before I've begun.

Marigold pops up beside me. "Jack, your lunch is being served." She points to a server placing a plate on the table in front of his empty chair. "Turkey and stuffing. Isn't that your favorite?"

Jack swivels his bald head towards his chair, then licks his pale tongue over dry lips. Without another word he scuttles off as fast as his bow legs will take him.

"I see you decided to stay," Marigold says.

"What the hell was that all about?" I whisper.

"Don't worry about him. It's Jack Belgrade. Likes to scare the employees. Used to be a CEO of a company and still thinks he's in charge. Next time just keep doing your job and eventually he'll leave you alone."

"As in Belgrade Conglomerate? That Jack Belgrade?" I gaze towards his table. He's sitting with his back to me, his spine rounded with age, not looking at all like the once CEO of the biggest private corporation in the country. As he digs into his turkey dinner, I feel my anger turn to pity. "Sold his business years ago. I thought he was dead. Made a lot of savvy investments. Grew that company to one of the biggest in North America. Owned everything from airlines to farm equipment distributors to grocery stores. He was an important guy in his day."

"Weren't we all in some way or another? I'm sure you'll meet more than one person in the next few weeks who will surprise you." Marigold points to the empty carafes I still have to fill and distribute. "And I take my coffee black when you make your way to my table." She looks at the floor. "He's right, you need to mop that up before one of us does slip and break a hip."

I retrieve a mop from the broom closet and clean up the spill, then begin filling carafes. I rattle my way to the front of the dining room until I remember Mrs. Crockett said to start at the back. I quickly make my way to the back before another resident gives me heck.

As I move from table to table, I hear jokes that would make my old co-workers at the post-office blush, and jokes that would amuse my five-year-old granddaughter. I listen to people advise me that if I want to keep this job I'd better learn to be quick, and I tolerate cold shoulders from others as they let me know I'm not worth acknowledging.

I come across Rachel from this morning's teeth argument. She looks up at me with such rheumy eyes I'm unsure if she can even see. "You're new," she says. "Saw you talking to Alma this morning."

"Alma?"

"Mrs. Crockett. Alma Crockett. Caretaker of us oldies. Guess she hired you."

"She did."

"Well, my name is Rachel Johnston. I'm a retired school teacher and I always drink tea. Coffee gives me the runs. I'm sure next time you serve me you'll be able to remember that bit of information, won't you?" She peers over her glasses at me.

"I'm sure I will." I pour a cup and place it in front of her. "Next time, Mrs. Johnston, I will remember to serve you tea without asking."

She pushes her glasses up her nose and nods, confident she's taught me an important lesson.

For the next half hour, the words, "Coffee, tea, or decaf?" become my mantra. When I'm finished, I wheel the cart back to the table under the watchful eyes of the last of the residents who didn't get their beverages until long after the meal was done.

"Mrs. Hawkins needs a plate brought up to her," Mrs. Crockett says when I meet her in the lobby. "She's not feeling well today. Go to the kitchen, the cook will have it ready for you. Room 204. You can take the elevator not the stairs. She's a bit deaf, so let yourself in then call loudly at the door that you're there. Don't want to frighten her by walking in unannounced. When you come back down, help yourself to a plate in the fridge, Dave makes extra, then sit in the dining room to eat."

I enter the kitchen and smell turkey. My stomach growls. Two large stoves sit at the far end of the room, both covered with dirty pots. A double door fridge is on the opposite wall, and on the front wall, under the window, two stainless steel dishwashers stand with their doors open, an industrial sized sink, between. A woman stops what she's doing to say *buenas tardas* to me, then continues with her chore of scraping plates and stacking them by the sink. A man with an apron tied around his thick frame who I assume is Dave, is rinsing the plates before he loads them in the dishwasher. He has ear buds wedged into his ears and I hear Ben Webster's saxophone emanating from them. I stand behind him — he smells of cigarette smoke — and clear my throat. He does not turn around. I step into his line of sight. His face is long. A bandanna pulling his hair back exposes a wide forehead. His nose is hawkish and his lips are thin. He's probably around my age, although with his angry demeanour, he appears older.

"You have a plate for me to take upstairs?" I say, hoping he speaks English.

"I do," he says keeping his eyes on his task.

I wait, thinking he'll tell me where it is, but he says nothing and I have to ask. "And where would that be?"

Instead of answering, he lifts his hand out of the sink and points a soapy finger over his shoulder towards the side wall. A plate, covered in foil, sits on the counter next to the refrigerator. I say *thank-you*. He doesn't respond. I pick up the plate, wondering why this man is being so rude, then leave, passing two of the women in the hall whom I saw serving lunch. They're deep in a conversation.

"Just about choked," one of them says in a thick accent I can't place. "Forgot to put her undies on. Could see all the way up to her hoo hoo when she bent over and picked up her napkin off the floor."

"If I ever get that forgetful, shoot me, will ya?" They cackle in unison.

I walk past in total agreement.

A scrolled metal plate that frames two buttons, well-worn from years of prodding fingers, is attached to the wall beside the elevators doors. I push the top button and a motor somewhere in the belly of the building comes to life. The dial above the doors, like a large second hand, begins to tick down from number three towards the ground floor, the elevator moving more quickly than I'd expect from something so old. The doors slide open and I enter. Then the ancient beast whooshes me up faster than the elevator in a new condo.

I stagger into a hallway and begin down the narrow span. The walls are decorated with everything from family pictures, to amateur paintings, inspirational quotes; *you can do it if you believe* and wreathes of all shapes and sizes. I stop in front of room 204. A wooden plaque with two birds saying welcome to each other, sitting on a paper wreath with fake orange leaves, hangs beneath the suite number. A mat with animated renderings of a dog and cat with big eyes sits on the floor in front of the door. *God save me from crap like this.*

I knock and wait, but hear no footsteps. I knock louder, still no answer. I turn the knob. The door is unlocked and I enter her apartment.

"Mrs. Hawkins? It's John Davies. I have your lunch." It's quiet in here, with only a glow coming from the end of the hall. I take a few steps then call louder. "Mrs. Hawkins, I have your lunch." I begin to slow my gait, hoping on my first day I haven't encountered someone who's passed on. I turn the corner and come face to face with Dr. Oz on the largest TV I've ever seen. The sound is muted and I watch as his silent lips give advice to a woman in the audience. When I first retired I tried to watch daytime television, but most of it was so mind-numbing I would fall asleep. I do not need someone telling me how to eat healthier or how to have a good relationship with my wife.

A chair is pulled up in front of the television and a tuft of blue hair is poking over the back. I step in front. A diminutive woman is seated there with her cane resting between her knees. She appears to be asleep; her head is tilted back and her mouth is slightly open. I breathe a sigh of relief when I see her chest rise and fall.

I turn around the room. Photographs cover every available end table, sofa table and coffee table, crowding around the television, pushed into the table lamps, surrounding the knick-knacks, threatening to fall off the edges wherever they sit. Kids, adults, babies, dogs, cats, horses, houses, mountains and lakes. People swimming and hiking, gathered around Christmas trees, grinning bridal parties and birthday parties with cakes and candles in the foreground. There's even one where everyone is dressed in black and looking sombre; a funeral, I suppose. Her entire life is framed and set out. I squeeze her plate onto the coffee table then turn when she stirs.

"Mrs. Hawkins," I say gently, "I've brought you lunch. Mrs. Hawkins?"

Her eyes pop open and she tries to stand. Her cane gets caught between her legs and she pitches forward towards the coffee table where I've set her lunch plate. I reach for her, knocking the plate to the floor, and push her backwards. She lands in her chair and her legs rise in the air — thank God she has on underwear — then plunks her feet down hard on to the floor. She gives her head a shake and I step back, afraid she's going to grab that cane and start swinging.

"Are you all right?" I call from across the room.

"Who the hell are you?" she says as she struggles to sit straight and pull her dress down over support stockings that are bagging out over her knees.

"John Davies," I yell. "Are you all right?" I say again.

"What the hell are you doing in my room?"

"I knocked. You didn't hear." I point to her plate lying upside down on the floor. "I was trying to bring you lunch. I'm sorry if I startled you." Because of the heat in this stifling room and fear that I may have injured her, sweat pours down my brow and stings my eyes. My shirt is soaked, my hands are damp and my socks feel wet in my shoes. I kneel down and begin to scrape the food back onto the plate.

She squints at me. "You're new."

"I am."

"You look like my dead husband. He was always sweating too. Shirt was always wet, just like a God damn dishrag."

I wipe my forehead and stand, ruined lunch plate in my hands. "You must miss him."

"Miss him! Good God no. Crazy son of a bitch. You're not a crazy son of a bitch, are you?"

"Never been told I am. I'll just go and see if I can get you another plate of food."

"Not hungry." She opens her mouth to say something else but stops.

"I'll be on my way then," I say.

"Thought I saw him standing right where you are, then when you appeared the hell out of nowhere, well, I thought it was my time."

"That would be startling," I say, "to think you were seeing your deceased husband." I take a step towards the door but stop when she starts to say something else.

"No, not him. The other one. The one that comes to those who," she flicks her eyes at me then looks quickly away, "you know."

Again, I begin to walk away. "I'm sorry, Mrs. Hawkins, I didn't mean to scare you."

"You ever seen someone die?" she says to my back.

"I haven't," I lie.

"Then you've probably not seen him."

I turn around. "Pardon me?"

She looks at me as if she's talking to a remedial child. "Are you thick-skulled? Wouldn't surprise me, husband was thick-skulled too. I'm talking about the one who comes when someone dies."

I'm confused.

"The man in black, angel of death, the grim reaper, for God's sake. Not ready yet," she mumbles. "It's not my time. Saw him this morning down the hall when they came to collect Ed. Then now, standing right there, where I saw you. You can bet Ed's dead. They just haven't told us yet."

I remember Melanie telling me this morning there's someone living here that sees the grim reaper in her room. "Mrs. Hawkins, it was just a dream. There's only you and me in this apartment."

I let myself out, glad to be out of the hot apartment and away from this crazy old lady, hoping this isn't an indication of what everyone here is like. Mrs. Crockett isn't at the front desk but I can hear her on the phone in her office. I wait in the hall for her to finish before I pull the door open.

"Ed Brown died," she says.

"Mrs. Hawkins just mentioned him."

"He's the man I was called away for during our interview. Sad affair, that," but she says no more about him. "You'll get used to it. We don't get immune, just used to it. It's still upsetting. Just because someone's old doesn't mean it's not a sad thing when they die." She sees the smashed plate of food in my hands. "You were gone a long time," she says.

"Had a little mishap." I pull my head out of the office, then turn back. "Have any residents ever mentioned seeing someone?" I trail off not knowing how to finish my question without sounding as crazy as Mrs. Hawkins.

"Seeing someone?"

"Yes, you know, when someone dies?"

"Oh, you mean the grim reaper. Is that what took you so long? Mrs. Hawkins saw him?"

"Came at me with her cane. Thought I was him and I'd come for her."

Chapter three

One good thing about starting work at seven-thirty in the morning is by mid-afternoon, I'm done for the day. Much like working at the post office. For thirty-five years I would be home by two-thirty in the afternoon then lie on the couch listening to Elaine bustle around as she helped the kids with homework, or stirred pots on the stove preparing supper. Comforting sounds to be sure.

Mrs. Crockett shooed me out of The Wheaton at three on the dot after telling me to get a good night's rest and she'd see me tomorrow afternoon at three-thirty, ending with the words, "Tomorrow's bingo, John," following me out the door like a threat. I left, looking forward to some quiet, a beer, and giving Clementine a hug.

Barbara's car is parked on the driveway and my anticipation to be home wanes. *Selfish of me,* I think. *It's my daughter.* I should be happy to have her visit, but I'm in no mood to talk, especially to her. She has a way of making me feel guilty even if I have nothing to feel guilty for. She'll think I'm sidestepping my life by going back to work, that my sole motivation is to avoid being a parent and grandparent. I'd be too easily swayed and the last person I want to sway me is her; someone who always thinks she's right. I'd argue the sky is red with her.

It must be because she's the oldest of our three kids. The answer to her mid-life crisis was to take the welfare of Elaine and myself into her own hands; reminding us about dentist or doctor's appointments, sending Colin, my oldest grandson over to help me shovel the snow, making sure we took vitamins. An efficient person, even as a child. I remember once, she was around twelve or thirteen and we hadn't seen Elaine's parents for a couple of weeks — I never got along with Elaine's dad — and Barbara decided it was time we had them over. "They'll be dead and gone in just a few years," she said as she dialed the phone and invited them for supper. "We have to make some memories before it's too late. I'll cook a casserole; it'll be fun."

I pull up beside her silver Lexus, wishing I could have my house to myself. I stay in my car, stalling the inevitable and I'm reminded of Mark, our middle child, slouching out of the house in a huff, only to sit in his beat up Supra because I wouldn't allow him to do something I considered unwise. He'd stay there for hours by himself mad at the world, and I'd want to tell him I was only trying to do what's best for him and one day he'd thank me for it. I wanted to shake some sense into his teenage brain but at Elaine's request, I'd stay inside. *He had to work it out on his own* she'd say and *my forcing myself on him would just make him rebel more.* She was right, as usual. I've always been the last one to figure things out.

I'm sure I'm getting attention from Barbara only because since her mother's death, she thinks I need help. But she has to understand I've managed to make it this far in my life. I don't need her constantly watching over my shoulder to make sure I'm okay. I just don't know how to tell her this without sounding angry. I had many a lecture from Elaine over the years on how to be diplomatic with our children, you'd think I'd have perfected it by now.

I drag my weary body inside. Immediately I smell Elaine's perfume. Her scent floats lightly on the air as if she just walked through the front door. Her mark is everywhere, from the white sheer curtains, to the colour of paint on the walls. Even though my paycheque bought just about everything we own, this was definitely her house more than mine. I never told Elaine I always felt like a guest in my own home.

Barbara greets me. "You look tired, Dad." She turns her back to me as she rearranges the couch cushions, plumping them up and placing them in strategic positions.

My voice is sharp, "Why are you here, Barbara?"

She freezes, pillow in hand. I touch her arm.

"Sorry, Barb. Just tired. It's good to see you."

Her smile is forced, breezy. "On my way to the gym. Have to teach an afternoon spin class so I can't stay long. Brought you some cabbage rolls."

"You didn't need to do that."

I hang up my jacket then Clem and I follow Barb to the kitchen. Me for a beer, Clem hoping for food.

Barb picks up the dishrag and begins to wipe crumbs from the sandwich I ate last night for supper into the sink. "I let Clem out. Bounded off the deck like she hadn't peed in hours. Where've you been?"

"Trying to keep busy." I stall, not wanting to tell her but knowing sooner or later I have to. "Got myself a job."

Her head spins around to face me. "You what?"

"Got a job, at a seniors' place."

She stops wiping for a moment then turns back to the sink. "Why am I not surprised," she says just loud enough for me to hear.

"I have to do something, Barbie. I can't spend the rest of my days sleeping on the couch."

She bends down and pets Clem on the nose. "Poor puppy." She looks into Clem's eyes. Clem wags her tail, happy for affection, not understanding Barb's using her to make me feel guilty. "Guess your walking days are done." With her face snuggled into Clem's fur she says, "I thought you were helping to look after Mark's kids when Deanna goes back to work? Her mat leave is just about over. And Colin and Julie would be happy for a visit from their grandpa any time."

"Don't worry about Clem. I plan on walking her after work. She'll still get her hour a day, just at a different time. And Mark and Deanna told me they would rearrange their schedules if something came up. Maybe it will still work out; the job is only part time. They'll understand. And I'm sure, being his mother, you know as well as I do that Colin is a teenager now and visits from his grandfather are tolerated, not relished."

I don't tell her that the last time we were together I overheard her forcing Colin to come and sit with me. Whether it was because he's a teenager or because I was grumpy, I don't know.

"So, it's part time?" She stands and places the cabbage rolls in the fridge.

"Yes. But for the next week it's every day until I'm trained."

"Trained? Can't be that much to learn about looking after old people, can there?"

"Can we do this another time, Barb? I'm tired and I still have to take Clem for her walk."

"Oh, yeah, sure Dad." She folds then places the dishrag on the tap. "Have to run anyhow. Colin has a basketball game at five and Rob can't make it home from the office to drive him. Then Julie has a piano lesson right after. I have to teach this class then drive her in rush hour traffic. Talk to you tomorrow."

Clem and I stand at the door and watch Barbara's car back out of the driveway. I wish I'd been able to say what I really thought; that I'm no good at this parenting thing, that family obligations were her mother's domain and she's right, going to work will give me a reason to tell them I'm busy. That I don't want to babysit all the time, or go to every family dinner and reminisce about their mother. She's dead and gone and no amount of talking about her will bring her back or make me feel better. And besides, I still have a few good years left. Many people nowadays work until they're sixty-five or seventy so it's not entirely out of avoidance that I took the job. But that wouldn't be the way Elaine would have handled it. She would have patted Barb on the arm and told her *thanks for thinking of us.* She'd have told her we couldn't ask for a more considerate daughter, then given her a hug and a kiss on the cheek, sending her on her way feeling good about herself.

One down, two kids to go. But Barbara's the toughest. Perhaps I'd mellowed a bit by the time Mark and Janet came along; they don't seem to hold as much resentment towards me as Barb does. When she turns the corner, I feel my energy for walking Clementine fade. I grab a beer and sit on the couch, Clementine at my feet, happy to have me home.

1979

"You're pregnant?"

"It's ok, John. We'll be fine."

"How am I going to feed another mouth? I barely make enough for the two of us?" I throw my lunch box onto the counter. "And anyhow, I thought that doctor said you wouldn't get pregnant after you lost the baby last time?" I peel my jacket from the security company off and toss it on the chair. It falls to the floor. "God almighty, Elaine, how could you let this happen?"

She picks the jacket up and I can tell from her movements I've made her upset. She makes light of the situation. "Do I have to explain the birds and bees to you, John?" She tries to give me a kiss and I turn my face away. She talks to my back. "The doctor did say that every case is different and with time, I might be able to get pregnant again. I guess he was right." She reaches for my arm. "You'll see; things will work out."

"How are you going to keep working when you're pregnant? You can't be standing at that cash register all day when you're as big as a house. And what about when I work nights? I won't be able to sleep during the day with a God damn baby crying."

She rubs her stomach in the way I've seen other pregnant women do, but that doesn't stop me.

"They won't hire you back after the baby's born," I continue. "They'll be afraid you'll get pregnant again."

She shrugs. "Maybe I don't want to work after the baby's born. Maybe I want to stay home and be a mother, not let someone else raise my kids while I spend half of my salary on day-care. Why don't you answer that ad I saw in the newspaper? The one for the post-office. They're looking for letter-carriers."

"Me and a thousand other applicants."

"You've just as much chance as anyone else. Good salary. Pension. I think it's something you might enjoy. Get to be outside on your own, no boss breathing down your neck."

"Quit being so naïve, Elaine. We can't afford a baby, even if I get a job as a mailman or whatever the hell they call them now. What's the matter with you?"

Her face drops. She turns towards the oven and takes out a casserole. I want to reach for her to comfort her, but my feelings are swirling and I don't know how I feel.

***

My eyes pop open with the words *I'm sorry* on my lips, and the sounds of Elaine in the kitchen preparing supper in my ears. It's so real I just about shout, *what's for supper*, but when I sit up, I realize it was only a dream. Clementine is staring at me, wagging her tail with a hopeful expression on her face. I take a sip of warm beer, put on my running shoes, grab the leash and we head out the door. The days are getting shorter; it's only five and the sun is already close to the roof tops. Neighbours are cutting their lawns for one last time, and kids, with the school day ended, are getting in the last few days of riding scooters, bikes and skateboards before the snow flies. Soon I'll have to start putting Clementine's boots on so she won't get ice wedges stuck between her pads. She hates her boots and it's always a struggle to corner her and push them over her dewclaws, then get them done up tight enough so she won't lose them in a snowbank. Elaine used to do that for me. I didn't have the patience. Just one more thing I've had to learn to do on my own and not for the first time, my anger at Elaine for dying surpasses my grief.

Chapter four

The roofline of The Wheaton is blurred with clouds, the walls veiled with rain. The building looks like a mirage shimmering in the mist as I run from the parking lot, only stopping when a car pulls up beside me. I stand under the overhang by the front door and look into the face of the man Melanie drove away with yesterday. He rolls down his window.

"Hey, bud, you work here, right?"

He's chewing juicy fruit gum and I back away. "I'll get Melanie for you."

"Weather's got me a bit behind this afternoon, just makin' a delivery. Mind doin' me a favour?" He grabs a bag from the back seat before I've had a chance to answer.

I draw a wet hand down my face, pulling water off like a squeegee.

He shoves the bag out the window. "My arms are gonna break, mister. Ya gonna take it or not?"

"What am I supposed to do with this?" I say, taking the bag.

"For the Brighton woman. Melanie'll show ya."

"What is…?" I ask but he's already left me choking on his exhaust. I pull open the door and enter the lobby. Like Walmart greeters, the same people that sat here yesterday are here again today.

"Told ya," one of them says. "Knew this was the day."

"Yup. Delivery every five days like clockwork."

I peek inside the bag; vodka, gin, and two bottles of bourbon nestle against each other. I turn and bump directly into Melanie.

She's pulling on her coat and looks over my shoulder at the rain-soaked driveway. "Where'd he go?"

"Gave me this bag of alcohol."

"He gave you the bag and left?"

"He did."

The Walmart greeters have stopped talking and are poised to listen. I get the distinct impression that fireworks from Melanie happens quite often, and they enjoy every minute of it.

Melanie yanks off her coat then jams it on the coat rack. She stomps back to the reception desk and picks up a magazine. The greeters slump into their chairs with disappointed looks on their faces.

"Said he was running late because of the rain," I say.

"Whatever." She begins flipping through a magazine.

I can feel water dripping down the nape of my neck. "This is a regular occurrence? Her getting alcohol delivered?"

"Always the one you'd never expect," she mumbles.

"What do I do with this?"

"Room 205. Brighton. With her money, you'd think she'd have the show suite. Spends it all on alcohol. Must have a lot of demons."

I look at her with a puzzled expression.

"Retired lawyer. Ruthless, they called her. All they call her now is a drunk." She nods towards the elevator. "Get up there, wouldja? I gotta go." Her voice has risen to a whine.

My wet shoes squeak on the tiles as I clink my way to the elevator.

"And don't let her talk you into anything," she instructs. "Just hand her the bag and leave. No sense giving her the wrong idea from the beginning. Best to nip it in the bud."

I push the elevator button wondering what a feeble old lady could possibly talk me into.

Her apartment door is ajar and I lift my hand to knock. The door swings open as if she were expecting me. A woman in a grey suit, white blouse, pearls and high heels stands inside, an unlit cigarette in one hand and a coffee cup in the other. She looks the furthest thing from feeble I could imagine.

"That for me?" she says.

I nod.

Without introducing herself, she turns and walks into her suite before I can hand her the bag. I stay outside her door, thinking about Melanie's instructions to not let her talk me into anything.

She looks behind her. "Bring it in then, don't just stand there."

I step across the threshold and follow her down a short hall, emerging into small galley kitchen.

"Set those here." She slaps a counter where a microwave and bar fridge sit on either side of a tiny sink. Save for a coffee pot and a kitchen chair pushed up to a small table, the remainder of the room is empty. Even the counter tops are bare. I put the bag down, then having done as I was told, turn to leave.

"Just a minute," her voice is deep and notched. She steps into the next room, which is inches away. "Gather the empties and take them to the recycling bin," she presses a bag at me. My nostrils flare and I linger a beat by the counter before taking the bag from her hand.

All that defines this as a different room is the furniture. A bed dominates the space and is made to perfection. The small dresser is free of clutter, its top gleaming as if it was just freshly dusted. A pair of slippers are wedged under the edge of a nightstand, and I presume the closed door next to the bed leads to a bathroom. It's the apartment of a woman who is under control, or trying hard to show the world she is. The only thing out of order in this miniature living room/bedroom setup is a coffee table, laden with empty liquor bottles. The piece of furniture is squeezed between the bed and an open window which leads to a balcony the size of my linen closet. How she manages to live in a space so small without going crazy is beyond me.

"Call me a drunk. Suppose you've already heard that," she laughs. "Gossip is the mainstay of the staff around here. Gossip and rumours. Small minds, most of them."

I don't make eye contact.

"I don't care what any of them think. I like to have a drink now and then," she waves her unlit cigarette at me, "but I'm no drunk."

Her eyes are bloodshot and her make-up, heavy, probably hiding a vein riddled nose. I saw many letter-carriers' noses peppered with red streaks over the years. The ones who would spend their afternoons — after they rushed through their routes — in bars. I had more than one invitation to join them but never fell into that particular trap. I always had my music, and besides, Elaine would have killed me.

"You don't believe me," she says.

"I have no reason not to," I say.

"Diplomatic one, aren't you? More than the rest." She touches the cigarette to her lips, then pulls it away. "Not supposed to smoke in here, not even on my own balcony. Supposed to go down to the gazebo." She says gazebo like she's sucked on a lemon. "I pay good money for this apartment," she waves her cup around the room, "if you can call it that. Should be able to do as I God damn please." She steps into her kitchen and sets the cup in the sink, then turns on the tap and begins to wash it. "As if I'd want to sit down there with all those grannies, knitting and gossiping. Talking about gardening and grandkids, and what it was like back in the good old days. Listen to who's visited whom, what their families are doing. If I hear one more story about how great-grandson Johnny can already read and he hasn't even begun school yet, or that old crow Rachel brag about her granddaughter, Breanna, because they put her on the front page of the paper for saving that person who fell in the river, I'm going to puke." Placing her hands on the edge of the sink, she leans on her arms and shakes her head. "It's like a God damn competition."

I continue placing bottles into the bag.

"They want everyone to believe they get visitors all the time, want everyone to believe their families haven't forgotten about them." She faces me, "but I hear things, I see things. I know everyone isn't as happy as they claim."

I keep my eyes on my job.

"You probably think I'm ranting." Then more quietly, "Suppose I am, but it's the truth. Just ask Ed Brown."

I stand, bag in hand. "Ed Brown?"

"You know him?"

"No, no. Just, I heard, I think, yesterday…."

"Spit it out. You heard, you think what?"

I stop for a moment to consider what the protocol is for informing residents of other's deaths but then plough ahead. "He was taken away in an ambulance yesterday. I believe he might have passed on."

Tears well up in her eyes and she swallows hard. Her voice is thick. "Need a light bulb changed. Kitchen, if you can call it that. Light above the sink. Blew last week. Tried to get someone here to change it but no one wants to come to my apartment." She points to the kitchen chair. "You can use that to stand on."

I drag the chair to the sink. She turns away to wipe her eyes.

"I'm sorry about the death of your friend," I say.

"I have no friends."

"It just seemed like…."

She interrupts, "Ed was an acquaintance. No more than that."

I set the burned-out light on the counter then take the new bulb from her.

"You've worked before." she says. "This is a retirement job. You were some sort of blue-collar worker. You take direction but you bristle with each of my commands. Like a man who's worked under supervisors who don't know their asses from their elbows."

I look at her, surprised at her insight.

"Know a government worker when I see one. Saw lots of people like you when I practiced law. What's your name?"

"Davies. John Davies."

"Well, Mr. John Davies, I'll be sure to ask for you next time I need anything. You're different from the rest." Her voice gets louder. "I see them snicker when they think my back is turned. I was *somebody* once upon a time, respected and feared. No one dared make fun of me. Like to see them when they're my age, then let them talk.

Don't make judgments without hearing the entire story," she stumbles a bit. "Lesson I should have learned."

I step off the chair then walk down the hall with my bag of empties.

"Regrets. That's what does it to you. Regrets will change your life."

I put my hand on the doorknob.

"Be sure to come back when you can stay longer. We can have a drink…."

I close the door on her voice.

"Where do the empties go?" I ask Melanie who hasn't budged since I went upstairs.

She lifts her eyes to me, then lowers them back to her magazine. "I see she rooked you into helping her," she licks her thumb and turns a page. "Out the back door off the kitchen. Recycling bin is beside the garbage. Hurry, wouldja? You were gone a long time already."

Over the course of my career I encountered many people like Melanie, ignorant, lazy types who worked only the bare minimum. Taking the advice of a seasoned postal worker, I count to ten and leave her to her magazine.

The same cook I saw yesterday is standing by the sink peeling potatoes. "Just taking out some recycling," I say.

He doesn't respond. I hear Charlie Parker's rendition of *East of the Sun* coming out of his ear buds. I dump the empties outside and am about to leave the room when he pulls the ear buds out.

"Think you're pretty smart, dontcha?"

"Pardon me?"

"Think you're pretty smart gettin' two paycheques."

I've heard of the occasional pensioner being harassed for getting a second paycheque but always thought those claims were exaggerated. "How is that your business?" I say.

"I'm strugglin' to make ends meet and you get a pension and a salary. Probly got a cute wifey waitin' for you at home. Grandkids clamourin' to sit on your knee. Why don't you and your kind just stay home? We don't need you here."

I forget my advice to count. "If I'm taking a job away from you, just say so, but if my working here doesn't affect you, mind your own business." I walk out, seething with anger.

"What's the matter with that guy?" I ask Melanie.

"Thinks he's had it tough. Was adopted. Family was religious nuts in some sorta church, or cult or whatever. Said that's where he learned to cook. Tried to tell me some stuff when he first started working here but I put an end to that. Got enough problems of my own without having to listen to his." She steps into her rain boots then drags the sleeves of her coat on over her bulky sweater and pulls up the hood. She's so well camouflaged in this outfit, it's difficult to tell if she's a man or a woman. "Can't stand here talkin' all day. Already missed one bus, don't wanna miss the next."

I lose sight of her now large outline in the rain. A list of chores for the shift manager is on the desk, something Melanie neglected to show me yesterday. Only a couple have been checked off and I spend the next hour folding the supper napkins then placing them in the dining room, opening a new box of chocolate bars and putting them in a basket under the dais, and taking the towels out of the dryer, then folding them and placing them on the housekeeping cart.

The elevator opens and a group rushes towards me. Everyone's talking at once. I hold up my hand. "One at a time, please."

They're all beginning to look alike and a woman I can't remember if I've met or not, speaks first. "He reached out and touched her arm." She tsk's her tongue at the man beside her. "Fell right across the threshold, out of that pink scooter she rides, nothing else we could do." She pats the top of her well-sprayed hair. "Had to leave her there. It's time for supper, we couldn't stand about lollygagging."

"What are you talking about?" I say.

"She fell, Darlene. Right across where the door opens and closes, you know, the threshold. We had no choice."

"Someone fell?"

"Upstairs in the hall," she looks at the man beside her. "Told you not to touch her. But no," she draws out the word, her lips pursed in a perfect zero. "Sixty years together and you're still as stubborn as the day I married you."

He grunts, "Only wanted to make her shush-up, Irma. Thinks she knows everything about everything. Enough to make your ears bleed."

"She is a bit of a know-it-all, I grant you that," Irma says. "But to touch her, well that only made matters worse."

"You need to tell me what you're talking about." I rub my hand across my forehead; this constant prattle is giving me a headache. "Do I need to go upstairs? Is it an emergency?"

"She'll come around, long as no one touches her again. Never breaks anything when she falls, just plops to the ground and lies there till she wakes up. Weirdest affliction I've ever seen."

The woman beside her speaks up. "There was a girl I went to school with, had the same thing. Couldn't be touched or she dropped on the spot like a bag of potatoes. We used to touch her just to watch her faint."

"That being said, Deardra," Irma scowls at her friend, "Darlene fell right in the way of the elevator door so we nudged her," she pushes her toes forward, demonstrating what she did.

"You nudged her?"

The elevator opens again and another large group steps off.

"Rolled her out of the way with our feet. What else could we do? Nettie stayed with her, she's on a diet anyhow." She peeks nervously at the group shuffling past. "Can't stand here talking anymore, have to get going before all the good seats are taken. Don't want to sit with old Mr. Bickers. Picks his nose while he eats, thinks no one sees him. Pickers Bickers, we call him."

Mrs. Crockett emerges from the hall.

"Mrs. Crockett…."

"Don't you think it's time you dropped the formalities, John. Call me Alma, please."

"Uh, Alma, there's a woman, she fell, apparently someone…."

"Touched her? Yes. That's Mrs. Carillion. Darlene Carillion.

Don't know what that's all about, just don't ever touch her. She faints. Rides a pink scooter around the place like Evel Knievel. Surprised you haven't met her yet. She's leaving on a trip tonight. You probably won't meet her now for a number of weeks." She looks at her watch. "Plane leaves in a couple of hours. I'd better go and make sure she gets there on time." She points to the dining room. "Supper time."

I look at the clock on the wall. "I have to take a plate up to Mrs. Pearce. She called yesterday while you were out, said not to be late."

"Get that plate before you begin to pour coffee. Christine's a diabetic, needs her food on time."

I slip into the kitchen and grab the plate without talking to Dave. Mrs. Pearce snatches it from me with only two words, and they're not *thank-you*.

Yesterday when I followed Alma into the crowded dining room, I was so nervous I didn't notice the odour. Tonight, the moment I walk into the room, the smell hits me like a punch in the face, and I feel my stomach turn.

Over the last two months of Elaine's life, the hospital cafeteria became my escape from the constant dinging and beeping of the machines that were hooked up to her morning noon and night. At the time, it was a relief to smell food, even bad food, rather than medicine, vomit and pee, but now I find the smell of institutionalized food nauseating.

Mrs. Carillion must have got up off the floor and be on her way to the airport, as Alma's here filling bun baskets and schmoozing. She looks my way and nods towards the row of coffee and tea urns. I march to table, avoiding the gaze of Jack Belgrade. If I had a run in with him tonight, I'd quit on the spot. I stop at Marigold's table and place a cup of black coffee in front of her.

"You're moving with more confidence after just one day."

Deciding the only way I can work here is to stay aloof, I smile, then roll my cart to the next person before she can say any more.

She lifts her cup, then says to no one in particular, "We never know until we try, like most things in life."

Tonight is bingo, just as Alma promised. Chairs slide across the floor as people rush to grab the last of the seats and I hear, "This seat is saved," and "Over here, Ester," and "I hope I'm luckier this week than last." Everyone has two bingo cards in front of them, and everyone, as usual, is talking. Packages of daubers are cracked open and passed down the tables.

Years ago, when our kids were in high-school, they raised money for school trips by working at bingo halls. It's how Barbie managed to go to Disneyland with her school band, something we could never afford to do on my salary. Elaine would take them to the bingo nights, and when they came home they'd sit at the kitchen table eating cookies and drinking hot chocolate while they laughed and gossiped about the people they'd seen there. There was the woman who wore purple from head to toe. Slacks, blouse, socks and purse. Barb said even her hair was dyed a light mauve. Then there was the man who loudly repeated each number after it was called. Elaine said no one ever told him to stop, said everyone liked the repetition.

I was always jealous of the intimacy Elaine had with our kids, but that didn't prompt me to volunteer to help. My excuse, *I was too tired from work*. And I was, but in reality, the thing that stopped me more than exhaustion was my fear of not being able to do it as well as Elaine. Of not asking the right questions, or having one of them say, "Oh, Dad!" My fear of failure ran that deep and old.

Once, when the kids were small, Elaine went out for an evening with friends, something she had never done before the kids were tucked in bed. Janet, who was only two at the time, wasn't happy. She clung to Elaine's leg as she tried to leave the house. Elaine gently peeled her off and told her she'd be back as quick as a wink and her daddy would make supper and read her a bedtime story. Janet sobbed and nodded at each of her mother's words, but as soon as Elaine left, she threw herself by the front door, crying so hard her small body shuddered with each breath. I picked her up and tried to console her but she fought me, squirming and kicking until she managed to get off my lap and run to her sister, who rocked her until she calmed down. Angry at my inability to help my own daughter, and angry at Janet for humiliating me in front of my other two children, I slammed around the kitchen for half an hour preparing supper. I didn't look after the kids without Elaine around again until they were much older.

A bingo cage stands on a table and a microphone is attached to a dais. As Alma steps in front, a hush comes over the crowd. The tension in the air is palpable. Not in all the years I delivered mail was I as anxious as I am right now.

"Everyone, this is John, the new shift manager, and this evening he's going to call the numbers."

Groans. People shake their heads and the words, "He'll never get it right," ring in my ears.

Alma spins the cage. "You crank the handle then take out a ball and read the number. First game is a straight line. Second one is an X. Third one is a blackout." She pulls the basket of chocolate bars from the shelf under the dais where I placed them a few hours ago. "Winner gets to pick which kind they like. But they only get one per game, except blackout. For that they can have two."

On my first spin of the cage I forget to close the door. I hear, "Told you he'd flub it up," as bingo balls fly everywhere. My face burning, Alma and I, with a little help from a few of the more agile residents, crawl around the floor and in under ten minutes we have all of them picked up. My second spin is more successful.

"Under the B, thirty-two," I call out.

"Under the B thirty-two?"

"That's what I said."

"How in the hell can thirty-two be under B?" someone shouts at me.

I glance at the ball. "Oh, sorry. I meant under the N thirty-two."

"Put your glasses on," someone mutters.

"This is gonna be a bust," a third person says. "Even that girl Melanie does a better job."

Before anyone else can comment on my ability, I pull out another ball. "Under the O, seventy-one."

"Can't hear you, sonny," a man at the back of the room says.

I lean into the microphone – it squeals. Hands clap over ears and I pull my head back. "Under the O, seventy-one."

"What did he say?" a woman asks her friend.

"O seventy-one, Mabel," her friend shouts.

"O seventy-one. Don't have it."

"Yes you do, it's right there." Her friend daubs out the number then attempts to pick up her table-mate's cards. "Why don't you let me play your cards?"

"Because if I win, you'll take the prize."

"I would not."

"Last week you took my chocolate bar."

"Last week you didn't win, Mabel."

A man in the front row says to me, "What are you waiting for? We're going to die before we get to blackout. *Antiques Road Show* comes on at nine."

"*Antiques Road Show?*" the lady beside him says.

"From Rhode Island."

"I like those picker shows," another woman with a head of blue hair resembling fiberglass insulation, says. She's one of the women who sits in the lobby like a Walmart greeter all day. "You know, where those two guys go from house to house asking if anyone has antiques they'd like to get rid of? They had a Canadian version a few years back, but it was pulled. Don't know why: I kinda liked that Sheldon guy. The long-haired cowboy was a bit of a know-it-all. I used to own all kinds of things like that. Kids made me have a garage sale when I moved. Sixty years of possessions laid out on my driveway for all to see."

I open my mouth to call the next number but she continues to talk as if there's no one waiting on her to be quiet.

"Kids thought they were doing me a favour. I remember my son telling me I didn't need my things anymore. Said I wouldn't be spending that much time in my room anyhow, too much to do here." She rocks her head back and forth on her neck. "Called it downsizing, as if my things were meaningless. Memories all gone for a few dollars in my hand."

Her table-mate pokes her in the shoulder. "Ivy, shush now."

"That's what I like," Ivy says under her breath. "Those picker shows."

Around the room, heads nod as if remembering belongings scavenged by people who had no idea of the meals eaten and homework done around that dining room table or the laughter shared or dreams spoken of while sitting on the couch. Years of history moved into someone's basement or cabin at the lake.

Finally, the group and I get into a rhythm and they settle down to daubing and complaining and repeating each number as I call it.

"I've got it!" Ivy, the lady who likes the picker's shows, shouts. "I've got it, I've got it!"

"You've got what?" someone says. "The flu? An idea? What are you talking about?"

"Bingo, I mean, bingo!"

I take the basket of chocolate bars to her table.

"You have to make sure she got it right," I'm told by a helpful person in the front row.

I hesitate.

"On the master card, you know, the one that has all the numbers on it? You did place the discs on the master card as you called out the numbers, didn't you?"

"No one told me I was supposed to."

She shakes her head. "Guess you've never played bingo before. You have to fill your card with all the numbers you call then check her card to make sure she didn't cheat."

"You think she'd cheat?"

"Some of the people here'd do anything to win a chocolate bar."

I say to Ivy, who's not said one word in her own defense, "You didn't cheat, did you?"

She looks at me, her eyes clear and bright. "Never cheated at anything in my whole life, have no intention of starting now."

I hold the basket of chocolate bars out to her. She takes two.

Chapter five

The night shift is no one's favourite and Melanie arrives in a bad mood. I leave, thankful it's her and not me. I stomp in my front door and call for Clem. She doesn't come and my throat tightens. I know she's getting old but not now, I think.

"Clem," I say more forcefully. "Come here." Her nails click down the stairs. "There you are. You scared me." I bend down and give her a hug. "Gotta get those nails trimmed. I've been shirking my duties." She piddles on the floor. I take her to the backyard where she finishes her business. "I know it's been a long haul, but I'm trying to make things better for both of us." I hold her face in my hands then kiss her nose. "How come labs have such apologetic faces?" I give her ruff a shake and we go back inside. "Let's get something to drink, girl."

I turn on my phone and there's a message; it's from Mark. *Shit. Now what.* Clem's at her water bowl lapping it dry as I read Mark's text about wanting to visit tomorrow. I text back, talking myself through the same tired excuses: I have to work, so he'll need to make it short.

Clem lies by my feet resting her chin on the toe of my shoe. She opens her eyes and looks up. "Well, Clem, your human brother wants to talk to us." I sit on the floor and pull her head into my lap. "We need to show him we're doing fine, okay? No peeing on the floor when you see him." She gives me a kiss. "And for God's sake, don't look at him with those lonely puppy dog eyes. He'll just tell Barbie and she'll never leave us alone."

1979

"I found a crib, John. Will you come and look at it?"

"Too tired." I kick my shoes off then pad to the kitchen; Elaine follows.

"You need new socks, John. Your heels are bare."

"Yeah, well, we can't afford any."

"Now you're being silly."

"I'm not being silly, Elaine. You don't pay the bills. You don't know anything about the finances involved around here. And now you want to buy a new crib?" I yank open the fridge.

"Our baby has to have something to sleep in. If it's the money, I've been careful about spending."

"I said I'm tired, Elaine."

"The crib is second hand, only twenty-five dollars."

I slam the refrigerator door, then pop my beer. "A used crib. No new furniture for you, kiddo. You get a piece of junk because it's all your father can afford."

"John. It's good as new, I talked to them on the phone."

"How gullible are you, Elaine?"

She places her fingers on my lips. "Hush, they had a miscarriage."

In anger, I turn my head, forcing her to remove her hand. "What if you miscarry again? Hey, maybe that's what we could do to make extra money. Buy shit from the classifieds, then sell it for more."

Her eyes flash. "Now you're being ridiculous. I was less than three months when that happened." She rubs her stomach. "Why are you being like this? You've had over eight months to get used to the idea." She grabs my hand, placing it on her swollen belly. "John, she's kicking! It's going to be soon, I can feel it. Maybe she'll be born on my birthday!"

I've peeked at her stomach when she's putting on her nightgown or getting dressed for the day — at the skin pulled tight across her abdomen, at the angry stretch marks forming, at the blue veins crisscrossing her belly — and have turned away, repulsed by her changing figure. I've tried to process the fact I'm going to be a father, that we're going to be parents, but every time I try to imagine what it will be like, all I can think of is the years of debt and responsibility ahead.

Something pushes from beneath her skin and I lift my hand off her stomach. "How do you know it's a girl?"

"Just a feeling. What do you think of Barbara for a name? And her second name could be Grace, after your sister. Barbara Grace Davies."

I walk to the living room annoyed over being pressured about something that hasn't happened yet.

Elaine follows. "Anyhow, the doctor said I should have no trouble delivering, which you'd know if you came to the appointments."

"Don't you dare give me heck for not coming to the appointments. I'm working, for Christ's sake. I've a family to support."

She touches my arm. "I know you're overwhelmed. But everything's going to be great, you'll see. Won't you come and give me a hand?"

"How many times do I have to tell you no? It was your idea I get a job where I have to get up at five. Quit nagging."

"But I need help loading a crib into the car."

I pick up a pillow then slap it into the thread-bare arm of the couch, tired of arguing with her. "They're selling it, surely to God they can carry the damn thing to the car."

"John, please. Just this once…."

I step towards her, shaking my beer in her face. "That's the trouble, Elaine. It won't be just this once. It's a crib, then a stroller, a playpen, and a highchair. And that's before the kid's even in school. Then what? Clothes, cars, education? It's not just a crib and you know it."

**

Rather than coming to the house, the next morning Mark asks if I'll meet him at The Roastery. Turns out he doesn't have much free time, and this coffee shop is close to his office. I'm not much of a going out for coffee kind of guy. One has to make conversation in coffee shops, but I agree to go.

Instead of taking the short route down Eighth Street, I take the long way around. I tell myself there's less traffic, and it's a spectacular fall day to see the trees by the river that cuts our city in half, when actually, in my heart, I know I'm stalling. Still, I arrive first.

The place is packed and I turn around to leave but when a couple, probably no older than sixteen, vacate a table by the window, I nab it. Brushing the crumbs off, I save the spot with my jacket, then take my place in line. I begin to peruse the menu knowing by the time I get to the front, I still won't have a clue what to order. The menu always confuses me. Grande, Venti, Trenta. Espresso, Latte, Macchiato, how the hell am I supposed to pick one? Elaine was the one who liked going out for coffee. She liked the crowds, the constant hum of conversation, the smell of roasting coffee. It excited her to be with people socializing, laughing, and working on their laptops. I liked being home, sitting alone with my jazz and a beer. I order a black coffee and sit at my table. Ten minutes later Mark saunters in. Like Barbie, he's tall and good looking, only with brown eyes. Elaine used to tell me Mark's temperament is much like mine, but I've never been able to see that.

"Sorry I'm late, Dad. Got a last-minute phone call. Can I get you a refill?"

I clamp my hand over my cup. "Nope, time for just the one."

"You're looking good," he says when he returns with his own black coffee.

"You too."

He pulls his hands through his hair. "Tired. Juggling a job and two kids. Raising a family isn't easy. You know how it goes."

"Was there something you wanted to …."

His phone dings and he raises his hand to me. "Have to get this." He finishes typing and waves the electronic device in my face. "Sometimes these things are a nuisance." He slides it back into his pocket. "Nothing in particular, Dad. Just thought I'd touch base with you. Barbie said you got yourself a job."

"I did."

He nods, swallowing a gulp of his drink. "You're enjoying it?"

"Sure."

"And Clem, she's ok?"

"Misses me, but I still walk her every day. How's your job? I heard your company got the new high-rise downtown. Are you drawing up the blueprints?"

"Me and some other architects. Job's too big for one person."

"That's great, Mark," I say, trying to be supportive. "Proud of you. It's good your salary is enough so Deanna can stay home with the kids."

"Economy sucks but we're making ends meet."

"You know you can come to me if…"

"Damn it." He pulls out his phone again. "Sorry, Dad. I gotta run. Can we do this another time?"

He stands and holds out his hand.

"For sure, Mark. Another time," I say as he gathers his coat and briefcase.

I arrive at work half an hour early and sit in the parking lot, taking my frustration for not having a better relationship with my son out on the steering wheel.

Chapter six

Elaine did most of the errands. I wouldn't get home until mid-afternoon, then I'd shovel snow or cut the lawn, do the recycling and take out the garbage; look after the never-ending chores Elaine expected of me around the house.

Promising Clem I won't be long, I leave to get groceries. I circle the parking-lot three times before I'm able to squeeze my fourteen-year old Honda into an empty space on the other side of the mall, opposite the Safeway. I hurry towards the nearest doors, feeling the pressure of having to rush home to the dog.

I'm a big man and it takes a lot to knock me off my feet, but the moment I enter the mall, I'm pushed back by a wave of people, the majority of them old, all heading in the same direction I want to go.

"The flyer said 'buy two loaves, get the third one free,'" a man says as he and a woman hobble past, each on a walker.

"I know Myrtle will get there first, she doesn't have a husband to slow her down," another lady says to the man lagging behind her. "Probably take all the good bananas and leave me the spotted ones."

I step between two of the slower moving groups and am immediately sucked into the procession.

"Hurry up, Abe. They never have enough asparagus spears when they're on sale," a woman in front of me says. The man I assume is Abe, rolls up behind me, increasing the speed of his scooter and bumps my leg as he passes.

As I'm pulled along in this stream of human decay, shoppers begin to veer off towards rest stops serving juice and cookies set up on either side of the entrance to the Safeway.

Suddenly I realize what this is; senior's day, the last Tuesday of the month. All groceries are ten percent off if you're sixty or older. Deciding I can do without my coffee creamer for another day, I push my way out of this convoy, sidestepping walkers, oxygen tanks and wheelchairs.

A man, who was once as tall as me, stops at one of these social gatherings to help himself to a cookie. Remembering all the times my mother told me not to slouch or my back would freeze that way, I pull my shoulders straight then plaster myself against the wall, waiting for a break in the traffic so I can turn and go against the current. A reedy voice calling my name cuts through the din of the mob.

"Mister Davies, oh, Mister Davies."

Flapping hands reach over the crowd as three of the ladies from The Wheaton begin weaving between shoppers. I duck my head and pretend I don't see them, but soon they've circled me, hemming me in. I smell baby powder and mothballs.

"Mister Davies, so good to see you. What are you doing here?"

I use the excuse of having to leave to grocery shop. "Picking up a few groceries."

They don't take the hint. "Isn't that sweet," Mrs. Chambers says, "a man doing the grocery shopping."

Mrs. Hopkins, wearing a dress that shows too much cleavage, nods at the wedding ring on my hand. "My Bart would never go for the groceries. Your wife is a lucky woman," she titters.

"Well," I say as I step forward, hoping they'll part so I can leave without having to squeeze between their sagging breasts. "Better get to the Safeway before everything's picked over."

Mrs. Flannigan, still retaining a touch of her youth, and the only one of the three wearing slacks, touches my shoulder. "We try to get to the mall at least once a week. Go for coffee, buy a scarf." She says in a confidential tone, "You wouldn't happen to know where we could buy a pair of socks, would you Mr. Davies?" Her breath smells of medicine.

I breathe as shallowly as I can. "Perhaps Mark's Work Wear-house?"

"Of course," she says. "So nice to have a good-looking man around to give advice."

"Will we be seeing you later today?" Mrs. Hopkins says.

I keep my eyes averted as she dabs at her wrinkled chest with a tissue. "I have the day off."

Groups of people are streaming around us but the women don't seem to notice. "Oh dear. That's too bad." She bats her eyes.

"Sorry, in a rush," I say. "Like to be home with my dog on my day off." Again, I step forward and try to get away.

They tighten their circle. "Isn't that sweet," they croon.

With a serious face, Mrs. Flannigan says, "It's a good thing we saw you here," she looks at her friends, who both nod at her to continue. "We were hoping you could help us." She places her pale fingers on my forearm and leans into me. "Do you know what Arthur McIntyre did today? He took a jig-saw puzzle piece from the thousand-piece puzzle I've been working on and pounded it in with his fist. Just stuck it in where it obviously didn't belong and hit it until he made it fit, frayed the edges completely. Put a piece of sky in the water. Totally different colour of blue."

I stare at her for a moment wondering what the heck this has to do with me, before realizing the reason she's telling me is so I'll do something about it. "I'll see what I can do."

She beams. "We certainly appreciate you helping us. He doesn't listen to us at all. But if a man like you told him, I'm sure he'd pay attention."

"We never have him for happy hour anymore," Mrs. Chambers says as she takes her purse off her shoulder then reaches inside her sweater and adjusts a bra strap. "He would drink four glasses of wine before anyone had finished their first glass."

"You have happy hours?"

"Close to a dozen of us in the group now. He joined but never took his turn. Always said he wasn't feeling good, or had an appointment, or forgot to buy wine. We had no choice but to not invite him anymore." She hikes her purse back onto her rounded shoulder.

"He's just downright mean," Mrs. Hopkins says. She looks up at me and again bats her wrinkled lids. "Not like you at all, Mr. Davies. And you're welcome to come to our happy hour any time you please."

After five more minutes of fluttering hands, clothing adjustments, and batting eyes, the three of them leave, turning to giggle as they walk away, "Bye-bye, Mr. Davies. See you at bingo." As people smile at this exchange, I scurry to the Safeway, pretending it wasn't me they were talking to. Since I made it this far I may as well buy my meagre list of groceries.

I lug the grocery bags to my front door where Janet, my youngest, is waiting for me on the step. She has her red hair tied back in a ponytail, the same way Elaine wore hers.

"Hey, Dad," she holds a casserole dish out to me. "Barb sent me over with this."

She leans in to kiss my cheek. I turn away and begin to fumble with my keys.

"Three visits from three children in less than a month," I say.

"Don't be a smart aleck. How are you doing? I see you aren't starving."

"I'm not totally helpless like your sister seems to think." I stop myself before anything else inappropriate pops out. "What brings you here? Thought you taught a class this afternoon. Isn't it Contagious Disease Statistics on Tuesdays?"

I open the door. Clem greets us with jumps and kisses and, in lieu of me, Janet bends down and kisses the dog's nose.

"Wow. I'm impressed. I do teach that class today, but I still had time to drop by and see my dad."

I lead the way to the kitchen, placing the bags on the counter. "You mean, you still had time to drop by so you could tell Barbie how I am." I close my eyes. *Be nice, John*, I tell myself. I put the crackers, which were the last box on the shelf that I managed to nab just ahead of an old man, into the cupboard.

Janet keeps talking as if I'm not being an ass. "We're planning a birthday party for Barb. We're hoping you're available on Friday."

My back stiffens.

"It's for Barb mostly. It is her birthday too, not just Mom's."

"Think I'll pass."

"You can't pass, Dad. You already missed last year's. We can't have it without you forever."

I pull the mayonnaise out of a bag and notice I bought diet instead of regular. Elaine would never buy diet anything, said *why would she pay good money for something that substituted water for ingredients?*

"Please come. It'll make Barb happy and make me look good."

I look at my youngest, who's the spitting image of her mother, and suddenly I miss Elaine so much, I don't know how I can go on. *God damn it*, I think, *why did you have to die? Why did you have to leave me to do all this alone? It's not me the kids want, it's you, for Christ sake.* If they're trying to fill the void in their lives with me, they're in for a fucking big disappointment.

"I'll check my work schedule and let you know," I say, keeping my eyes averted.

She leaves me alone in the kitchen. "I'll text you tomorrow to see if you're available. We'll pick you up at six," she calls before closing the door behind her.

After she's gone, I sit on the couch nursing a beer, finally tossing the empty across the room where it dents a hole in the drywall.

Janet and her latest boyfriend, a doctor named Sean something or other, picked me up in his brand-new BMW to take me to Barb's thirty-sixth and Elaine's sixtieth birthday party at Joe's Pub and Steakhouse. Janet got out and moved the seat up so I could climb in the back. Then I sat, wondering at the practicality of this car that probably cost two year's salary at the post-office, as my knees bumped into the back of her seat all the way there.

The restaurant is situated in one of the newer communities that sprang up during the last couple of years of Elaine's life, in what used to be farmland on the edge of town. The new subdivision now sits surrounded by condos and pocket parks, strip malls, and houses crowded onto lots so narrow, they're all built straight up with not a bungalow in sight. I've taken Clem walking in a few of these new communities to see if it's an area I might consider downsizing to after Clem is gone, and have noticed many of the people living here are immigrants. Elaine said even though she liked the city better when it was smaller, growth was progress and there was nothing she could do about it. Besides, she enjoyed meeting people from other countries. She would recipe swap with co-workers at the library and more than one night a week she would serve food so foreign to me, I'd have to sneak out to A&W after supper to get enough to eat.

The lot is jammed with cars and Sean parks far from the main entrance in order to prevent having his doors dinged by careless drivers. We're the last to arrive and are led to tables pushed together to make room for twelve people. I squeeze into a chair at the far end.

From seven seats away, Barb leans forward and peers at me. "This is nice, isn't it, Dad?"

I scan the booths with dim lighting lining the walls. I see the bar in the middle of the room, surrounded by bar-flies barely old enough to drink and the rest of the floor around the bar, squeezed with as many tables as minimal elbow room will allow. I hear music I abhor, and watch as waitresses in short skirts and high-heels struggle to bend forward with their orders. "Sure," I say, surprised that Barb doesn't know me better than this. "Good choice, Barb." Near the entrance a heavy door leads to a separate lounge that I long to be sitting in.

"Thought you'd like to eat out. Not that you're not getting out lately, what with your new job."

I smile, and for the sake of everyone around us, pretend my daughter and I have a close relationship. "The chef at work is excellent and you know how I like to eat."

"They have really good steak at this place. Cook it to your specifications. Did you and Mom ever come here?"

By this time, everyone's eyes are on me as our conversation volleys back and forth making it impossible for other people to talk. "She liked home-cooked meals," I say. "Said there was too much cholesterol and salt in restaurant food."

I look at the faces glued to mine and realize I've insulted my kids' plans. Without Elaine to nudge me, I seem to plough through one faux pas after the other. Barb pulls her head back and leaves me in peace.

Elaine's parents are here and her dad, a man named Frank Brindle, whom I've never got along with after he told me I wasn't man enough to marry his one and only daughter, and if she wasn't pregnant, there's no way in hell he'd allow this charade to take place, sits in a wheelchair at the other end of the table. Frank's lips are drooping and he has a tic under one eye. His hands are in his lap, the fingers bent into claws, and he stares, not recognizing anyone around him. I heard he had a stroke the month after Elaine died, but I didn't contact my mother-in-law to find out how he was doing or offer to help. Patricia gives me a grim little smile.

My grandchildren, Rose, age five and who belongs to Mark and Deanna, and Colin and Julie, Barb's and Rob's kids, ages thirteen and eight, sit together playing a raucous game of rock, paper, scissors. Mark and Deanna's new addition, a baby girl named Amanda, just six months old and who I've only seen twice, is snuggled in her mother's arms.

"Would you like to hold her?" Deanna asks me.

I cross my arms over my stomach. "Oh, I don't know, Dee, it's been a while. Don't know if I remember how."

"It's like riding a bike," she says. "You never forget."

"Maybe later."

Elaine would have already gone and asked if she could hold the baby and probably held her for the entire meal, a proud grandma.

The waitress arrives. "What can I get everyone to drink?"

"I'll have a Shirley Temple," Julie shouts.

"Me too," says Rose.

"Inside voices," Barb says.

If Barb, Mark and Janet had been as outspoken to a waitress as my grandchildren are being, they'd not be brought to a restaurant again for a long time, even though eating out was something we could afford only two or three times a year. We order our drinks and food and I lean back, not contributing to the conversation.

I don't know how anyone can hear, the noise is so relentless. In the past year, continual noise of any kind has begun to bother me. I can't have a bedroom fan anymore, preferring to sweat out my nights rather than have to listen to the whirring, and the defroster in the car drives me round the bend. Our food arrives and the talking stops for a few moments.

Barb leans forward. "What did you order, Dad?"

"Fish."

Suddenly, Frank, who I assumed couldn't understand what was being said let alone speak says, "Who orders fish in a steakhouse? Only a fairy'd do something like that."

"Frank, hush," Patricia says.

At the sound of his wife's voice, Frank goes quiet. But those few words were enough to silence everyone at the table.

Rose climbs out of her chair and squeezes onto my lap. She puts her arms around my neck and whispers in my ear. "Don't worry about what Great-Grandpa Frank said, Grandpa. I love fairies."

I peel Rose's arms away and pat her on the head as I place her back on the floor. At the end of the meal a cake is brought out and the waiters and waitresses, people we don't know from Adam, gather round and sing. Rose, someone who barely remembers her grandmother, tacks on Grandma's name at the end of the line, *happy birthday dear Barbie*.

No one seems to mind when I excuse myself.

The noise of the restaurant becomes muffled the moment the heavy door of the lounge closes behind me. I stand in the entrance and listen to Oscar Peterson playing *Canadian Sunset* out of hidden speakers. I spot an empty booth, but instead, settle at the bar and order a beer. A tall blond woman slides onto the stool beside me and the smell of strawberries wafts my way. She orders tequila with lime and salt, then glances at me.

"Hey," she says.

"Hello." Not knowing what to say next, I keep my eyes on my beer and let my mind wander.

1979

Having been up since one in the morning, and figuring we both would benefit with more sleep, I went home immediately after Elaine had the baby, not stopping at the nursery to hold or even look at this supposed bundle of joy. Five hours later I'm back, my eyes heavy and nerves raw. I ride the elevator up with two other men clutching flowers, and wonder if I should have thought to bring a bouquet as well.

The moment I disembark I'm confronted by corridors leading in all directions and begin to make twists and turns, becoming so disorientated I just about step back on the elevator, which I've now passed three times, and call it a day. I have no choice but to stop at a nursing station. Without lifting her head from a chart she's staring at, a nurse in a pink smock points the way.

Three other women share Elaine's room and each of them smiles as I pass. I find Elaine asleep in the last bed. My eyes slide down to her still protruding belly and I imagine the stretch marks and scars hidden under the gown. I remember before Elaine became pregnant, how I loved the look of her body, how it excited me and I wonder if I'll ever want to touch her again. The room is hot, and smells I can't identify linger in the heavy air. A machine behind Elaine's head beeps and a clamp is attached to her finger-tip.

When they wheeled Elaine away, because I had declined to take the course that would enable me to be in the delivery room with her, I sat in the waiting room with three other men who must not have taken the course either. Gradually, over a period of five hours, the room emptied as the doctor announced the birth of each of their babies. Every time the new father was told, he jumped up and shook all of our hands. When the doctor finally arrived and told me I had a daughter, with no one left to congratulate me, it felt sur-real. Until now. A see-through bassinet on wheels is parked beside Elaine's bed. A baby lies inside, swathed in a blanket so tight, all I can see is a tiny pinched face.

Elaine opens her eyes. "John, you're here," she grasps my hand. Her fingers are cool to the touch, the skin pale. "We have a daugh-ter. The best birthday present I could ask for."

The baby stirs and my legs go weak. I pull my hand from hers.

"Would you like to hold her?" Elaine asks.

"I don't know how," I whisper. The women in the other beds are watching and I'm acutely aware of my youth and my inexperience.

"Just cradle her in your arms. She won't break."

I sit on the edge of the bed, my back stiff and my arms extended as I allow Elaine to place my daughter in my arms.

"Barbara Grace Davies," Elaine says. "I'd like you to meet your father."

I hold the bundle against me; her small body is hot. I pull the blanket from her face and she opens her eyes, they're blue, like Elaine's. Her fingers curl and uncurl against her cheek and the sweet smell wafting from her obliterates any bad smell the hospital has to offer.

"She looks just like you," Elaine says. "I'm sure her blue eyes will turn brown in no time."

I rub my calloused finger across her cheek, it's soft as velvet.

"The doctor said she's strong and healthy. I should be home in fewer than four days."

"Four days?" I feel my panic rise. "Shouldn't you stay longer? I mean, what if something happens? What if you need help?"

Elaine laughs and my face heats up.

"It will be fine, John, you'll see. I'll show you how to change a diaper and how to bathe her. It's not difficult. We can't stay here till she's grown."

I give my daughter to Elaine and I don't come back until it's time to take them home.

***

"Looks like you and I are here alone," the blonde on the bar stool beside me says.

I turn to face her. She's youngish, long legs, more than good looking. "I'm sure someone will come and find me eventually," I say. "Can't hide forever." I stick my left hand, which still bears my wedding ring, under the bar.

"That's imaginative. A man hiding out in a bar."

The bartender solemnly places a shot of tequila, a salt shaker and a slice of lime in front of her.

"My daughter drove, and she's not ready to leave, so…." I stop when I realize how lame I sound.

She slides the salt shaker to the left. "You can't leave." The tequila gets moved to the middle. "You're trapped." The lime goes on the far right. "That worked out well."

I look into her eyes. They're brown with amber flecks. "Worked out well?"

"Drinking and not driving. I'm doing the same thing."

"Drinking and not driving, or hiding?" I can't believe this gorgeous woman is flirting with me.

"Both."

"Who are you hiding from?" I look at the door expecting a bruiser to come barrelling through any moment.

"Nosey cousins with two and a half kids wanting to know my marriage prospects," she salts her hand. "Cheek-kissing aunts," she licks it off. "Ogling pubescent nephews," she downs the shot of tequila. "And ancient uncles who get their giggles slapping my bottom," she sucks the lime. "Family reunions, I hate them," she says through a grimace.

"I don't think I've seen that done for thirty years." I nod at the trio of used drink accoutrements lying on the bar.

"Been told I'm an old soul. Reason I like older men," she looks me in the face, and cocks her head. "Reason they like me."

I pull my hand through hair that I'm sure was thick just this morning and find a bald spot. Dinah Washington begins to sing, *You're Nobody Till Someone Loves You*, and we both listen to the song's end.

"Is that the truth? You're hiding from your family reunion?" I ask searching for anything to say.

"Sad excuse for a Friday night, isn't it?"

"Won't you get in trouble for leaving?"

"No one will notice."

"I doubt that," I say.

She lifts her eyes to mine. "I knew a good-looking man sitting alone in a bar had to be sweet. Most women come to a bar looking for the bad boy so by the time they're all taken there's only the sweet ones left. Or the pervs. And you don't look like a pervert to me."

The bartender smiles in my direction and I know I'm out of my league. Even in my youth, women like this could spot my innocence. Though, being married at such a young age, I didn't have many years to develop any kind of style. "Can I buy you another?"

"Don't see the point of being in a bar without a drink in front of me."

The bartender brings me a beer and her another shot.

"What brings you to this yuppie, I'm-a-grown-up-now, kind of joint?" she asks as she again aligns her drink order.

"My daughter's and my wife's birthday."

"Your wife's?"

I stammer, "Oh, uh, well, she died a year and a half ago. My daughter and her share the same birthday. The family thought it would be a good idea to celebrate both birthdays here tonight."

"That's cool," she sucks the lime and presses it into the empty tequila glass.

"It's ok."

She looks at me hard. "Your wife was a lucky woman." The scent of lime mixes with the strawberry aroma that floats in the air around her and I breathe deep. "A year and a half and you're grieving like it just happened." She nods at my hand. "Still wear your wedding ring. You must have loved her a lot. I mean, most men have remarried before a year is up."

I shake my head. "No," I say.

"I'd give anything to have someone love me that much. Two husbands and I still haven't got it right. Yup, she was one of the lucky ones."

"Don't know if she considered herself lucky."

"No?"

"I guess I could have told her more often I needed her."

"So, your grief has something to do with what, guilt?"

"What are you, the bar psychiatrist?"

"Just a woman who's been propositioned by too many married men."

I shrug.

"I notice you haven't propositioned me yet," she jiggles her leg, red toenail polish glints in the lights.

The restaurant noise swells as the door opens. I lean back and watch Mark enter. He scans the room then locks eyes with me before I have a chance to pull my head out of sight. "I think I've been found," I say.

She glances behind her. "Too bad, just when we were getting to the good part."

"Perhaps it's time for me to leave," I say.

"It's ok, you know."

"It's ok?"

"To be seen with me," she slides her fingers down my thigh. "You're not cheating on your wife." She slips off the stool and her heels click towards the exit.

Mark perches on the barstool she vacated. "Sorry about Rose," he says over his shoulder as he watches the first woman that's flirted with me since Elaine died, leave the bar.

"Rose?" I touch my leg, still feeling the heat of her hand.

"She made you uncomfortable."

"Just needed some space for a while. Crowds get on my nerves lately. Absolutely nothing to do with Rose."

He orders a beer. "Someone you know?"

"What?"

"C'mon, Dad. That beautiful woman that you and every man in

here watched walk out of the bar."

I feel myself blush. "Just shooting the breeze with the person on the stool beside me."

"Ah. Like me."

I finish my beer and carefully place the bottle down on the bar. "I'd better get back, Janet must be waiting on me."

"Jan's gone, Dad, and so has everyone else. Deanna drove the kids home. I told her you and I could catch a cab. No pressing meetings until tomorrow morning." He picks up his beer. "Do you have time to shoot the breeze with your son?"

Chapter seven

"You got a ton of messages," Melanie says the moment I enter the lobby. She licks her thumb and begins leafing through a handful of notes. "Fiona Brighton, Marigold Blossom," she sniffs, "Marigold Blossom. What kind of a name is that? Phoney as a two-dollar bill."

I tune her out as I hang my jacket on the coat rack by the door. It's a coat Elaine bought me the first year she went back to work. Black leather with a brown collar. Said it made my brown eyes pop.

Melanie continues flipping through more messages. "Ester Flannigan, Irma Chambers. Quite the fan club, Davies." Her voice is full of sarcasm. "These three," she waves the dog-eared notes, "probably want to invite you to one of their happy hours. But Brighton, she must actually need something because she wouldn't share her bottle with anyone. What the hell are you doing, flirting with them? Gotta watch that around here, they'll take advantage of us all if you start bending over backwards for them. And I for one don't have the time for that."

I want to smack her.

"These little old ladies, they're plain goofy over any man they think is half-way good-looking." She tries to hand me the mess of papers but I keep my hands in my pockets. She scatters them on the desk. "Brighton said she needed you as soon as you arrived. I gotta be outta here in ten so don't dawdle."

I knock on Mrs. Brighton's door. It opens a crack at my touch. "Mrs. Brighton, you wanted something?" I call from the threshold.

She doesn't answer so I step in further. "Mrs. Brighton, are you here?"

It's a short walk to the living room where she's standing beside her bed with her back to me. She picks up a glass of amber liquid and drinks it dry, then slips a wig over hair that looks like it hasn't been washed in a while. I tip-toe back to the door and call again.

She steps around the corner. "Mr. Davies. Sorry, I was in the bathroom."

I try not to focus on her hair. "You need something?"

"Another light bulb. Can't seem to reach them myself. Sense of balance seems to be compromised."

"Sure, I could do that, though you could have asked Melanie."

She waves her hand. "Won't have that woman, if you can call her that, in my room."

"Oh?"

"Asks too many questions. Snoopy. Caught her with my watch in her hand once. Said she found it on the floor. I know it was on the table; I'd only just put it there."

"Did you report her?"

"No one would have believed me."

I know this is probably true, but I don't voice my opinion.

"There you go being diplomatic again. Have to watch that. Been told by the best that holding things inside isn't healthy." She points behind us, "Bulb in front of the door." She grabs the chair and as she does, I notice her wig shift a little on her head. She quickly adjusts it but sees me watching. "Bad hair day," she says. "Got used to wearing them when I was working. Vanity runs deep."

I slide the chair under the light and climb up, pressing my palms against the narrow walls for balance, then unscrew the bulb as she hands me the new one.

"Practiced law for forty years," she says, her head craned back watching me. "I was what they called me in the later years of my practice, an innovator. Can you imagine that? An innovator. Not what they called back in the day when I was fighting for women's rights. Any man who pushed his way through like I did would have been called a go-getter, a man with vision. Me, I was a loudmouthed bitch. Took me twice as long to gain their respect, just because I don't have a penis."

I step onto the floor and look her in the eye. She gives me a smile and I can see how she would have scared men back in the day. Not only was she strong, smart, and outspoken, but she would have been very handsome. Still would be but for the ravages of alcohol etched on her face.

She leads the way to her tiny kitchen. "Because they discounted me, I was able to slip past without them noticing. Won some big cases, got myself promoted, and before they knew what hit them, I'd furthered my career. Even in school I knew I had to learn the law better than the men. No one would have hired me just because I have breasts."

She presses a coffee cup towards me. When I don't take it, she says, "Suit yourself," and pulls the cup back. "I'm sure that lazy girl, Melanie, told you to hurry."

I take the cup and put it to my lips; the coffee's hot and strong.

"Not that I'm a man hater, far from it. I simply wanted the same respect the men in my profession, or any profession dominated by men, seemed to get only for the fact they had that Y chromosome."

I blow on my coffee.

"You've never told me what you did before this," she says.

"I was a letter-carrier." Her outline flickers through the cloud of steam I'm blowing from my cup. "Thirty-five years."

"Ah. Another breakthrough for women. I'm sure you saw a lot of harassment in your day."

"I did."

"And I'm sure you weren't one of the people doing the harassing."

I don't tell her I didn't do much to stop it either. Not because I thought what was happening was right, but because I didn't want to get involved.

"You have kids, John? Is it ok if I call you John?"

"Sure. Yes. Three. I have three kids. Two daughters and a son." Someone's toilet flushes in the apartment above.

"Do they visit or are they as obnoxious as mine?" She reaches behind her and grabs a bottle, then pours some bourbon into her cup. She holds the bottle out to me. I shake my head. She takes a deep drink.

"They have lives of their own," I say. "Jobs, kids, spouses, but they try. My youngest is still at university. Going for her Ph.D. in epidemiology." I hear Ivy in the hall calling to someone about coming over for coffee.

"Another woman with brains," she lifts her cup to me. "I wish her luck."

I toss back a large gulp of the scalding liquid, burning the roof of my mouth and grimace, plastering my tongue over the burnt spot.

"You give birth to them, feed them, clothe them, educate them, then they abandon you." She shrugs her shoulders. "But that's the life of a parent," she takes a swill of her coffee then seems to change the subject. "I hope my death is quick," she says, her gaze on the floor. "Don't want a long drawn out affair in the hospital where your kids sit by your side waiting for your demise even though you know they wish they were someplace else." She pauses. "Perhaps that's what Ed was thinking when he made the decision he did."

"What decision was that?" I ask.

"Ed killed himself," she says. "No one told you?"

"No one said anything to me."

"Took an overdose of his heart medication. His daughter told me. Knew her dad and I were acquaintances, I suppose." She swirls the last of the liquid in the bottom of her cup. "Not something I'd ever consider," she says, finishing the drink. "Life may be a bitch, but we're stuck with it until it's over."

"Well, Mrs. Brighton."

"Fiona, please."

"Fiona. Sorry, need to leave. Melanie's in a hurry."

"Ha, I knew it. Too busy thinking about going to bed with that boyfriend of hers to care about anyone living here."

"She's young."

"Youth isn't an excuse for ignorance. And for some people, as I fear is the case with Melanie, it's something she'll never grow out of." She takes my cup from me, "but if you have to leave, then you have to leave. Next time, maybe you can stay longer."

When I get to the end of the hall I look back; she's pouring herself another cup of bourbon. I close the door. *It's her life, she can do what she wants.*

The morning passes quickly with answering the phone, sending visitors to the right rooms, settling a spat over a double booking of the community room, and making sure Mrs. Crawford doesn't monopolize the elevator. The first time I saw her ride down without getting off, then ride back up, I was on my own. When she repeated this behaviour, I approached the elevator and asked if she needed help, but she just pushed the button and closed the doors in my face. Marigold says she's looking for her husband who died ten years ago. The family has her name on a list for a nursing home, but the wait could be a few more months. Most of the people here are sympathetic, but some, I've heard, call her Crazy Crawford behind her back.

A woman on a scooter has exited the elevator and is riding between residents, shouting, "Stay back," and, "Look out," and, "Clear the way." She brakes at the desk. The scooter is bright pink with flecks of gold embedded in the paint making it shimmer as she speeds through the lobby. She's painted up as well, with pink lips, gold glitter above her eyes, and eyebrows so perfect, they look like tattoos. I've been told she's in her nineties but the taut skin around her eyes and mouth make me think she's had work done.

"You must be John Davies, the bloke all the ladies are talking about. I see why. Left on a holiday to Thailand the day you started here. You know Thailand?"

"I don't."

"Beautiful place. Small people. Darlene Carillion. Won't shake your hand. Have a fainting problem. Actually, the medical term is syncope, pronounced, sing-ko-pee." Her shiny lips move in an exaggerated motion. "You know what causes that, don't you?"

"I don't think…."

"Lack of oxygen to the brain. You ever fainted?"

I shake my head.

"You'll know when you're about to. Spots in front of your eyes and a kind of sinking feeling. Doctors don't know why I faint when someone touches me. Been doing it…."

The landline rings. I make a note about taking someone's lunch to them.

"For years," she says when I hang up.

"Pardon me?"

"For years. Been doing it for years. Had one doctor tell me I'm being fashionably frail. Fashionably frail, my ass! What era do they think I'm from?"

"Excuse me, Mrs. Carillion, I have to…."

"It's about time they hired someone with a half decent person-ality. That girl Melanie is a waste of space, if you ask me, and all the cook is good for is cooking. Although I guess you don't need to have a pleasant personality to make a decent meal. But the people who work with the residents, they should at least be able to carry on some semblance of a conversation. Asked Melanie once how her day was going and she stared at me as if I was speaking in tongues. Girl's as bright as a used floor mop. Going out for lunch today. See you later."

As I watch her speed past the windows, the phone rings again. Someone's toilet is plugged.

Five empty boxes have been piled behind the reception desk when I return to the lobby from taking Mrs. Hawkins her lunch plate. She didn't see the grim reaper today and she engaged me in a reasonable conversation about being married. She claimed it was tolerance that kept her and her husband together as he was an ornery cuss. I ar-gued that there must have been some kind of love or she would have left him years before he died. When I left she was rummaging around the top shelf of her closet, searching for a picture of him.

I'm stacking the boxes out of the way as Marigold comes in the front door with another box in her hands.

"John, just the person I'm looking for. I left you a note but Melanie probably didn't give it to you."

I don't argue.

"We're picking the rest of the vegetables today," she sets the box down with the others. "Would you like to join us?"

"No thanks."

"You sure? Or maybe your kids would like to pick some tomatoes or corn?"

"They're pretty busy, probably don't have time. And I should get home to my dog."

She points to the empty boxes. "Can you help me carry these outside before you go?"

I haven't been to the garden since Alma toured me around the building a few weeks ago. Tomato plants are covered in fruit, and corn stalks are six feet tall. Cucumbers of all shapes and sizes lie under prickly leaves, and the back fence has sweet peas of all colours climbing over the top. The air is honeyed with their scent.

Marigold and I set the boxes down and even though I said I had to get home, I'm drawn to the plot of land. I pop a cherry tomato in my mouth and the taste takes me back to Elaine's crop. The whole month of September she'd make batches of relish, pickles and tomato sauce for pasta. Her garden was as wide as our backyard and took up the last ten feet, large enough to plant every vegetable she desired. She first began in order to have fresh vegetables for pureeing baby food for Barbie. Then she discovered she loved digging in the soil, so every year, right to the year before she got sick, she planted vegetables. Said it renewed her soul. I was never interested in helping, but I sure scoffed down everything she made. I watch the seniors pulling tomatoes off the vines and breaking cobs of corn from the stalks, and for a moment, wish I'd been more attentive to Elaine's hobby, wish I'd not felt what she did was less important than what I was doing. I was always good at that; making her feel everything I did was necessary and what she did was only because she wanted to.

I lift my face to the sun.

1980

"We can't afford to buy a house," I say.

Elaine has stopped at the top of the basement stairs, her arms wrapped around a basket of freshly laundered clothes. I reach forward and pull a wisp of red hair from her mouth then take the basket. Our hands touch and the heat of her body makes my skin prickle.

"Yes, we can," she says. "If we're careful about what we spend our money on. I've found a two-story and they're asking sixty-nine." She opens the fridge and stirs something, then dips her finger in and has a taste. "But that's what you have to spend to get a larger house in a new neighbourhood," she says as she licks her lips. "There are kids Barbie's age, and a school at the end of the block."

"Where do you want this?" I hold out the basket.

"On the couch," she races ahead to clear the mess away.

I toss the laundry onto the sofa, then go to get a beer. "I don't want to move," I call from the kitchen. "Maybe in a few years, but not right now."

I hear the snap of a diaper being folded. "I think now is just the right time; while we're still young enough to pay it off before we're in our fifties, and before our family gets any bigger."

I stop in the kitchen doorway. "What did you say?"

"I want at least two, maybe even three kids," she smooths a pair of sleepers than folds them and puts them onto the stack. "And I want a house big enough for all of us."

"But that's not what I want," I say.

She turns towards me. Her engorged breasts swing under her thin blouse. "Why is everything we do based on what you want?"

I touch her arm. "Don't get mad. Anyhow, you and I both know you were lucky to get pregnant with Barbie. If you don't get pregnant and we end up with only one kid, there'd be just the three of us rattling around in a big house."

"What are you saying?" she's stopped folding laundry and is standing with her arms crossed tightly across her belly. Her waistline has flattened close to what it was before she was pregnant, just a tiny bulge left.

"I'm saying," I emphasize, "I do not want to buy a house." I take a swig of beer, then look over my shoulder towards the kitchen. "What's for supper?"

"What were you planning for our lives then?"

"I don't want to buy a house, Elaine."

"I asked you a question, John."

"We'll be in debt for twenty years."

"If not kids and a house, what did you have in mind when we married?"

"I don't know," I yell. "Just not all this mess." I wave around the living room of our tiny rented house now cluttered with baby gear. "It isn't what I'd planned."

The music next door begins to thump, something we've had to put up with since the new renters moved in.

Elaine carefully chooses her words. "I'm sorry you're disappointed in how our marriage is going and I'm sorry for all this *mess* as you call it. I do my best to keep it tidy and out of your way. I certainly don't want to impose on you, the working man." She turns her back to me. From this angle, I can't tell she's even had a baby.

"Don't you think one kid is enough?" I say as I reach for her hand. She pulls away. "You already work hard looking after Barbie. We need our own lives too."

"That's a selfish way to live," she says under her breath.

"You asked. If you don't want to know, then don't ask."

"I was pregnant when we were married and you said you were happy. Was that a lie?"

"I married you, didn't I?"

She faces me and I notice a wet spot on her chest. "Out of duty," she says.

"I did not marry you out of duty."

"The thing is," she pulls her hair back and ties it into a ponytail, then looks directly in my face. "I'd have married you whether I was pregnant or not."

I pause. This is something I've always known, felt safe in knowing. "I said I didn't marry you out of duty. What more can I say?"

"So, after I lost the baby, were you happy or disappointed you married me?"

"Don't ask stupid questions."

"Answer me."

"This conversation is getting blown out of proportion. I'm glad I married you, I'm sad you miscarried and I'm happy we have a daughter. Satisfied? What I don't want to do is get into debt for the next twenty years." I return to the kitchen and place my empty beer bottle under the sink then slam the cupboard door. "God, five years and you can't let a subject drop. I came home in a good mood and you have to turn it into this."

"You're right," she says. "It's too late to be arguing about that now."

When I wander back into the living room, she's picked Barbie up off the blanket and is sitting in the rocking chair, her blouse open, nursing her. I move the laundry basket to the floor then stretch out on the couch and close my eyes.

All is quiet for a few minutes until Elaine says, "Do you agree this house is too small for the three of us?"

I keep my eyes closed. "God damn it, Elaine. Quit it."

She adjusts Barbie to the other side. "You're the one always complaining we have too much stuff. You're the one always saying there's just not enough room anymore."

"Ok, so the house could be bigger." I open one eye. "We could rent a larger house."

"No, it's time to move forward with our lives, not stay kids forever. Buying a house is the grown-up thing to do. And, if we buy a new house, we could put all this stuff in the family room," she says. "And a bigger garden would be great. And lawn, and a swing set. Maybe even a sandbox."

"I don't have time to do yard work."

"We both agree we could use more space and the prices are only going to get higher. You know this is the right time to buy, you just don't want to admit I'm right, you want me to make the decision for you." She strokes the silky smoothness of Barbie's hair. "If you want me to decide, then fine, I'll decide for both of us. I've phoned the real estate company and they're sending a man over to take us to see the house. He'll be here in ten minutes."

She passes me Barbie then goes upstairs to pack a diaper bag. I'm not surprised she took it on herself to hire an agent. She knew darn well if left up to me, we would grow old and die in this house. I put Barbie's face to mine and breathe in the sweet smell of both of them on her skin. I whisper in my daughter's ear. "Your mother is a take charge kind of woman, so get used to it now."

***

My mother liked my sister best. I know all kids say their mother liked their sister, or their brother, their cousin or even the next-door neighbour's kid best, but this time it was true. I looked like my father, I talked like my father, and according to Mom, I had the same personality as my father, which, as I grew into a man, annoyed Mom to the point she could barely stand to be in the same room with me. I would see her body stiffen whenever I did something that reminded her of him. "That's exactly the same asinine thing your father would have said," she'd say, or "You always make the wrong decisions. The wrong choices, just like your father." Her anger and hurt at Dad leaving her to raise two small children on her own, always just inches from the surface, just inches from me.

So, in that sweeping assumption I was my father's son in every way, including ways of the heart, Mom did not approve of Elaine. She said she was too bossy and too pushy. Truth be told, I married Elaine for just those strong personality traits. I'm happy to surrender authority to her; less for me to do, to worry about getting wrong. As I've matured, I've come to realize that a portion of my doubts are because I feel there must have been something I did or said that caused my own dad to leave, but that hasn't changed the way I think.

Marigold is watching me. "Did your wife garden, John?"

"She did. Was really good at it too. I'd better get going. Still have to walk Clementine today."

"Maybe next year you'll be able to stay and have a glass of wine with us."

"Maybe," I say. "If I'm still around."

Chapter eight

It's Thanksgiving, but anyone who didn't get picked up this morning before the storm began has had to stay put today. As a consequence, the dining room is full to capacity this evening. Only five of the residents who left the building early in the day are able to spend Thanksgiving with their families, but they have assured us they're safe and sound and won't attempt to return to The Wheaton until tomorrow. Dave has made a Thanksgiving meal of roast pork, applesauce, creamed carrots and mashed potatoes, with lemon meringue pie for dessert; everyone's favourite in his repertoire of meals, myself included.

The wind is moaning between the limbs of the pine trees and the snow is being lashed so forcefully against the window, all you can see out the glass is a violent dance of flakes, with a backdrop of trees bending to the power of the wind. The forecast is for the storm to continue all night long with an accumulation of ten centimetres.

I thought of calling one of my children before I left for work to ask them if they'd mind checking on Clem this evening, to make sure she's not too scared, but I dismissed the idea as soon as I thought of it, not wanting to be indebted to them. Anyhow, I'm sure if they were able to get through the storm, they'll be gathered at Mark's house for Thanksgiving dinner.

The tables nearest the wall of windows are always the most sought after because of the natural light offered during the day, and tonight, even though it's as dark as pitch, is no exception. Chairs have been pushed in where they don't belong and residents sit elbow to elbow, watching the storm while they tuck into their meals. Voices are muffled, not by the noise of the blizzard, but by the residents themselves, the reverence for Mother Nature silencing their tongues. I rattle my way around with the coffee and tea, stopping occasionally to look out one of the windows along with everyone else.

Elaine loved storms. Many times, I'd get up for work and find her with one or two of the kids, curled up on the couch, sound asleep under a quilt from one of their beds after they stayed up all night watching the snow fall. I would hear them downstairs in the night, talking in hushed voices so as not to disturb me, and there were times I wanted to tell them that I too have an adventurous spirit, that I wasn't always a working husband and father. But I never defended my position. It felt childish somehow to have to explain to them that I was the one who had to get up at five in the morning to plough through the snow so they could have a roof over their heads and food on their plates.

I pull my trolley up beside Alma who's standing at the window.

"Snow's early," she says. "It's going to be a long winter, I fear."

As much as snow is inevitable in our corner of the world, it always comes too soon. "You'd think at my age, I'd get used to this cold," I say. "Too many years working outside."

We watch as the wind bends the trees and I wonder how much they can take before branches begin to snap. As if my thoughts have influence, a limb from one of the tallest of the trees breaks off and begins to hurtle through the falling snow towards the windows. I think there's no way it's going to make it this far, the distance is too great. But the wind keeps it airborne longer than I would ever think possible, and I yell at the residents nearest the windows to take cover. Alma and I throw ourselves to the floor just as the branch hits. With a crack, glass and snow rains down on us as we cover our heads with our arms. At last the cascade stops and I stand, then help Alma up. Quite a few of the residents have managed to hide under the table but many are physically unable to perform such a feat.

"Is everyone ok?" I shout. "Look around you, is everyone alright?"

The wind is howling like a banshee through the broken window and on top of that, some of the residents are screaming.

Marigold shouts over the din. "Everyone close to me is fine, John."

Ivy does the same. "Everyone's good over here, too."

A voice near the back of the room starts to yell, albeit in a calm, matter-of-fact voice. It's Rachel Johnston. "I believe someone may be in trouble over here," she calls.

Jack Belgrade, who was seated away from the windows, is slumped forward into his plate. I rush to his side while pulling my phone from my pocket to dial 911 then I lay him on the floor and loosen the tie he always wears. I put my hand to his neck and check for a pulse; it's strong. The EMS worker tells me to stay by his side and the paramedics will be here shortly. A few residents gather around, though many continue to finish their meals. The paramedics arrive, then amidst grumbles from the residents who haven't yet got their pie, lift him onto a gurney, race past the crowd, and out into the storm.

Chapter nine

A gust of wind blows me inside and the paper turkey that's been sitting on the reception desk since Thanksgiving, tumbles to the floor. It turns beak over tail feathers, finally stopping at the other side of the desk, its paper beak now pushed into its paper head.

The music of choice today is Gene Autry with his rendition *Rudolph the Red Nose Reindeer*, and Ivy and Beatrice stop singing long enough to greet me. Ivy pats her hair and takes the lead.

"John, you should have been here. It was something to see."

I step behind the reception desk and put on my glasses to rifle through the messages Melanie has begun leaving for me after her shifts.

"Just stood there in the middle of the lobby and proclaimed he'd been to the other side." She snorts, "Like that old bugger'd ever make it into heaven. He's more a Scrooge than Scrooge himself was."

Carl wanders out of the dining room. "Who are you talking about?" he asks as he takes his usual spot at the end of the couch.

"Jack Belgrade," Ivy points to a spot in the middle of the room. "Stood right there not an hour ago and said he died when he had that heart attack and fell face first into his Thanksgiving dinner. Said he went to the other side and talked to Ed Brown."

"But Ed's dead, is he not?" Carl says.

She frowns at Carl. "Hence the reason Jack had to go to the other side to talk to him, Carl. Went to Ed's funeral myself." She shakes her head, "Catholic church wouldn't bury him on account he killed himself. Plus, he was," she whispers, "a homosexual."

Carl sits forward in his chair and blurts, "He was gay?"

"Yup," Ivy says.

"I liked Ed."

"When some of the people here found out that he," again she whispers, "liked men, they snubbed him. Not his choice to be born like that. Was buried in a plot with the other so-called heathens and only four people watching. Me, the minister, the caretaker, and some stranger the caretaker says goes to every burial the cemetery holds. Not that the church wouldn't bury him because he was a homosexual, the caretaker explained to me, only because he committed suicide. But still, it's kind of a slap in the face. He was a good practicing Catholic. Never missed a Sunday service. Family all lives out west. Never came to visit him, not surprised they couldn't be bothered to come to his funeral. I believe in paying respect to all my friends no matter what kind of life or death they had. Think I've only missed one funeral in all the years I've lived here and that was because I was sick. Been to funerals in rainstorms, heatwaves and blizzards."

Beatrice clucks her tongue.

"I was sure Jack was a goner when they took him out of here that night of the storm; grey as an unwashed sheet, he was. Though I suppose it could have been the mashed potatoes smeared on his face." She wags her finger at Beatrice. "Have a DNR in my will, with my doctor, and stuck to my fridge. So, if you're around when I kick the bucket, do not resuscitate me."

Beatrice nods her assent.

"I want to blink out like a light, not lollygag about waiting for someone to revive me like they did Jack. When the Lord says it's my time, just let me go."

Again, Beatrice nods.

"Jack says he can't wait to die again," Ivy continues. "Bea here," she points her thumb at her friend, "asked him why he bothered coming back if he can't wait to die again, why didn't he just stay dead? Jack said he needed to come back to get some things right."

"I'm confused," Carl says. "Who went to the other side and came back, Jack or Ed?" He straightens his bow-tie then rubs his hand over his bald pate shinning in the overhead light.

"Jack of course," Ivy says. "Ed may very well be on the other side, but he certainly can't tell us about it."

I pick the paper turkey up and fluff out the beak, then place it on the desk. Alma is by the window, perched on top of a ladder peeling a picture of the horn of plenty off the glass and replacing it with a picture of a Christmas tree. Each of the windows around the room has a picture stuck to it: a nativity scene, a Christmas tree, and a sign that says *Merry Christma*, the '*s*' missing after, I presume, years of picking the display off at season's end.

"I think Jack got used to all the nurses fawning over him," Beatrice says. "Concocted a story so everyone would listen now that he's home."

"Could be," Ivy continues. "He always has liked being the centre of attention. But you heard what he said this morning. Described what Ed was wearing the day he died and Jack wasn't even in the building. I saw him leave with my own eyes not half an hour before they carted Ed out," she waves her hands in the direction of the doors. "Last I saw of Ed was those old brown shoes he always wore. Sticking out the end of the sheet as he lay on the gurney. He was a tall man."

"Ivy, you know as well as I do that Ed wore the same clothes day in and day out. A green shirt, and tan slacks. Never without those same brown shoes." Beatrice says. "Anyone could have guessed that."

Carl chimes in, "I've been to the other side myself."

My ears prick up but Ivy and Beatrice pay no attention and continue with their own conversation.

"But not purple socks, Bea. Saw them myself when they wheeled him past the window. Noticed because they were so out of character. If ever there was a staid man, it was Ed. And Jack specifically said Ed had on purple socks."

"Saw things no living person should see," Carl shakes his head with a sorry look on his face.

"Funny," Beatrice says, "him wearing his own clothes like that.

You'd think they'd give you something to change into. Not keep you in the same clothes you died in." She shivers. "What if you had some horrific accident and were covered in blood? Would they make you wear those the rest of your days?"

Carl continues, "Wasn't peaceful at all."

Ivy leans across Beatrice to speak to Carl. "What did you say, Carl? You died? I don't remember you being carted off in an ambulance."

"Wasn't. Fell from a ladder when I was twelve." He nods towards Alma, "Be careful up there, Alma."

She waves down at him. "Always, Mr. Gibson."

"When I woke up I remembered everything. Floating in the air, seeing my body in Mom's arms." He rubs his chin. "Funny thing happened. Had a ball I got for a birthday present. They were called super balls back then because they bounced really high."

"I remember those," Beatrice says. "I had a white one."

"Mine was red," Carl says. "I always kept it under the bush by the back door. One morning I went outside and it was gone. I searched that backyard a dozen times but never did find it. Figured it was stolen. When I fell off the ladder and was floating through the air I saw the ball on the roof of the house. After the dust had settled and I'd come back from the dead so to speak, my younger brother confessed he'd thrown it up there months earlier on account he was jealous he didn't get one too. Forgot all about that till just now. Tried to tell everyone but no one wanted to listen to a kid. Thought I was making it up. Learned to keep it to myself, didn't want to be labelled a loony."

"I suppose it's like those people who claim to have been abducted by little green men; they don't talk about it much either," Ivy says.

"I've heard about that," Beatrice says. "Boy that would be something. To be taken on board a space ship. Meet people from another planet?"

"But they do strange things to you, Bea." Ivy's cheeks have turned pink. "Prodding and probing. Poking in places only my doctor, and my long dead husband," she makes a sign of the cross, "have ever seen. There's no way on God's green earth I'd ever want to be abducted by aliens."

"Never even told Elsie." Carl laces his fingers over his belly. "Fifty years of marriage and she went to her grave not knowing I'd died long before her."

"Were you afraid?" Ivy asks.

"Not at first. But when the shadows began coaxing me to follow them, I was terrified. That's when I woke up. Figured I must have been sent to the wrong place. I suppose mistakes happen. Tried to live a good life since."

Alma climbs down the ladder, interrupting this conversation. "John, would you go to the basement and bring up the rest of the Christmas decorations?"

"Basement?" I say.

"I asked Melanie to get them last night but that girl shirks more duties than you and I do in a day. They're in a plastic bin, says 'Christmas decorations' on the side in black marker. Might be by the furnace or I may have moved them to one of the rooms."

"Careful," Carl says. "The stairs are steep."

"And don't let the boogey man get you," Ivy says.

I pick up the turkey to take it with me.

"And leave that turkey there," Alma says. "It's a crossover decoration."

I open the basement door and daylight from the kitchen partially illuminates the staircase. A musty smell wafts up. I imagine old potatoes and gunny sacks, seeping walls, and spider-webs bigger than my hand. I flip the switch on the landing but the bulb is dead and the basement floor remains hazy in the gloom ten feet below. With only the light from the kitchen to guide me, I inch my way along, trying not to think about what could be lurking down here in the dark. When I reach the last step, I flip the switch and squint into the sudden brightness.

To my surprise, the basement is finished, though the lathe and plaster have seen better days. Cracks as wide as my thumb zigzag from floor to ceiling and cobwebs hang low from the ceiling beams. One long wall is lined with closed doors, and a gigantic furnace sits in the far corner. Pipes snake out of this monstrosity in every direction, then crawl along the ceiling, ending at ducts which lead to the floors above. The name for this type of heating system is an octopus furnace and was most likely installed using oil, though it must be years since it was converted to gas. Except for whatever lies behind the closed doors, the rest of the basement appears empty with no Christmas decoration bin in sight.

The furnace roars to life and I jump. Those people and their stories about crossing over have spooked me. I begin to open doors in search of the elusive ornaments.

The first room, except for a few rusty lockers heaped along the wall, is empty. The breeze from the opened door flutters the peeling paint like dead leaves on a winter tree.

In the next room, I find a fully equipped kitchen, the stove so large you could fit three giant pots on top and still have room to spare. What looks like a walk-in freezer takes up space in one corner, its door propped open by a small bronze cat. Copper pots hang above a wooden butcher block, with graduated tin canisters lined up on the counter. A kitchen most chefs would be envious of, but no chef has cooked here for years. Spiderwebs string between the pots like tattered prayer flags and the tins ooze rust from their rotting seams. The butcher block is gouged with clefts so deep it looks like something has been dismembered on it, and stains, which I can only guess are blood, now aged to a dark shade of copper, drip down its sides. Tumbleweeds of dust spin around the floor, propelled by a draft from God knows where. I quickly turn off the light and move on.

The last room is crammed to the ceiling with junk. Lamps lean against dog cages, china cabinets have toilets balanced on top, and chairs of all shapes and sizes are stacked seat against seat as they tower their crooked way to the ceiling. A wooden table is turned on its side and leans against one of the piles, and plastic bins labelled Thanksgiving, Easter, Canada Day, and Christmas, are stacked in front. I step inside the room and flip the switch. Without warning, something hits me on the back and I sprawl face down on the floor. The door bangs shut and I spring to my knees and turn, holding my arms in front of my face ready to defend myself. But there's no one there. I climb to my feet and wrench the knob, it won't open. I pound and yell, hoping my voice will rise up the duct work and someone not as deaf as Mrs. Hawkins will hear the racket. I yank the knob again and this time it pops opens as if it's never been stuck. Marigold is standing on the other side.

"John, what's wrong? I heard pounding and yelling and didn't know what to make of it."

"The door," I say. "It wouldn't open." I peer around Marigold and scan the room.

"What do you mean, it wouldn't open?" She turns the knob. "It seems to be working now."

I mumble, "I'm sure it was stuck." I reach out and rattle the knob.

She looks over my shoulder. "Are those the Christmas decorations?"

I nod.

"Alma was on her way to see if you were having trouble finding them, but the phone rang and she was called upstairs. I said I'd check, make sure you're not lost down here."

I swallow the lump in my throat. "Did you see anything?"

"I don't know what you mean."

"Was someone in the basement when you came down?"

She turns, looking behind her. "I didn't see anyone, John, did you?"

I pause. "No, no, I didn't see anyone, I just…. I thought someone pushed me."

She points at a box lying on its side, its contents spilling out onto the crumbling cement floor. "Perhaps that fell from the rafters? Places like these can play tricks on the mind. Let's get out of here. My old bones don't like the damp. Just stay right behind me on the stairs and give me a push if I start to tip backwards, would you?"

Chapter ten

1980

"What's this?" I ask, my hopes for a nap after work, dwindling.

"A Christmas tree," Elaine says.

I hate it when she teases me. "That isn't what I meant and you know it. I didn't think we'd have a tree this year. What if Barbie pulls it over? She's walking now. What if she breaks the ornaments and cuts herself?" Barbie's sitting on the floor draping clumps of tinsel on the bottom branches.

"Don't be silly." She hangs the ornament she bought six years ago near the top. It says *Our First Christmas* in silver glitter. "If she pulls it over, we'll just put it back up."

One Christmas when I was three or four, before Dad left, he bought us a tree. In my excitement, I knocked it over. "How much did it cost?"

"It's a straggler. That's what the Christmas tree guy called it. Only ten dollars. There's a bald spot right there." She points to the back of the tree. "But you'll never see it against the wall." She climbs onto a chair she's placed beside the tree. "Hand me that star, would you?"

"We don't have money for extras," I hand her the star.

"You may call a Christmas tree an extra but I don't." Her voice bounces off the ceiling as she pushes the star onto the top branch. "I call it an essential. You know I like real trees, not those artificial things everyone's buying now-a-days. And I want a real tree to celebrate our first Christmas in our new house." I hold her hand and she steps back onto the floor. She plugs in the lights. "There, isn't that pretty, Barbie?" she says.

I pick Barb up and give her a kiss. She wraps her chubby arms around my neck and I snuggle my nose into her hair. So far, being a father is not as difficult as I'd imagined, though there are still days I question my ability to raise her to adulthood. I whisper in her ear, "If you knock the tree over, I promise I won't get mad like my dad did."

"Pretty," she says then carefully touches a prickly branch with her chubby finger.

"Just like you." I poke her tummy and she giggles. I attempt to pass her to Elaine. "I'm going to rest. Lots of Christmas mail today. I'm tired."

Elaine doesn't take Barb from me and instead places the tinsel in my free hand. "I have to finish making supper. You," she gives me a kiss, "and you," she kisses Barbie, "need to finish decorating the tree. I'll call you when supper's ready."

I sit on the floor with Barbie and together we finish hanging the tinsel.

***

"Dashing through the snow, in a one horse open sleigh. O'er the fields we go, laughing all the way. Bells on bobsleds ring, making...."

I close the music room door on mouths open wide, and cheeks pink with excitement, muffling voices cracked with age. With the old standards blaring out of the lobby speakers all afternoon, and now the residents practicing every evening for their Christmas concert, I've had enough festive music for one day. The moment I'm back behind the reception desk checking off my list of chores, the door to the music room opens and Marigold emerges. I hear a surge of *O Holy Night* before the door closes, cutting Ivy off as she's warbling towards the high notes.

"John, come join us. We could use some more male voices," Marigold says. Her eyes sparkle with delight and I'm sure a glass or two of wine.

"You have Ezra, Julio, and Carl," I say. "And I spotted a couple of other men in there as well."

She counts off on her fingers. "Carl's tone deaf. Sounds like a wounded cow every time he opens his mouth. And Julio's Spanish accent is turning all the 'merrys' and 'Christmases' into nothing but flying spit. No one wants to stand near him. Harry complains every chance he gets that he didn't move here to sing in a third-rate choir, although I think he secretly loves it and simply likes to complain. And Ezra and Milt sing in old man high pitched squeaks. Ezra's mind keeps wandering and he wants to reminisce about when he was a boy at Christmastime in the country."

"I can't sing either."

"I've heard you hum along with the music in the lobby. You know all the Ella Fitzgerald, Artie Shaw, and Dinah Washington songs. As a matter of fact, I think you're something of a jazz aficionado."

"Just because I know when to bebop, doesn't mean I can sing." I bend my head to the list of chores hoping to find one more.

"Anyone can sing better than who we have in that room now. Do me this favour. If you hate it you can leave. If you can't sing we'll ask you to leave," she winks. "There's shortbread. With sprinkles. And I've seen you wolf down a few of those in the past month."

"Thanks, Marigold, but I'd better not, too much to do tonight."

She persists. "Just two songs. Hell, just one. For me." She presses the music to *Oh Come All Ye Faithful* at me, then takes my hand in hers.

"Alright," I say. "Just one song." I look at the page. "This is my favourite carol."

"Karma," Marigold pushes open the door. "Everyone," she says as we enter the room, "John has a real ear for music. He's going make us sound better than ever."

"Marigold," I begin to say, but the group is already regarding me as if I'm Les Brown. I stand between Harry and Ezra. Ivy begins to pound the keyboard and we launch into their rendition of *Oh Come All Ye Faithful*. By the time we finish, my ears are ringing and my jaw is clenched.

"Harry," I say. "Why don't you stand over there?" I point to the other side of the piano. "You're more a tenor while Ezra here is an alto. You'll be able to hear what you're singing better if you're separated. And Milton, perhaps tone down your part a tad. The melody needs to come through more, which is Marigold's part." I look at Marigold. "Right? You are singing the melody, are you not?"

"I am, John." She raises one eyebrow and the corner of her mouth twitches.

"Carl, join Marigold in the melody if you can. Give it that strong male voice, if you know what I mean. Now Ivy, on the count of four, let's try again."

Half an hour later Ivy strikes the last chord of *Jingle Bells* and my teeth rattle. "Time to get back to work," I say. "Still have a list of chores to finish before Melanie gets here. She doesn't like it when I leave things for her to do."

Marigold follows me out. "You off work tomorrow evening?"

"I am."

"Join me for a beer at my place?"

"You want me to come for a beer? At your place?"

"Just a Christmas drink. I'm not propositioning you, John." Her eyes twinkle.

"Like to stay with Clem once I'm home."

"Bring her. The more the merrier. After supper, around seven?"

"I can't promise anything."

She weaves her way across the lobby and opens the music room door. Ivy begins pounding the piano again; they seem to be getting better, or perhaps it's the glass of wine Marigold forced on me.

"Come on, Clem. You're lagging behind." I tug at the leash, Clementine tugs back. "What's the matter with you today? You getting old on me, girl? You're supposed to be my motivation, not the other way around." I pat my burgeoning stomach. "I need to lose a bit of weight and so do you." She slows to a walk. "Don't blame me if you never lose that roll."

We stop at the top of the Broadway Bridge and I look over the side railing. It's only four in the afternoon but the sun is already beginning to set and the street lights are blinking on. Two people are on the trail below that meanders through the city adjacent to the river. They're staring at the sunset and Clem peers between the slats in the rail as if admiring the same thing. She looks up waiting for me to say something important.

"How'd you like to go for a visit this evening? Nice old lady. Loves dogs, or so she says."

She wags her tail, which in dog language can mean anything: I'm hungry, I have to pee, I need to sniff that thing on the path down there. But as all dog owners do, I interpret her body language as meaning what I want it to mean; she understands exactly what I said and is excited to do anything which involves doing it with me. So, with Clem on the seat beside me I drive to the Wheaton, glad I don't have to go alone.

Elaine used to tease me about being able to engage young women in conversation just by having Clem by my side. *What a cutie! Can I pet her? What's her name?* they'd say as they bent to the sidewalk to kiss Clem on the nose, and like a proud Papa, I'd gladly answer. But it doesn't work on Melanie and all she says is, "What are you doing here?"

"Marigold invited Clem and me for a drink."

"And you accepted?" She flips the page on her magazine. "God, this is the last place I'd want to be when I'm done work, especially to have a drink with one of them."

My eyes linger on Melanie for a moment and I wonder if I was this immature when I was her age. Elaine and I were married so young, with a baby by the time we were twenty-four, we were forced into adulthood before many people nowadays are even considering marriage. I have a vague recollection of taking Elaine and Barbie to a family gathering from Mom's side of the family when Barbie was just a toddler. I sat with a cousin I used to hang out with when we were kids. He'd not yet married or had a family and though we were the same age, he seemed much younger than me.

At the elevator Clem and I wait beside a man I don't know. He squats and looks into Clem's eyes; she wags her tail. "Love golden labs. Had one when I was a boy." He stands and holds out his hand. He's tall and big boned and appears to be first nations, though he has blue eyes. "Albert Rutherford. Just heading up to Mom's. I mean, Marigold's."

"We seem to be going to the same place, Mr. Rutherford," I say, trying to hide my surprise.

As the elevator doors close, Melanie lifts her head from her phone and looks me in the eyes. She has a smirk on her face.

Marigold's door is open wide and Christmas music and laughter spill into the hallway. People mill everywhere, a drink in one hand and a plate of goodies in the other. It seems many more besides Albert, Clem and I have been invited this evening and for a moment I balk at the door.

Clementine, always the party animal, pulls me inside. The air is warm and filled with the scent of savory mixed with sweet. I'm sure she can smell the food; strings of drool are already dripping out of the corner of her soft mouth. Marigold meets us at the door and gives Albert a hug. She sees Clem and me stalling our entry.

"Don't just stand there, come in, you two." She bends to Clem, "And you must be Clementine. I've heard a lot about you. So good to finally meet."

Clem lifts her paw.

"Aren't you the smart dog? Come, I've a special treat just for you." Marigold looks up at me, "If that's okay with you, John."

"She'll be your friend for life if you give her a cookie."

Marigold leads Clem to the kitchen and I'm left to face the crowd alone. Elaine was always my anchor in situations like these. She could talk to anyone about anything. I'd rely on her to begin conversations, then take over so no one would know I was the shy one and she was the extrovert.

I look around the room. It's beautifully decorated with comfortable furniture. Elaine always wanted to redecorate the house, but I resisted. I told her we needed to save money for my retirement because my pension would only be enough to live on, not any extras.

And since being a housewife didn't garner a pension, we couldn't afford to redecorate. I suppose, in hindsight, it wasn't the most sensitive thing I'd ever said to her.

Jack Belgrade, the man who suffered the heart attack at the Thanksgiving dinner, is chatting the ear off Carl Gibson. Darlene Carillion is munching on a bowl of pretzels, enlightening the woman beside her on where Christmas trees are grown. Beatrice Fielding is huddled by the Christmas tree snuggling with her dance partner, Allan Cummings. They're staring into one another's eyes and I wonder at this love having blossomed at such an age.

Ernestine Hawkins is hunched in a corner chair and being shouted at by Rachel Johnston and Ezra Adelman is standing by the window, his fingers wrapped around his lower back. Ivy McDonald is at his side. I look out the window to see what they're watching. A dog is romping through snow in the park that backs Marigold's apartment and I long to be out there with Clem.

Ivy turns from the window and approaches. "Are you going to join us in the concert this evening?" she waves her glass in the air and keeps on talking. "Well, we call it a concert. More like sing-a-long. The old standards we practiced last night. You have a good ear; made us better than we usually are. One year all the staff sang with us. Mind you, we didn't have that girl Melanie at the front desk at that time. Last year Marigold tried inviting her to join in the choir, but if I remember right, she actually laughed in Marigold's face. Thought it was a joke or something." Again, she waves her glass. "Who knows what she thought," she slurps her wine. "Alma said she'd try to make it up if she doesn't get too busy. Last year she came dressed as Santa Claus. Passed out cookies she baked herself."

"Marigold's done this before?"

"It's the shindig of the year. She and Ernestine buy all the drinks and snacks, won't let us pitch in."

Marigold returns minus Clem, but with a beer for me. "She's the hit of the party. Well trained dog. Mingling in the kitchen like an old pro."

"Elaine's doing. I can't take any credit for that. You do this every year?"

"Spread the joy, that's my motto. Invite the whole place though some are out of town with their families for the season, but almost everyone else shows up. If there's one thing we elderly like to do, it's party!"

"Fiona Brighton doesn't attend?"

"I'll keep trying," Marigold says. "One year she'll give in. It's easier to be happy than mad."

"She is a loner," Ivy says. "Lord knows I've tried to get to know her but she likes that bottle better than she likes people." She takes another gulp. "Figure something must have happened to her to make her so standoffish. I've invited her to bingo, to card games, shuffleboard, even over for a cup of tea, but she's always declined. Managed to get myself inside her apartment a while back. Asked if I could borrow a cork screw, figured she'd probably have one kicking around. Snooped a bit while she searched through some drawers then she scuttled me out of there the second she found the thing. Said she had someplace to go, though I'm sure that was a lie. Not much to see in that apartment anyhow. If there ever was a minimalist, it's her." She stares into the bottom of her glass. "Time for a refill."

Jack Belgrade's voice booms over everyone else's. "Saw my brother. Said he holds me no grudge. Didn't see Mom. Talked to Ed Brown for a moment."

"Come on, Jack, you don't really believe that do you?" Neil Elliot, a man I've only ever served coffee to, says.

"What else could it be?"

"The last remnants of life, your brain dying, seeing what you want to see."

"You'll believe me when you die, Neil."

"What did Ed say to you?" someone else asks.

Heads turn Jack's way and he stumbles with his words. "Well, his voice was muffled. As near as I can make out he said he had prepared himself to go to hell. But, he said, it was hell on earth, it didn't matter to him one way or the other." He pulls on his earlobe.

"I was just about to ask him where he's spending all eternity, when I woke up."

"That was convenient," Neil says as he turns his face away from Jack.

"Seeing my brother, though," Jack shakes his head, "wish I could've talked longer."

"He's trying to ease his guilt," Marigold says as she puts her hand on my shoulder, ushering me to the kitchen. "Jack's brother drowned. His mother had gone to answer the door and left the two of them alone in the tub. His brother was three, Jack was five."

"Oh my God," I say. "That's awful."

"Jack said his mom never forgave him."

"But he was just a kid."

"Couldn't face blaming herself, I suppose."

A voice, louder than the rest, echoes down the hall. It sounds like Fiona and I turn.

"How am I supposed to sleep with all this racket? Geez Louise. Aren't I good enough for you? Leave me sitting alone in my suite while all of you party your asses off." Her words are slurred and she's hanging onto the doorframe for support. I hurry to her side.

Her make-up is blotchy, and her wig is crooked as if she's slapped it onto her head in a hurry. A housecoat hangs loosely tied at her waist. "Come on, Fiona, let's get you home." I put my arm around her. Her breath smells like scotch and cigarette smoke.

She bends her head back and squints up at me. "Is that you, John? You want me to leave? Why can't I stay and have a drink with everyone else?"

The party comes to a standstill. Some people whisper behind hands, others say nothing.

"It's ok, Fiona, I think you've probably had enough to drink. I'll just give you a hand back to your place." She doesn't resist and I help her out of Marigold's suite and down the hall.

Ivy rushes ahead of me to open Fiona's door. "You go back to the party, John. I'll get her to bed," she says.

"Thanks, Ivy."

"Won't take but a minute. Don't start the carols without me."

I lie Fiona on her bed and Ivy removes her slippers and pearls. Fiona moans and turns to her side while Ivy takes the wig and housecoat off. I close the bedroom door and return to the party. I grab another beer and Clementine follows me to the window. Together we watch the dog romping in the snow.

Marigold wanders over. "Is she going to be alright?"

"Ivy's putting her to bed. Probably won't remember anything tomorrow."

"That's the tragedy of it."

Ezra creaks his sore back forward and gives Clem a pat. "No wonder you're always so anxious to get home, John." He kisses Clem's nose. "If I had this to go home to, I'd be in a hurry to leave too."

I want to tell him there was one time I wasn't in a hurry to leave, though I wish I had been.

1982

Elaine is shouting at me over someone's high-pitched laugh. "It's time to go home. Barbie will be awake in a few hours." She pulls our coats from the pile on the bed.

"Not yet, Elaine," I say.

"What?"

"I don't want to go home. Not yet."

"John, please." I follow her down the hall towards the front door. She starts to root through the pile of boots. "You know how early Barbie gets up and you know it's me who has to get up with her." She holds my coat towards me. "It's time to go."

Two neighbours squeeze by us and grab their boots from the pile. "The Jensons' always throw a good party, it's a shame to leave," the husband says, "but the morning comes awful early. Merry Christmas, you two."

"Same to you," I say.

His wife opens the front door and Elaine's red hair shimmers in the glow of the Christmas lights hanging over the porch.

Jingle Bell Rock, the Bobby Helms version, not the Brenda Lee version, begins to play and I pull our coats from Elaine's hands and toss them to the floor beside the boots. I take her by her waist, now engorged with pregnancy, and twirl her down the hall and into the party. "You're beautiful, Elaine. Turned my head the first time I laid eyes on you." I stop under the mistletoe and give her a kiss. "I guess I don't tell you that very often."

Her body surrenders to mine and I pull her closer. For a moment, I see the hint of a smile, glimpse the carefree look that drew me to her only a few years ago. As suddenly as she's yielding, she stiffens.

"You're drunk." She pulls my arms from her waist. "It's after midnight, the babysitter is waiting."

"No, Elaine." I reach for her but she pushes me by the shoulders and I stumble back.

"John, it's time to go home," she hisses. A few people look, but turn away as the music swells around us.

In anger, I place my hand on her back and push her ahead of me towards the door. We stand on the shovelled back step and I lean into her; there's resentment in her blue eyes.

My breath puffs around her face. "I'm not going home, Elaine. I'm an adult and I can decide for myself when I want to leave. That's all I ever do. Go home to shovel snow, go home to take out the garbage, go home to look after the kid. Go home to sleep so I can start all over again the next day. When was the last time we had fun without worrying about getting home to Barbie, or spending money, or going to work?"

A siren blares on the freeway and the dog next door, whose owners are at the party, barks at the sound.

"Aren't you tired of making meals and cleaning the house? Changing diapers and clipping coupons?" I give her shoulders a shake. "C'mon, stay out with me tonight. Be something else besides a housewife and a mother."

She cracks open the back door but doesn't enter. I hear the music change songs to *Jingle Bells* by Duke Ellington and a conga line snakes past the dining room window.

"You're right," she says. "Maybe I do need to loosen up. Maybe I do need to stay up all night and howl at the moon. But you know, John, being a parent means something and the sooner you figure that out, the sooner you'll quit blaming everyone else for your restlessness."

Tiredness comes over me. "It's not restlessness, Elaine. I need to feel like I still have some life in me. I don't want to grow old before I am old."

***

"Come, John, join us at the piano."

I shake my head.

Marigold touches my arm. "Don't be such a stick-in-the-mud," she says. "Whatever happened in the past is over and done. Time to forgive yourself and move on. Life is passing you by."

A wedge of guilt breaks free and it's such a relief, my legs feel weak. I stand beside Julio and Clementine joins me. She sits quietly for most of the songs until the end, when, along with Ivy, she howls the high notes of O Holy Night.

Chapter eleven

The snow is deep for December and the going is tough as I slog my way towards her plot. When we were first married, Elaine would drag me to country cemeteries like this. She'd rub her hands over the weather-worn names on the oldest of markers, fascinated by the people buried there. She was like that; attracted to other people's lives and at times I found myself jealous, her interest in others seemingly more intense than her interest in me. I kneel and brush the snow off her headstone.

Though most of what I did immediately following her death is a blur, I remember the day I ordered this piece of granite. I told the salesperson who was eagerly showing me pictures, that it had to be the colour of amber. His face morphed into what I mistook in my grief as pity, but now realize he was only worried about losing a sale, then said he doubted he could find anything that came in the colour orange. I insisted, not orange, amber.

"I know I haven't been for a while, working more than I thought I would." I trace my finger over her name carved in the orangey-brown stone. "You'd like that. Wouldn't be hanging around the house bugging you. You always warned me I'd become a hoverer when I retired." I stop to pull a weed that has survived the snow. "Had Barb's birthday party at a restaurant; kids planned it. Can't believe we have a thirty-six-year-old daughter. Clem's doing ok. Getting old, the same as all of us. I'm sure she misses you, but dogs live in the moment, like you always said." I hunch my shoulders against a cold wind blowing through the trees that serve as snow-fencing.

"Job's ok. Fills the days. Lots of characters living there; we would have had some chuckles over a bottle of wine. There's this one woman, Mrs. Carillion, faints if you touch her. Drops to the ground the minute anyone lays a finger on her. And I'm sure I've told you about Marigold. You'd like her. Guessed I was a widower without me telling her. And yes, I know, I should tell people, but you know me, don't want anyone to know my business. That was another of your pet peeves about me; too private." I laugh. "I think some of those old ladies have crushes on me. They're always asking me to come for tea or join them for happy hour. Mostly I say no. Don't like to socialize without you, though I did go to a Christmas party at Marigold's. It was ok, took Clem. Missed having you by my side. Did I tell you Janet's hosting Christmas this year? Her first time, but I suppose you know that. She said I couldn't spend the day alone like I did last year." I pull a tissue out of my pocket and blow my nose. "Cold out here today, sweetie, gotta go. Working this afternoon and I still have to take Clem for her walk. I'll be back after Christmas."

I arrive at Janet's house by two in the afternoon. She greets me with a spoon in one hand, a carrot in the other, and a frantic look on her face.

"You'll never peel that carrot that way," I say.

"Funny man. Barb's going to be here soon and take over if I don't look like I know what I'm doing," she waves the carrot under my nose. "There's an entire pot to peel in the kitchen."

We peel the carrots and potatoes to the sounds of *Silver Bells, Have Yourself a Merry Little Christmas* and *Winter Wonderland*. I hum along to *Rudolf*, as I lift the turkey out of the oven, and dig the stuffing out of the bird to the tune of *White Christmas* while Janet makes the gravy. We're putting the finishing touches on the table to the beat of *Rockin' Round the Christmas Tree* when the rest of the family barrels through the front door. With a kiss on my cheek and, "We make a good team," whispered in my ear, Janet pushes me to the living room to socialize.

Her place is a one-bedroom apartment with a small dining

room and even smaller living room crowded with a loveseat and matching chair. Elaine and I couldn't afford to pay for her university education and the only way she could get a loan was to move out of the house, the government citing she was still a dependant and her parents made enough money to pay her way. Elaine and I give her a bit of money to help cover costs and I suddenly remember, it's been a while since I've given her anything. She must be going to her brother or sister for help.

The kids sit on the floor while Barb drags a dining room chair in to sit on and I squeeze on the couch between Mark and Rob, Barb's husband. Deanna and the baby have the chair.

Rose climbs on my lap and whispers in my ear. "It's ok you didn't bring us presents, Grandpa. We got enough already."

I blush and realize I completely forgot. That wasn't my job. No one else mentions my faux pas.

Barb's oldest, Colin, who's now thirteen, has brought the video game he got for Christmas and asks me to play.

"Oh, Colin. I don't know how."

"Go on, Dad," Mark says. "I'll bet you'd be good at it. You used to play the guitar, I'm sure your hand eye coordination is pretty decent."

I look at Mark, surprised he knows that about me. I slide off the couch and sit cross-legged on the floor beside Colin. He hands me a control and explains the game. After a few false starts, I manage to shoot some sort of fire breathing dragon out of the air while avoiding getting eaten by a dinosaur before Janet calls me to carve the turkey.

We crowd around the table. I'm at the far end against the wall, with Mark, Deanna and Amanda's high chair, up the side of the table, effectively blocking me in. Rob is at the other end with Barb, Rose, Julie and Colin down the other side.

Mark raises his glass. "Thanks for cooking, Jan. Looks like it turned out better than I thought it would."

"Hey!"

"Just teasing."

We enjoy a delicious Christmas dinner — Janet's freckles turn red when everyone says it's as good a meal as Mom made – and drink a couple of bottles of wine with more than a couple recollections about Christmases past.

"Remember the time you ran your remote car into the Christmas tree, Mark?" Janet says. "Knocked that thing over before we'd even had time to open the rest of the presents."

"Thanks for reminding me," Mark says. "And remember what Mom did? She grabbed her camera, made us gather round that fallen tree, and snapped a whole roll of pictures. Said it was part of this Christmas and be damned if she wanted to forget."

Everyone laughs.

"That was Mom alright," Barb says. "Always making lemonade out of lemons."

"Remember, Dad, the time the oven quit in the middle of cooking the turkey?" Mark says. "You and Mom had a living room full of aunts, uncles, and cousins, and a raw turkey in the oven."

"What did Grandma do?" Colin asks.

"She took that bird out of the oven, chopped it into pieces, dipped it in flour and spices and deep fried it. Told everyone we were having a Cajun Christmas."

No one mentions how angry I got both times.

"Your grandma, Colin," I say, "was a brilliant woman. Always knew exactly what to do." I wave my glass at him, "Always came out the other end smelling of roses. Me, I always came out the other end smelling of…."

"Dad," Janet takes my wine from me. "I think you've had enough."

"You're right Jannie. I have had enough. I'd better go call a cab, leave you guys to enjoy yourselves." I stand then realize the only way I'm getting out of here is if everyone else vacates their own chairs. I plop back down to my chair.

"You're not the only person who lost someone, Dad," Mark says.

"Mark," Barb says. She shakes her head at him.

He ignores his sister. "I know you were her husband, and I can't imagine how hard it would be if I lost Deanna," he squeezes Deanna's hand, "but we lost our mom."

"I know you did, Mark."

"I don't think you do, Dad. I'm sorry you're having a hard time, but so are we. Do you know we've gotten together like this every couple of months for the past year and a half? Talking about Mom, remembering all the good stuff. We've thought about asking you to join us, but we knew you'd say no. It seems like we not only lost our mom, we lost you too."

Chapter twelve

The usual greeters meet me this cold January morning: Carl Gibson, Ivy McDonald, and Beatrice Fielding. They sit side by side on the couch, looking out the windows at the snow sparkling in the sun and for some inexplicable reason, I find myself happy to see them. This morning Ezra has pulled up a chair and he speaks to me before Ivy is able to get a word out.

"If you ever need a dog sitter, John, I'd be more than happy to give you a hand. Enjoyed your dog's company at Marigold's party a few weeks ago." He seems excited, not his usual unruffled demeanour.

"I might take you up on that sometime."

"What kind of dog is it again?" He snaps his crippled fingers as he tries to remember.

That's an odd question. He spent most of the party sitting with her, and a good portion of his life as a vet. "She's a golden lab named Clementine."

"Oh yeah, yeah, now I remember. Clementine. Golden lab. Don't meet many dogs named Clementine. And you call her Clem for short?"

"I do."

He chuckles. "Great name, John. Great name. Over the years I met many dogs with names like Blackie, or Ruff, Spike, or even Sweetie; you know, ordinary names." He snaps his fingers again and I cringe in sympathy. "That dog of yours, John."

"Clementine," I say.

"She's something special. Never heard a dog named that before."

"My wife named her. When she was a puppy her feet looked too big for her body. In the song the line goes, *Oh my darling Clementine, and her shoes were number nine,* or something like that. Wife thought it fit."

"Thought it fit?" Ezra asks.

"The dog's name. Clementine. Good name for a dog with big feet."

"Oh yes. Of course. Your dog, the golden lab."

"Are you alright, Ezra?" Carl asks.

"Very good. You?"

"I'm good," Carl says.

"Good, good," Ezra says and sits back in his chair.

The sun streams in the window and I put on a CD hoping it will distract everyone from the bizarre conversation with Ezra. I discovered the CD player tucked in the bottom drawer of the reception desk about a month after I began working here; something Melanie neglected to show me. Probably because when she's working she turns it off. Says she can't abide the old geezer music; gives her the creeps thinking about what they do with each other, whatever that means.

Today I've put on the mellow sounds of Stan Getz. His music has always reminded me of warm places, and on this minus thirty-degree morning in the middle of January in the middle of the Canadian prairies, we need something warm to boost our spirits. Ivy, Beatrice, Carl and Ezra start tapping their toes and bopping their heads the moment the music begins, perhaps remembering times long ago spent on far-away beaches.

The five of us are still enjoying the music, looking out at the sun-dappled snow, imagining it to be the Caribbean or some such place, when Melanie returns.

"When will that crazy woman hurry up and die?" she says popping our daydream.

"Melanie, that's a bit harsh." I nod towards the four residents whose average age is at least eighty.

She doesn't falter. "That's twice this week I've had to check for an intruder in that Hawkins woman's room. How am I supposed to get anything done when I have to keep running upstairs? God almighty, these people are loonier than my grandmother."

"Be quiet, Melanie," I say.

She whips her head towards me. "Pardon me?"

"You talk too much."

"I what?"

"These people," I wave at my audience now sitting on the edges of their chairs and hanging on to every word, "as you call them, deserve respect. Just because they live here does not mean they're stupid." I clamp my lips together, wondering what just came over me.

She steps closer. Her breath smells sour. "How dare you talk to me like that. I've worked here longer than you. I have seniority. I'm writing this one down, Davies. All your shenanigans; cavorting with residents, doing God knows what up there with that drunk, Brighton. And the Blossom woman, bit more than a working relationship there, I imagine." She points her finger in my face. "I told Crockett the day she hired you, said you're old enough to be checking in, not working here. They see you as one of them, not as an employee."

"Go home, Melanie," I say, pushing her hand away and wishing I'd never said anything.

She grabs her coat. "I have to go, and not because you told me to. Tomorrow, Davies, tomorrow I'm talking to Crockett. You'll be outta here before you can say sayonara." She tugs on her boots and the five of us watch her run down the driveway then get into an idling car. The driver speeds away, his arm around Melanie and her head on his shoulder.

"My God, John," Beatrice whispers, looking at me like I could leap tall buildings in a single bound. "That was fantastic. It's about time someone stood up to her."

Kicking myself for my big mouth, I say, "Shouldn't have said anything. Don't like to cause trouble. Too many years with a union." I think of all the times I turned my head when one of my co-workers did something inappropriate, like sluff mail, or run through their routes. All it did was make our supervisors add on to our walks when they decided the rest of us were going too slow. I remember one postie who hid mail in the front porch of his mother's house for ten years. Cheques, and bills, magazines and even passports were discovered when she died and the house was renovated!

"Don't worry, John. We were here. We know what went down."

"What went down, Beatrice?" Carl says. "You've been watching too many reruns of *Starsky and Hutch*."

Beatrice waves her hand at Carl. "We heard exactly what happened. Don't you worry about a thing, we'll stick up for you" she says to John. "You didn't make employee of the month for no reason."

"I doubt she'll go to Alma," Ezra says. "She may not be the brightest apple in the cart, but she's smart enough to know she could be fired for wishing a resident dead. She does nothing but paint her nails and read magazines all day long."

Ivy, who's been unusually quiet, says, "I wonder why the grim reaper hasn't already taken Ernestine. She must have seen him ten times in the last few months."

The four of us stare at Ivy as *The Girl from Ipanema* plays in the background.

"Because there isn't such a thing as the grim reaper?" Carl says.

"I know that, Carl Gibson, don't patronize me. What I'm trying to say is, Ernestine's a shrewd woman, knows how to run a business better than most men. Surely she must wonder, if she truly believes it to be the grim reaper, why he hasn't taken her yet?" She taps her chin and scowls out the window. "She's seeing something, that's for sure. She's deaf, not blind. I've seen her spot a dime on the floor from across the room."

"Most of us in this place could claim that talent, Ivy," Ezra says. "Spendthrifts we aren't." He gets a faraway look on his face. "Remember when a dime could buy a cup of coffee?"

Ivy ignores Ezra. "It has to be something, don't you think? And if it isn't the grim reaper, then who or what the hell is it?"

"A shadow, a reflection, any number of things," I say. "She has a large picture window in her living room, it could be the sun glinting off all those photographs she has sitting around."

"Too many people staring at me in that apartment." Beatrice shivers. "Was up there for tea last week. Even the amaretto she put in our drinks wasn't enough to make me stay. Had to leave after just one cup. No matter what chair I sat in they followed me with their eyes."

"Clementine," Ezra chuckles. "Beautiful name. I had a golden lab called Goldie and a Jack Russell called Jack. Wife was always telling me I had no imagination."

The elevator door opens and the group that every day greets the letter carrier steps off. My day has begun.

Chapter thirteen

Over the past week and a half, I've had a dozen invites from the widows, and even from some whose husbands are still alive, to the Valentine's dance. They stand by the reception desk, white hair sparkling in shafts of sunlight while tittering behind pink polished nails as they ask if I'd do them the honour of accompanying them. Not wanting to hurt anyone's feelings by choosing one over the other, I've turned down every one. This afternoon I'm hanging cupids and hearts in the community room as I watch the band set up. They're called The Bridge City Big Band and I've been told by Beatrice and Allan that they play a variety of music including big band, swing and jazz. I finish my shift and go home wishing I was staying.

As a kid, I listened to jazz even though my era was The Beatles and the Dave Clark Five, The Who, and the British invasion bands who should have influenced my musical taste. But I felt connected to jazz. Duke, Ella, Dinah, Chet, Django, Glenn, and Artie; they were my mentors, my heroes. I'd peruse the jazz section at the record store along with sun-glassed beatniks reeking of pot, and people old enough to be my parents and grandparents. I became quite knowledgeable, schooling myself for hours at the library about the lives of these artists. But the responsibilities of marriage and kids changed all that and I struggled to find the time to listen to my music. I never let it drop completely, much to Elaine's chagrin, as she would find me hiding in the basement with my turntable when I was supposed to be helping with one kid or another.

1983

Heart-shaped cookies with pink icing cover every surface in our kitchen and it's an effort to find a place to pour myself a cup of coffee. I push some of the sweet treats out of the way and set down my mug.

"Jesus Christ, Elaine. Who the hell are all these for? There's only the three of us to eat them, the baby doesn't eat cookies yet."

"Quit swearing, John. Barbie's preschool class. I'm hosting her Valentine's party." She wrinkles her nose. "And I'd appreciate it if you'd shower when you get home from work."

Before we had kids, on occasion when Elaine would pick me up from work, she'd open all the car windows to let the odour out. And if I offered a ride to another postie, she would breathe very shallowly until we dropped him off. Letter carriers, after a hard day's work, do not smell very good.

"Valentine's party?" I say.

She rolls her eyes and I know I'm about to get a lecture. "Tomorrow. Everyone's arriving at three-thirty. We'll have cookies, play games, pass out valentines. I told you this last week."

"Perhaps if you wouldn't tell me when I'm tired I might remember."

"Perhaps if you weren't tired all the ti...."

"Don't know why kids have to go to school when they're four," I say, cutting Elaine off before she can finish the sentence I've heard a thousand times. "You and I didn't start until we were six and we turned out alright."

"This isn't the fifties anymore." Her tone is sarcastic. "It's good for Barbie. Gives her confidence, something everyone needs in life." She hands me a cookie. "You should be home just in time to help."

"Might be late tomorrow," I say with my mouth full.

"What, lots of valentines to deliver?"

"Are you making fun of my job?" I take another cookie.

"I'm teasing, John. Don't be so serious. There'll be lots of mothers here to help. Just thought you might like to see your daughter handing out her valentines. There's this one boy she likes, Nathan

Fritz. Cute little guy. They always try to stand…."

"I'll see if I'm not too tired, Elaine." I leave her to go and shower, thinking I'll take some overtime tomorrow. A room full of twenty screaming four-year olds and their mothers is not something I want to come home to after a long day at work.

Of course, there isn't any overtime today and I drive home, spotting Brenda as she walks down the sidewalk in front of my house. Even though she's had a couple of kids, the belt of her coat accentuates her slender waist. After two babies, Elaine's body is getting plump, her waist thickening to the same size as her hips. Brenda's daughter is skipping beside her and together they climb the steps to my front door. Instead of parking, I circle the block before pulling into the garage, then shut off the ignition and stay in the car.

I'm sure she doesn't even remember, hell I barely remember, we were both so drunk. Why did Elaine have to leave me while she talked to the neighbour women? That damn clique stood in the Jenson's kitchen for an hour, cackling and gossiping. Can I help it if Brenda saw me sitting by myself under the Christmas tree? Can I help it if her husband left her last year to raise her daughter alone and she needed to talk to someone? I pound the steering wheel. "Why didn't I listen when Elaine said it was time to leave? Why didn't I put on my coat and go home to bed like a good little husband?"

Assuming everyone is in the living room, I slip through the backdoor, anticipating I'll be able to sneak in unseen and go to the basement to listen to some music. I really should build myself a jazz room in the garage, a man cave as I've heard my co-workers call them. Not sit in the unfinished basement like some banished teenager, on a fold-out chair under a single light bulb with the kids toys scattered everywhere. But my plans are foiled when Elaine, who is standing in the dining room and has a clear view of the kitchen, sees me trying to enter unnoticed.

"John, you're home," she yells over the horde of four-year olds.

I point upstairs. "I'm sweaty, need a shower," I mouth, positive telling her I smell will help me get away easier than telling her I'm going to the basement to listen to music.

"Come here," she mouths back.

I shake my head. "I'm going upstairs."

She weaves between the kids towards me. "We need your help," she grabs my hand. "We're having an inflation problem."

"Elaine," I protest. "I'm stinky and dirty. Just let me go and shower first."

"This will only take a sec." She drags my resisting body through the group of women standing around our dining room, making it impossible for me to continue saying no. A canister with a limp balloon attached to its spout sits in the middle of the table. Elaine giggles and so do the women. I get the feeling they've been into the punch.

Elaine extends her arm at the canister. "We can't seem to get this thing to work. We've been trying but it just stays like this." She pokes the sagging pink balloon. The women stifle guffaws. Brenda is in back of the group watching me.

I unclip a valve from beside the tap, pull off the balloon and attach the valve to the spout. I stretch the vinyl lip of the balloon over the valve, turn on the tap then squeeze the trigger, releasing the gas and inflating the balloon.

"Well," Elaine says. "We'd never have figured that out. I guess men are good for something."

I look up hoping Brenda didn't hear, but she's gone. I leave the group with an order from Elaine to bring down the extra flat of juice that's on the floor of the linen closet and escape upstairs to shower.

I smell Brenda's sweet scent before I see her. She's standing at the top of the staircase.

"Kids' parties," she says. "I can take only so much." Her lips are red and I remember the fullness of them pressing onto mine.

I squeeze by her. "Hey, Brenda. Just need to shower and change."

"Hey Brenda? Pretty cool reception considering last Christmas."

"I was drunk."

She licks her lips. "Seemed quite focused if I remember right."

I scan my eyes down a dress that clings to her narrow waist and hips. Mark's bedroom door is ajar and I assume he's down for his afternoon nap. I whisper, "I'm a married man, with two kids. And I love my wife." I pull Mark's bedroom door closed.

She touches my arm; her hand is cool on my hot flesh. "Not from what I've seen," she says. "Seems to me like you and Elaine are drifting apart."

Elaine calls up the stairs. "John, are you going to bring down the juice?"

"Just need a quick shower and I'll be right there."

"What's taking you so long? Thought you'd be done by now. Can't wait all day."

Brenda smiles and without a second thought, I push her into the bathroom then close and lock the door behind us. I press my mouth to hers and feel her teeth cut into my lips. I lift up her dress then force her against the sink. The bathroom doorknob rattles and someone knocks.

"You locked the door, John," Elaine says.

I place my hand on Brenda's lips. "Didn't want a toddler to walk in on me."

"I'm getting the juice. I need it now, not later."

"Fine."

"Are you alright?" Elaine asks. "You sound stressed. Everything go ok at work today?"

"I'm fine, work was fine. Just let me clean up and I'll be right down."

I turn on the shower and Brenda and I remain quiet until we hear Elaine's footsteps, weighted down with the crate of juice, descending the stairs. While I watch, Brenda strips and steps into the shower. I undo my buckle and let my pants drop to the floor.

**

Tears drip down my cheeks. Elaine and I wasted so much time being angry and feeling used, blaming each other for our unhappiness, becoming so involved with work and raising a family, for a few years we forgot to be nice to each other. I've often wondered if she knew I was hiding in the bathroom with Brenda, and not wanting to face such a scene at our daughter's Valentine's party, chose to ignore it.

I return to The Wheaton to the sounds of *String of Pearls* playing in the community room. For the next three hours I twirl Marigold, Ivy, and even Alma around the room.

Chapter fourteen

Alma hasn't approached me about talking to Melanie so I imagine, just as Ezra predicted, Melanie's smart enough to realize that complaining about wanting a resident to hurry up and die could be used as grounds for dismissal.

I'm folding napkins, restless to go home to Clem — Melanie's behind the desk, grouchy because she hates the night shift — when Ezra walks into the dining room. He's been doing that lately, thinking it's breakfast when it's eleven at night.

"Ezra, what are you doing here?"

"Where is everyone?"

"Supper's over, Ezra."

"Over?"

"You had pork chops, remember? I served you coffee?"

"That was last night."

"No, that was a few hours ago."

He pulls his hand down his face. "Oh dear."

"I'll take you back to your room." I touch his elbow.

"Can you stay for a bit, John? Could use someone to talk to tonight. Won't take up too much of your time."

I look at the clock and think about Clementine. "Sure. I'll stay for a few minutes."

I pull out a chair across from him and sit. While Ezra collects his thoughts, I hear Melanie in the lobby telling Mrs. Crawford, in not too empathetic a voice, to quit riding the elevator looking for a husband who died ten years ago, and go to bed.

Ezra starts to talk in a cracked voice. "I've had a good life. Found a loving woman to marry, kids grew up with no major problems."

"Some of us have been lucky, Ezra."

"Done a few things I shouldn't have, missed doing a few things I should have."

"We all have our bucket lists, good or bad. Can't get past that. We're only human."

He nods, not noticing I'm talking in clichés.

"If you live to be an old man," I continue. "and have things you wish you could do again, that's unavoidable: understandable even."

"Understandable," Ezra repeats. He holds his hands out in front of him, examining them as if they aren't his. "Don't recognize them anymore," he says. "Used to lift dogs that weighed a hundred and fifty pounds. Lifted them right up onto the examination table. Now I can barely lift a cup of coffee. How did the years sneak past? I don't remember growing old."

"You've lived a useful life, Ezra, helped a lot of animals, been a decent man. What more can anyone ask?"

"Decent." He massages his thumb into his palm.

I reach across the table and place my hand on his knuckles; they're knobby and swollen. "We can only do our best: that's all we can do. If we make a couple mistakes along the way, so be it."

"I killed a man once."

Thinking he's delusional I say, "I doubt that, Ezra," and pat his hand.

He begins to unfold and refold the napkin I've just placed there. "Had a client a long time ago. Roger. Roger Willingham. Owned a dog named Petunia. Chihuahua. He was a big guy, over six feet. Probably weighed two-fifty." He shakes his head, as if remembering the man and dog together. "Looked funny, him walking that little thing on a leash. But he loved that dog and that dog loved him.

"At one appointment when Petunia was getting older and having trouble with her kneecaps, something Chihuahuas are prone to, I mentioned to Roger that he looked like he'd lost a bit of weight and asked him how he was doing it; I needed to lose a couple of pounds myself in those days. He said he wasn't trying, it was just falling off. Being a doctor and sensitive to any sudden changes in health, I suggested he get that checked out. A year later when he brought Petunia in for her annual checkup, he looked worse. Told me he'd gone to his doctor and found out he had stomach cancer. Had done the whole chemo, surgery route but the cancer had come back. Said it was his time and he was at peace with it."

I glance at the clock; eleven twenty-five.

"Then he asked if he lived longer than Petunia, would I help him die. Said he didn't want to die before his dog as Petunia needed him, but once she was gone, he would be ready. Roger surprised me asking that, like he knew me better than I thought he did. But I told him my Hippocratic Oath wouldn't allow me to participate in any plan that would allow him to die sooner than the disease would take him. He didn't say any more."

The ice maker in the fridge clatters ice into the bucket and we both jump at the noise.

"Six months later to the day — believe me I remember everything about this — he came back with Petunia to have her put down. She was in bad shape, he had to carry her everywhere her legs were so bad. She was hardly eating, nothing left of her but skin and bones; she was going on seventeen. I knew it was her time and felt no guilt, though I did feel sad when I put that second injection into her, as I always did when I put down an animal. I used the two-injection method. First one puts the animal into a deep sleep, second one stops its heart. My animals never felt any pain. They died knowing they were loved." A tear rolls down his cheek. "That's how Cynthia died, me holding her hand and whispering I loved her."

He's quiet and I don't press him to talk. Sitting this close to Ezra I notice wrinkles around his eyes that I haven't seen when he's sitting with his cronies in the lobby. They cut out from the corner of his eyes and turn upward towards his temples. Elaine had them too; she called them laugh lines. Said she got them after being married to me for forty years.

"I never socialized with clients, made it a rule. But that afternoon, after I put Petunia down, Roger and I went out for a beer. It felt like the right thing to do. He talked about his life and how lucky he'd been. He told me he didn't want to become a burden to his wife, and just wanted to die with no fanfare. We'd had a few rounds by then and I confessed to him, even though I was a doctor, I thought there should be assisted suicide for people who wanted to die, that it shouldn't just be animals who we were allowed to be put out of pain. We parted and I thought I'd probably not see him again."

Ezra pauses and I shift in my chair, worried about where this story is going and not sure I want to hear the end of it.

"Roger called about three months later and again asked for my help. No, not asked, begged. Held me to what I'd confessed to him that afternoon in the bar. Told me he would tell his wife he was having a good day and she should take this chance to get out of the house for a while." Ezra blows his nose with the clean napkin. "Sorry, John." He holds the napkin out to me. "You need this for tomorrow."

"Keep it," I say.

He dries his wet cheeks. "I packed a bag and threw it into the trunk of my car. I had no definite plan of following through with Roger's request, but I took my bag just the same." He shrugs his shoulders. "I suppose it was subliminal. When I arrived, I could see he had a week left, two at the most. He must have lost over one-hundred pounds; was nothing but a skeleton lying in the bed. He said his wife had gone to dinner and a movie with her sister so we had at least three hours before she returned. He was in pain from not taking his morphine but he needed his mind clear to be able to talk to me, that's how badly he wanted this. Said even though his wife was glad for every day she had with him, he didn't want to bear the humiliation of having his diaper changed, or being sponge bathed anymore. The pain had worn him out and he was ready to die. I told him I'd administer the drug between his toes, but if the injection sites were found, there would be an inquiry. He said that's why he wanted his wife to have a damn good alibi. And because no one would know I'd been there, chances are they wouldn't think to look for injection sites as no one else visited or looked after him. Everyone would simply assume the cancer finally took him. The plan was perfect. As I listened to him talk about his life, preparing himself for the end, I knew in my heart what he was asking of me was the right thing to do. When he said he was ready, I opened my bag and removed the first syringe, the one that would make him sleep. I looked into his eyes as I injected him; his gaze didn't waver from mine. He slipped into unconsciousness. I pulled the second syringe out of my bag and without hesitation I injected the other foot, hoping the dosage was correct as I'd only ever given it to dogs and cats before. He was the size of a large dog, so I guessed the amount to use. I placed my stethoscope on his chest and listened as his heart slowly stopped beating and watched his lungs as they stopped rising and falling, just as I would do for one of my patients. I lifted his eyelids and saw no dilation; he was gone. I quickly packed up my things and left before his wife returned. I parked a few blocks away to catch my breath. My body was tingling and I felt alive, even though I'd just killed a man. A week later I saw his obituary in the paper. Never told a soul until now. Not even Cynthia."

I remember sitting with Elaine as she writhed in bed when the morphine would begin to wear off. Many times, she wished she would die, but I told her to hang in there, not to leave me yet, that I needed more time. I knew I was being selfish, that she was suffering, but all I could think of was myself.

Ezra massages his deformed hands. "Near the end of Cynthia's life, she asked me if I would help her die." He sighs a shuddering sigh, then mimics my thoughts. "To my shame I refused. Because of my selfishness, I allowed my wife to linger, doped up on painkillers. I didn't want to lose her, kept hoping for a miracle, yet I felt so guilty."

"You shouldn't feel guilty. There's nothing wrong with wanting more time with your wife."

"That's the thing, John. Any guilt I have doesn't stem from my wanting more time, or even from the fact I killed a man. My guilt is because I couldn't stand behind my beliefs when Cynthia wanted to die. I should have allowed her the dignity of dying when she wanted, not made her suffer needlessly. God almighty, I helped Roger, surely I could have helped my wife. I was a doctor, I am a doctor. I knew what to do. It's not difficult, even for a lay person.

"There are very few things we keep our entire lives," Ezra continues. "Be damned if I can remember my first Christmas with my wife, or my kids' first days of school. But the memories of Cynthia in that hospital bed waiting to die, I can't seem to escape."

I hear a noise outside the dining room and turn to see blue nail polish slipping past the doorway. "Ezra, let's get you back to your room," I say. "You'll feel better in the morning."

"Ok, John. Thanks for listening." He wipes his face with the napkin.

I put my hand under his elbow and escort him to his room, then leave with Melanie watching me walk down the path to the parking lot. That night I dream of the night Elaine died.

2014

I wake on the couch not to the sound of the phone, but to Clementine nosing my arm, something she does when she's confused. She's been nosing me for weeks now, ever since Elaine was admitted to the hospital. Without her mom around, she doesn't know what to do with herself.

I shuffle across the living room and pull myself up the stairs using the bannister. I flop on to the bed fully clothed and somehow manage to doze off.

When the phone rings I sit up and look at the clock. I know who it is. I left there an hour ago. The nurse said she'd call if there was any change. If I don't answer, nothing will happen, they won't tell me Elaine is dead. The ringing stops and I lie back down, momentarily relieved. Wrong number I tell myself. Five minutes later it begins again. This time I answer. It's Elaine's nurse.

"John. You need to come here now," she says.

"Now?" I say, knowing full well what she means.

"As soon as you can."

I hang up and with shaking hands, call Barbie. I ask her to call Mark and Janet then I leave the house without saying good-bye to Clementine. She whines as I close the door on her face.

I walk down the hall past the nurses' station. The smell of death is strong in this wing of the hospital and I cup my hand over my nose. Nurse Prentice approaches, "She's gone, John. It's over."

Barbie runs up behind me and without stopping, enters her mother's room. I hear her crying and try to pull my feet from the floor; I have to go in there, I tell myself, I have to be strong, I'm the one they're going to expect to lean on. But I stand in the hall outside Elaine's door unable to go any further. Instead, Barb comes out of the room to be with me. She holds me, her body shaking as she tries to find some comfort in my embrace. Over her shoulder I see Janet and Mark running towards us. As the four of us stand in the middle of the hall, my children clinging to me, I'm the only one with my arms by my sides.

Chapter fifteen

Not wanting Melanie to quiz me about my conversation with Ezra, each day when I arrive at work I avoid her by going to the dining room to do some chores, or I sit in my car and wait until I see her bulky frame exit the building. Using these tactics, I've managed to avoid her for an entire week. When I finally do bump into her, she corners me in the kitchen as I'm doing my rounds of checking to be sure all the appliances are turned off before I leave for the night.

She blocks the doorway, her hand on the frame. "That was quite the chin-wag you and Adelman had last week," she says. "Thought you always liked to get out of here ASAP."

I play dumb. "When was that, Melanie?"

"Last week. You and him," she points her thumb over her shoulder towards the dining room, "sat in there. Seemed to be something serious." She presses her blue fingernails into the frame, turning her knuckles white. "Thought maybe you'd like to share, is all."

"Oh, that," I say. "Nope. I'm good."

Her smile is forced. "Being the residents' friend isn't part of the job."

"It seems to me, Melanie," I say in a level tone, "that being their friend, that listening to what they have to say is part of the job. And since Ezra was speaking to me, not you, what he and I were talking about was meant for only me to hear. Anything you might have heard through eavesdropping was misconstrued." I don't stop there. "And I've heard some unsettling things about you."

She wags her finger in my face. "That's the trouble with gossip in this place. It gets passed along so many times between so many mouths it ends up being something entirely different than what it started out as. And often the people passing on these stories are light in the loafers in the first place. I wouldn't trust a word they said."

Tired from putting in my eight-hour shift and tired of dealing with Melanie, I push past her arm, grab my coat and leave. I want nothing more in the world than to quit and go home, put this job behind me and sleep the rest of my life away on the couch.

1968

"Ah, Mom, I don't know why we have to come here. It's not like she's happy to see us."

"John, mind your mouth." Mom pushes in the clutch, grinding the gears, then turns off the ignition. The car sputters to a stop and I pray it will start again when we leave. I do not relish the thought of having to ask the old biddy for cab fare home.

"Dad left so long ago I don't remember what he looks like, but I have to visit his God-damn mother?"

This time Mom reaches into the backseat and whacks my head. "You complain one more time, John Mark Davies, and I'll make you visit her every week for the next six months all by yourself. Now get out of the car and quit your whining. And you'd better be on your best behaviour in there, or I'll whip your hide when we get home. Some day she's going to die and if we play our cards right, she might leave some of her money to you and your sister. She definitely won't leave it to me and Lord knows I can't afford to pay for any education past high-school."

I climb out of the car and stand on a sidewalk so hot, I can feel the warmth through my worn-out shoes. I don't care about any education past high-school and I certainly don't care about this old woman's money, if she even has any, which I doubt. Dad wouldn't have left if she did. Once, I mentioned this to Mom and she gripped my arm so hard I thought she was going to break it. She shook me, saying I shouldn't speak of things I know nothing about and that I had no idea why Dad left. I've never told her I heard them fighting one night as their voices drifted up the register. In whispers, Dad said he doubted his mother would be living in a run-down senior's apartment if she was loaded and *he wasn't about to wait around for her to die to see if it was true*. Then he said something that made me slide down under my covers. He said *it was enough that you got pregnant once, but then you had to go and do it again*. Said, *raising a family was not something he had planned on doing and the only way he would ever stick around would be if his mother was going to leave him some money*. Said he was leaving, that he found someone else. I put my pillow over my head and stopped listening.

I mop my forehead with the frayed cuff of my dress shirt while Mom tugs at the hem of my sister's dress then plasters a cowlick down at the back of my head with her spit. A group of boys are playing a game of softball in the park across the street and their laughter makes me yearn to be with them. I close my eyes and wish — something I do a lot — that Dad had never left and we were a real family. I open my eyes and nothing has changed, as it never does. I drag myself towards a building I've been to twice a year for all of my life.

The one-story flat roofed affair sheds flakes of yellow paint off window frames that stretch down the block, seemingly to infinity. The sign, Willow-Gate Seniors Apartments, has seen better days as it tilts in the brown grass surrounding the weather-worn posts holding it up. The place looks like something out of a horror movie.

Every Christmas and every summer Mom, my sister and I arrive, gifts in hand, to visit the mother of my father, a woman I barely know, someone my father hasn't seen since he left when I was five.

Mom pulls open the door of the apartment block and a faint odour of overcooked food and body odour gushes out making me retch. Two old people sit in the faded chairs scattered around the lobby and turn their rheumy eyes our way as we stand on the other side of the threshold. Mom grabs my hand and jerks me after my younger sister, who is skipping down the hall toward the tiny apartment my grandmother calls home.

Nothing has changed since last time I was here, not even Grandmother. The wrinkles on her cheeks and forehead are so deep, I wonder if they hurt. Her nails are yellow and ridged, with a rim of dirt under the edges. A fridge hums loudly in the corner of the tiny kitchen, rust staining the linoleum around its base, and a hot plate is on the counter, a pot sagging on one of the crooked burners. An empty can of beans sits on the counter. In the living room, the same photographs that were here at Christmas clutter the coffee table, and the bathroom door on the far side of the living room is closed, because, as Grandmother has always said, you shouldn't air your dirty laundry in front of others. Grace and I are not allowed to use her facilities while we're here so Mom usually stops at a gas station before we arrive so we can take a whiz.

A mat lies on the floor by the front door where we're supposed to leave our shoes. I slip mine off and stand in my socks, tucking the hole towards the floor with my toes and leaving sweat marks on her linoleum.

Grandmother is sitting in a chair by the window in the living room with the same blanket she's used for years covering her knees. Her feet rest on a tiny wooden stool in front of her chair and are clad in lace-up shoes that I assume never touch the ground.

Mom slips off the high-heels she bought at Kresges in the discount bin, then walks in her nylon stocking feet across the floor to give her mother-in-law a kiss. "Happy birthday, Mom," she says and I wonder why she calls Grandmother, Mom, this being her mother-in-law. And even that's stretching it, considering she hasn't seen her husband for over eight years. When friends ask where my dad is I always say he's dead, which he could be for all I know, or care. My sister and I perch ourselves on the edge of Grandmother's couch.

"John," she cackles. "Come and look at the picture of your father."

I slouch over to look at the picture I've seen twice a year for as far back as I can remember. It's black and white with Dad kneeling on the front lawn of some childhood house, petting a long dead dog.

"Loved that dog, your dad did. He'd drive that truck he bought and fixed up himself down country roads, let the dog run behind.

Does a kid good to own an animal. Teaches responsibility."

"Yes, Ma'am." I glance at Mom and she shakes her head.

"Stand up straight, let me look at you," Grandmother says.

Mom pinches the back of my arm and I straighten my shoulders, bringing my eyes to the level of the fly specked window. A plot of land is in back, overgrown with thistles six feet tall. A wooden bench sags on the perimeter of this derelict piece of earth, its slats rotten and twisted from years of exposure to the elements. An old woman perches gingerly on the edge of the bench, her skin as weathered as the wood she's sitting on. She's looking longingly at the patch of weed-riddled earth that was once a garden and I understand her desire to be out there; anything is better than this.

"Look like your father, don't you?"

I pull my eyes off the view outside. "Yes Ma'am."

"Guess you gotta look like someone." She strokes the picture with a pointed finger.

"Yes Ma'am," I say for the third time. The picture must be twenty-five years old.

She pokes her nail inside her nose and picks something out then looks at it before she wipes it on a tissue she has tucked in the bosom of her dress.

"You should have seen your father when he was a boy. Took me shopping every week. Earned his keep, he did."

Until he took the coward's way out and decided to abandon everything that should have been important to him, his own mother included, I think to myself.

As Grace and I sit on the edge of the couch, not even swinging our legs because Grandmother would tell us to quit fidgeting, a mouse pokes its head out from under the old sofa, then sniffs its way between our feet towards her chair. Out of the corner of my eye I see Mom stiffen, but to her credit, she says nothing. At home, she'd already be on a chair, screaming for someone to kill it.

Grandmother spies the thing but she doesn't make any movement to let us know she's surprised to see a mouse in her house. Instead she sits perfectly still as the creature inches closer to her, then like a snake striking its prey, she reaches her shoe-clad foot forward and tromps on the mouse so hard, blood squirts out of its mouth and its tiny eyes pop from their sockets.

Mom, Grace and I are so shocked at the viciousness of the act that for a few moments we're frozen in place. Grandmother, as if this is something that happens every day, removes a paper bag from the drawer in the end-table beside her and orders me to pick up the mouse then throw it in the garbage can outside.

I sit, frozen at the sight of the mangled creature, until my mother, someone who should really be saying I don't have to do such a repulsive chore, says, "John, did you hear your grandmother? Get that thing out of here."

I stare at her — she looks like she's going to hurl — defying her, hoping she'll see the error of her ways and take Grace and me out of this hellhole. With her complexion turning greener by the second, I finally scoop up the mouse then, dragging Grace with me, I leave the room to take the gruesome mess to the garbage. When I'm finished with the task, I don't go back inside, but wait with Grace in the small square of shade next to the peeling wall of the building. Fifteen minutes later when Mom exits, she doesn't meet my eyes, nor does she give me heck for staying outside but tells Grace and me to get in the car then races away faster than I've ever seen her drive. For the next week she's cordial, giving me no chores to do and not bringing up the subject of the trampled mouse.

1969

"I'm home," I shout. There's no answer but I hear Mom in the kitchen making sounds that could be either laughing or crying. "What's so funny?" I ask as I walk into the room.

She's seated at the table with tears streaming down her cheeks. She shows me a letter she's ripped from an envelope that now lies on the table. It's addressed to my dad.

"This letter is for Dad?" I ask. I peer at the return address; it's from the law office of Pinder and Heathrow.

"It is," Mom says.

"But, how, why?"

She raises her palms then wipes away some tears. "We never divorced. He must not have got in touch with them after he left. I suppose they think he lives here."

I take the paper from her hands — she offers no resistance — and begin to read. The letter is informing us that Mrs. Dorothy Davies has passed away and has left her estate to Mr. Steven Davies. He's to book an appointment with the law office to review the conditions of the estate. If this letter fails to reach him within the next thirty days, the money is not to be left to anyone else and will be donated to charity.

I look at Mom. "She really did have money?"

"After you and Grace took the mouse outside that day, she told me she had no money and I shouldn't expect anything when she dies. She said if that's why I keep dragging my brats to visit her, then don't bother bringing you back."

"So, do you think this letter means she had money?"

Mom shrugs and looks me in the eye. "Doesn't really matter to us now, does it?"

"Do you know how to get in touch with Dad? Maybe he'll give us some."

"I haven't heard from that man since the day he walked out on me. For all I know, he could be dead." Then without hesitation, she takes the letter from me and tears it up into tiny pieces.

Chapter sixteen

Instead of quitting, which I vowed to do the day after my confrontation with Melanie, I return to work with the plan to be less personal and more professional. An invitation to join Mrs. Hawkins for tea this evening is waiting for me on the desk. So much for that idea.

She's been hounding me for two weeks; says she's taken a shine to me. Says she feels we got off on the wrong foot and wants to get to know me better. With each invitation, I've made an excuse — need to go for groceries, have a dentist appointment, babysitting my grandkids — but today I can't come up with anything so perhaps to test my ability to remain aloof or simply to check out Beatrice's theory, I sit in her living room, the last of the days sun shining through the large window, and see that Beatrice was right; I am being watched from every corner. I take a cup balanced on a saucer from her shaking hand. "Thank-you, Mrs. Hawkins."

"Darjeeling," she says. "Supposed to be good for you or some such thing. I hope you don't mind, but I put a drop of amaretto in it. And call me Ernestine, please."

She grins at me over the rim of her cup as we take sips in unison.

"When I was first married we bought our tea in the grocery store on the shelf right beside the coffee," Ernestine says. "Now there's shops that sell nothing but tea. Speciality shops for everything nowadays. Do you know I've seen stores that specialize in walking? Walking! Can you believe that? I've been walking since I was ten months old."

Again, I sip, nod and smile.

"Mind you, I was child number twelve in a brood of twelve. Had to learn to fend for myself. No one was going to look after me in that family, that's for damn sure. Except Dad. He had a soft spot for me, being the youngest."

"That's a large family," I say, feigning interest.

"All of them gone but a brother somewhere on the east coast. Must be close to a hundred by now." She shakes her head. "Bullied me night and day. I might have been the baby of the family, but I was never babied. Doesn't mean I was smart enough or old enough to marry a decent man."

"Oh yes?"

"Eighteen when I wed," she sets her cup down and passes me a cookie. "Considered young nowadays but back then, just on the cusp. No one ever told me I was too young. It was just accepted."

Pretty close to the ages Elaine and I were when we married. "How old was your husband?" I take a cookie.

"Ten years older than me, though he acted much older. But he was born old. Always pragmatic, too practical. Hell, he never let loose. His given name was Beverly. Don't know why a parent would name their son Beverly, but that's what his name was. Wouldn't let anyone call him that. Went by Walter. I used to call him Beverly just to get under his skin." She laughs and picks up her cup. "I was a bit of a rebel when I was younger. Got used to sticking up for myself when I was a girl."

"Your husband had no good qualities?" I don't want to believe Ernestine wasted her life in a loveless marriage.

"If he did, he hid them from me." She swirls the last of the tea in the bottom of her cup and peers in, as if looking for her husband's virtues in the murky grounds. "He was angry from the moment he got up till the moment he went to bed. Never cracked a God-damn joke, never even saw him break a smile. Found a picture of him a while back. That day you and I talked about marriage. Thought maybe seeing him again would remind me of the good times." She points to the end-table by my elbow. "There. Our twentieth-fifth anniversary. Someone snapped a shot and gave it to me. Cripes, don't know why they thought I'd like to have a picture of him. He died a month later. Fell down a well, broke his neck. I was a young widow, only forty-three."

I pick up the picture. It's a small photo, five by seven, but clearly shows his features. His face is long, with black hair slicked off his deep forehead. Narrow eyes stare at me above an equally narrow nose. He is not smiling. If anyone looks like the grim reaper, it's him. I can't imagine living with him for twenty-five years. "And did it?" I ask.

"Did it what, John?"

"Remind you of some of the good times when you saw his picture."

She wobbles her head. "Hells bells, not a one." She sets her cup down. "Don't know why I put the damned thing out. Had enough of him watching me for the twenty-five years we were married. I've a mind to put it back where I found it after you leave."

She shuffles to the stereo and lifts the lid. It's the kind of record player that was considered a piece of furniture back in the day. Not like now where everyone plays music through their phones and listens with ear buds. I don't know how anyone can hear the individual instruments and their harmonies through pieces of plastic wedged in their ears.

We had one of these stereos when I was a kid. Mom said if I was going to listen to good music, it may as well be on something where I could hear the instruments properly. One of the few things she splurged on after Dad left. Once, I came home from school and found her singing along with Ella Fitzgerald, *Cry Me a River*. The music was so loud she hadn't heard me enter. I stood for a few moments, listening to her mimic Ella, until she sensed she was being watched. She stopped singing and turned off the music then told me to take out the garbage and make sure my homework was done before supper.

Ernestine pulls a record from its sleeve and places it on the turntable. Benny Goodman begins to play his licorice stick. She has an assortment of vinyl I'd like to peruse through. From here alone I can see Shearing, Cohn, Dorsey and Webster.

The combination of good music and spiked tea have relaxed me and I find myself curious about Ernestine's life. "Can I ask, Ernestine, if you didn't like your husband, why did you marry him?" I empty the cup, so dainty you can see the light shining through, then wipe my lips with the back of my hand.

She tilts her head to the side. "Women were supposed to marry back then. Marry and procreate. I may have been a rebel but I wasn't rebellious enough to want to be labelled a spinster. I was a plain girl…"

I try to object.

"No, no, John," she raises a hand. "I'm a realist. Probably what drew Mr. Hawkins to me in the first place; he knew he was hard to live with and figured a girl as homely as me would never stray. Like I said, he was a sensible man. Hindsight is a bitch sometimes."

"It is indeed," I hold my cup out.

She pours us each more tea then holds up the amaretto bottle. "Splash?"

I nod then ask about the pictures.

"Some are friends, some came with the frame." She pours in one dollop, then tops it up with another more generous than the first.

"Pardon?"

"Couldn't bear to have a family with that curse of a man so I have no family pictures to set out." She passes me the plate of cookies then pauses in mid-air. I take the plate from her sagging hand, the cookies now sliding to the edge. "Truth be told, I did give birth, a son. Just don't talk about it since my involvement in his life ended the moment he was born." We each take a cookie and I set the plate on the table. "I went to my oldest sister's house the last couple of months of my pregnancy without breathing a word to my husband of his impending fatherhood. Told him my sister needed help with her own family as she'd just given birth to her fourth." She takes a bite of her cookie, then talks around the crumbs while she chews. "Gave my son up. My husband never found out the truth. He thought I was just getting fat." She blows on her tea then slurps up a drink. "Knew I could fool him, he wasn't a bright man about women's private goings on. Most men back in that day didn't know much." She dunks her cookie and takes another bite. "Felt it wasn't necessary. We took care of the children and the home and they took care of the rest. Not like now, when the fathers go right in the birthing room."

I continue to sip my tea, surprised by Ernestine's confession.

"At first, when I found out I was pregnant," she says, "I wanted to wait and see if things were going to get better. But as the months passed and I got closer to my birthing date, I came to the conclusion that once a man is an ornery cuss, he's probably not going to change. Decided I didn't want to raise a child in the same house as him." She waves her cup around the room. "So, because I don't have pictures of family to surround me with, I keep the pictures the frames came with." She takes a sip.

"Wow, Ernestine. It must have been a difficult time for you."

"Well, I figured the child would have a better life. Forced myself to not think about being pregnant so never bonded during the nine months I carried him. Kept myself removed from the situation, so to speak. At least as removed as one can be when she's as big as a God-damn house. And my sister, God bless her soul, took him away as soon as he was born. Didn't even let me see him. Don't know if he had blond hair or dark, though I suspect my husband's genes came through and he had a headful of dark hair."

She stares out the window, lost in thought.

"Had the doctor do a hysterectomy right there and then. He didn't want to do it, said I was too young. But I offered him a healthy sum and he acquiesced. My husband may have been a son-of-a-bitch, but he was a wealthy son-of-a-bitch, always gave me a generous allowance." She lifts her face to me. "And on the bright side, I got a couple of months' reprieve from looking after Mr. Hawkins. Always wanted everything perfect. Whereas I couldn't be bothered keeping the furniture dust free or the floors gleaming." She shakes her head. "Jesus H Jerimiah, he was a finicky man." She peers at me over her cup and pushes thinning eyebrows together. "I've never told a soul about this, John. Don't know why I told you. Guess some secrets just want to come out, no matter how old they are."

"I won't say a word, Ernestine." I think about the secrets told to me in the past few months. "Your secret is safe with me."

She waves her cookie at me. "I suppose at this point in my life it doesn't really matter who knows. Everyone has skeletons rattling around in their closet. A woman giving up a child for adoption is nothing compared to some. I have a niece, got pregnant out of wedlock. She raised that child without a man in the picture. Back then it would have been a scandal." She pours us each more tea and amaretto. "My own father was a kind man and treated me as an adult. Never made me feel as if it was a chore to spend time with me. What about you? Did you get along with your dad? I know sometimes Dads can be hard on sons, even if they're not sons-of-bitches like Mr. Hawkins."

"My dad wasn't in the picture much."

"I'm sorry. That must have been difficult."

"I didn't think about it a lot."

"It's hard for a son to grow up without his father," she looks around her living room as she dunks her cookie. "Some people think I'm crazy, all these pictures of people I don't know. Old Mr. Merriweather, you know the man that lives down the hall with the nose so long you could open doors with it?"

The first time I saw him I thought he had on a fake nose.

"He came in here and told me I was a fool. Said I was living in an imaginary world and everyone thought I was nuts. Said that's why no one believes me when I say someone is in my room. I know it's kind of odd, but the pictures keep me company." She cocks her head and grins, "So good of you to come for tea, John. I like getting to know the staff, makes it feel less like a hotel and more like a home. Not that I'd ever let that girl, Melanie, in here. She is what, in my day, we would have called a dud. Wouldn't trust that one with a three-dollar bill, let alone to sit here eyeing up all my stuff." She blows on her tea. "And it's not like they're all pictures of strangers." She points, "There's Alma at a Christmas party with Ed Brown.

Several years ago, of course, since Ed died just last fall. I think that might have been the day I met you, if I'm not mistaken."

"You have a good memory, Ernestine."

"Everyone's got to be good at something. Never had the looks, but remembering facts, numbers, people, it's always been my strong suit. Kept the books for Mr. Hawkins without even going to school to learn how. Numbers and such just came natural to me." She points her cane to a picture tucked in behind the television. "There's Marigold and Carl Gibson at a dance we had a few months ago. We can't dance as spryly as we did twenty years ago but with arthritis and other old age maladies, we do what we can to keep moving. Except for Beatrice and Alan. Those two never seem to age." I pick up the picture. Marigold is smiling as Carl spins her across the floor. Ernestine points again, "And there's Rachel and Beatrice at a painting class we took last year."

Finding this more interesting than I would have imagined, I ask, "Are there more?"

"Ezra and his wife that passed, lovely woman. They're around here someplace. If you ever wanted to meet a couple that were suited to each other, it was those two. Took Ezra quite a while to bounce back."

I search for Ezra and Cynthia and find them on the coffee table behind the bowl of potpourri. Ezra looks happy. Beside him is a picture of Dave the cook.

"That's the cook, what's his name, Dave. Don't know why someone gave me a picture of him, but they did. Guess they thought I needed more pictures of people I know. Christ on a bike, he's an odd one."

A shadow flits across the wall and I look up. A bird, the size of a large cat, is sitting on the balcony railing just outside Ernestine's living room window. When it sees me, it flaps its wings and flies away.

"Raven," Ernestine says. "There's a difference you know, between a raven and a crow. Ravens are much bigger. Supposed to be bringers of death, or so my grandmother claimed. She was always saying things like that. I dared not shiver around her or she'd say someone just walked over my grave. And she'd box our ears if we didn't hold our breath when we passed a graveyard, said we'd inhale the spirits of the dead people if we breathed."

"If you believe such things," I say.

"As a girl, my grandmother scared me with her notions, but I didn't believe. Now I do."

"It's an old building, Ernestine. Lots of creaks and groans."

"Place was a hotel back at the turn of the century, probably a guest or two died in this very room. Could be a hundred ghosts roaming these halls."

"Ernestine, we just saw a raven on your balcony who cast a shadow on the wall he was so big."

"I'm not seeing shadows, John. Unless you call ghosts shadows."

Chapter seventeen

The cold stings my face and I jog from the car as quickly as the ice on the driveway will allow. If anyone were to see me burst through the doors they'd get the impression I was anxious to get to work. I stand inside stomping my sneakered feet, and clapping my gloved hands together, wondering why Melanie has neglected to lock the front door.

It's eleven at night and the door greeters are no longer here. The lobby is empty save for a dog, a border collie. He's standing by the reception desk, shifting his gaze between looking outside, and at me. I find this peculiar as normally dogs who are brought to visit don't wait in the lobby. And even if someone did bring him, it's awfully late to be visiting with a dog in tow.

I see no collar bearing identification tags and his fur is scruffy; perhaps he's homeless. There's a chance he could have activated the door himself – it wasn't locked – and come in to warm up; it is a border collie after all. They're supposed to be the smartest breed, although I like to think Clem is just as smart. I don't move, watching the dog before going any further, unsure if it's aggressive. When he wags his tail and sits, I step away from the electric eye, allowing the door to close, and kneel in front of him. He lifts a paw.

"What are you doing here?"

He doesn't answer, not unexpected, even from a border collie.

"Did your owners leave you in the lobby?" I look around. "Melanie is supposed to know better than this."

The dog whines, then steps under the electric eye, opening the door.

"You want me to follow you out?"

He wags his tail.

"I can't leave right now, not until Melanie returns. She probably had to run upstairs for a minute. Although she shouldn't have forgotten to lock up." I glance behind the desk. "Or take the phones with her. I'm sure your owners will be right back."

If I knew he was a stray I'd phone the pound to come and pick him up. I don't want to make him leave, it's too cold. After a couple more minutes of waiting on Melanie to return, I begin to get worried that maybe she's the one the dog is telling me to go outside and look for.

"Let's go and see what you want. Just not too far, ok?" I pull my gloves on and pick up the phone for the emergency pendants, leaving the other phone behind. I use the app to lock the door behind me and the dog and I walk into the night together.

It's a typical winter evening on the prairie; the air crisp, clear, and, as I can attest to from my short walk from the car to the lobby, very cold at minus 25. The kind of weather people in warm climates romanticize winter as being like in Canada. Where we go tobogganing and ride in horse drawn sleighs while drinking hot chocolate. One year over Christmas break, Elaine took our children on a sleigh ride. They bustled through the front door at the end of the day, rosy cheeked and in high spirits, and I regretted my decision to stay home alone.

I hear the crunch of winter tires on the nearby road, a noise that always sounds louder in cold weather, but I don't see another soul out walking. I take a deep breath and feel the cold scrape the inside of my nostrils and throat. I remember someone telling me that it's impossible to freeze your lungs; that the air would be sufficiently warmed up before it got that far to do damage. But I doubt that person was standing outside on the Canadian prairies in the middle of winter at night. I rub my chest and look down at the dog. He seems to be unaffected by the temperature and is calmly surveying the landscape along with me.

The snow lies unbroken the length of the front yard, and the moon, just beginning to rise, makes the shadows from the trees so black and straight, it's as if they're painted on the white backdrop. Like spider legs, they stretch towards me and up the side of the building, disappearing into the night sky when they pass the eaves. The dog does not run through this pristine snow, but turns down the driveway towards the parking lot and soon he's blended into the darkness.

"Hey," I shout. "I said not too far." He keeps going and the last I see of him his bushy black tail is disappearing around the corner of the building into the deepest snow. I turn to go back into the warmth of the building, thinking the dog has just conned me into coming outside with him, when he returns to the driveway and barks at me to follow. I look inside at the well-lit lobby; still no Melanie. "Ok," I say. "But wait for me. I don't have four-wheel drive like you."

I slip and slide down the driveway then enter the backyard and begin wading through snow up to my knees, the top few inches as crusty as a loaf of bread. My toes are beginning to feel like lumps of frozen flesh inside my sneakers and I wonder at my decision to come outside so poorly dressed. It's dark; the moon hasn't risen high enough to cast its light back here, and I can't see a thing, not even the dog.

"Where are you?" I call, "Come here."

I hear him breaking through snow and I begin to march in that direction, taking steps as tall as my hips. He noses my hand and I jump, then I grab his collar and allow him to lead me further into the yard. When we're about thirty feet from the house my eyes have adjusted to the dark and I look back. The majority of windows visible from this side of the building are lit, and shadows of residents are outlined in their golden glow. The rooms look cozy and welcoming, and I'm reminded of walking home from the rink or a friend's house on a winter's evening, looking in windows at families, imagining monopoly games, and movies and popcorn, wishing I could go inside.

It's deserted out here, the street so far away I can hardly hear the traffic. Just as I've decided to head back, the animal stops and begins to paw the snow. This is where the garden was planted last summer and I think he's probably digging up a potato that didn't get harvested. I pull my phone out and turn on the flashlight. Something odd is sticking out of the snow. It looks like fur. The dog continues to dig.

"You'd better not have brought me out here so I can help you dig up a dead rat," I say.

I push away snow and uncover what looks like a short, brown, wig. I reach for it but the dog moves on, sniffing and pawing his way across the yard. At the edge of the property, he jumps clear of the deep snow and stands looking down the ploughed alley. The light from nearby houses causes the snow to glisten on his black fur but he doesn't shake it off as most dogs would, instead he barks at me to follow. By this time, I can barely feel my toes and getting out of the snow, I figure, is a good idea. I leave the wig and follow his trail, stepping into the alley alongside the dog. He begins to circle me and bark, trying to herd me further down the road. In the light from the moon now peeking over the edge of the building, I see something lying on the ground. I move closer, curious as to what this animal is trying to show me. Splinters of moonlight glint off small objects, like marbles, scattered on the ground around a larger mass. I drop to my knees. Fiona Brighton is curled into a fetal position, her pearl necklace strewn on the alley around her. She's wearing a winter jacket and gloves, but nothing on her head and only dress shoes on her feet.

"Fiona," I shout. She doesn't respond. I pull off my glove and feel her neck — there's a weak pulse — then put my glove back on and push my numb hands underneath her back to scoop her up. She's thin from too much drink and not enough food, but still her weight is awkward in my arms and I struggle to regain my balance as I stand. The dog runs ahead, spinning and barking, and I realize he's leading me not through the deep snow of the backyard, but to the shovelled sidewalk. I stagger around the building and up the driveway then kick the buzzer to get Melanie's attention. She unlocks the door and I enter with Fiona in my arms. I rush across the lobby and lie her on the couch. When I turn and look behind me the dog has stopped and is standing on the driveway. He still hasn't shaken off the snow and it twinkles on his back in the glow of the moon.

"Come," I say, but he stays outside. "Call an ambulance," I shout at Melanie.

"What? Who's that?" she says. "And what's that dog doing out there?"

"Call a God damn ambulance, Melanie!"

She picks up the phone. I again look towards the driveway; the dog paces outside the front door, stopping occasionally to look at me. Melanie hangs up and begins putting on her coat.

"Get me a blanket," I tell her.

"I have to go home. My ride's waiting."

I shout. "Get me a fucking blanket, Melanie!" I point. "There's one in the community room on the back of the chair."

She pauses then throws her coat behind the reception desk and stomps to the community room. Outside the dog is still waiting, looking between the lobby and the road. Melanie returns and tosses the blanket my way. I spread it over Fiona, tucking it under her chin. I place the back of my hand on her cheek; it's cool.

"Where the hell were you?" I ask, keeping my gaze on Fiona.

"What?"

"How did Mrs. Brighton get outside?"

"How am I supposed to know? It's not my fault she's a drunk."

I turn my head. "Where were you, Melanie?"

"Someone called me upstairs," her tone is wary.

"You didn't lock the door before you went up."

She waves her hand at the desk. "That drunk must have unlocked it herself."

"How in God's name would she know how to do that?"

"You can't expect me to be in two places at the same time. And anyhow, you're not my boss, I don't have to answer to you."

"When I came in, that dog," I point outside, "was sitting in the lobby. He had to have come inside somehow, and if you locked the door like you said, you don't think he could unlock the door himself?"

She raises her palms, "Like I care."

I stand. "I waited for you then followed the dog outside thinking you were in trouble." Melanie begins doing up her coat. In frustration, I grab her arm. "I asked you where you were."

"Let go," she shakes me off. "I told you, someone called me upstairs and it took longer than I thought it would."

"Pardon my language, but bullshit, Melanie."

"You're calling me a liar?" her tone has changed from wary to challenging.

"If it wasn't for that dog, Mrs. Brighton would have frozen to death tonight and you can be sure it would have been your fault." I turn back to Fiona and touch her cheek again. She stirs but doesn't open her eyes.

"No one would have accused me. She wandered out by herself."

I take a step towards Melanie, she takes a step back. The dog barks and I look outside. The headlights of a vehicle shine up the driveway. I open the door and two paramedics enter pushing a gurney. I recognize one of them.

"John," he says. "Didn't know I'd see you here."

"Hey, Brian. Retirement job." I point to the couch. "Fiona Brighton. Wandered outside. I found her in the alley. Don't know how long she was there."

Brian feels for a pulse, then checks her eyes. "Pulse is weak, but steady. Pupils dilated," he says to his partner. He leans close. "Smells like she's been drinking." He checks her temperature and blood pressure.

"So, you changed careers?" I say.

"Not enough money driving a cab, though driving letter-carriers around was always a gas." He shakes his head. "Some of the stories I heard from your coworkers still make me laugh." He taps Fiona's cheek. "Mrs. Brighton, can you hear me?"

Fiona moves her head side to side.

"You're going to be ok. We're taking you to the hospital." He stands. "She's stable enough to move," he says to his partner.

They lift Fiona onto the gurney and I follow them outside. Melanie stays in the lobby getting her winter things on.

"Will she be ok?" I ask.

"Hard to say. But her heartbeat is stronger than I would expect in this condition. The alcohol lowered her core temperature pretty fast. I expect she hadn't been out there very long, maybe fifteen minutes, tops. If you hadn't found her she'd have been dead in a couple of hours." His partner gets behind the wheel and Brian climbs into the back beside Fiona. "Guess we both had a huge change in careers, hey?"

I shake his hand. "We did. Thanks Brian."

"Always looked forward to picking you up on your route. Glad to see you're keeping busy. Job suits you."

I close the back doors of the ambulance. As they pull away, I again attempt to coax the dog inside. Instead, he trots down the driveway, giving me one last look as he disappears into the night.

"I think," I say to Melanie when I go back inside, "you were somewhere you weren't supposed to be tonight. That's why you're being so defensive."

Her face gets very white. "So I forgot to lock the door. The person who called me said it was an emergency. Which it wasn't," she waves her arms in the air. "These people, they expect too much. Don't know what they're doing half the time. This isn't a nursing home. If they wander out on their own, then that's too bad, they shouldn't be living here."

"Who were you helping?"

"I don't have to answer you. You're not my boss."

"Who were you helping, Melanie? I want to know right now."

"Adelman. I was helping Adelman."

"Let's just give Ezra a call then and ask how he is," I reach for the phone.

"You can't. He's, he's gone to bed. He wasn't feeling well and wanted to talk, you know, like you talked to him that night. That's what took so long. Then he went to bed."

"We both know that's a lie, Melanie. These people wouldn't confide in you if you were the only employee here."

"It isn't a lie!" she yells. "He's so far gone; he wouldn't remember anyhow."

"Convenient."

"I don't have to take this! I'm leaving. Already stayed past my time."

"That's right, Melanie, you've already stayed past your time, something you always make sure to mention, don't you?"

"I guess in that regard, Davies, you and I are alike."

Chapter eighteen

In the morning, I call the hospital but the nurses won't tell me anything about Fiona – family only, they say. When I arrive at work, the greeters are waiting in the lobby. They jump up and one after the other give me hugs, even Carl and Ezra.

"I don't believe a word of it," Ivy says. She waves at the others. "None of us do."

"Oh?"

"Heard her complaining to Alma, telling stories, making things up to save her own skin. Don't let her walk all over you."

"Ok," I say, unsure of what they're talking about, though I have an inkling.

"I told Alma," Ezra says, "I never called Melanie to my apartment. I may be forgetful, but I sure as hell know I would never confide in her."

"Has anyone heard if Mrs. Brighton is alright?" I ask.

"Ivy and I visited her this morning," Beatrice says. "Took a cab. Cost thirty dollars! Can you imagine?"

"Get on with it Bea," Carl says. "John doesn't care how much your cab cost."

"Wasn't too fired-up to see us, but we managed to get into her room to say hi. Her hand was bandaged, think she may have frozen a finger but nothing that won't heal. Just have to be careful with it the rest of her life. There was cream on her cheek as well; frostbite," Beatrice says. "Discharging her today. Probably'd keep her longer on account of the hypothermia thing, but she was complaining about everything. No booze in the hospital I suppose."

Carl pats my shoulder and nods towards Alma's office. "She wants to talk to you. We're to send you in as soon as you arrive."

I knock on Alma's door and enter. Melanie is sitting in the chair.

"You can leave," Alma says to her.

As she's done since the day we met, Melanie doesn't meet my eyes but looks to the side of my face as she brushes past.

"Take a seat," Alma says.

I step in and pull the door closed, but not before I hear voices in the hall shushing each other.

"First of all," Alma says as I pull out the chair and sit, "you'll be glad to know Fiona is going to be fine. I'm expecting her back here late this afternoon."

"Beatrice told me. I called the hospital but no one would talk to me."

Alma stares at me without speaking. I brace myself for the worst.

"Do you recall your first day here, John?"

I remember the crowd in the lobby and to my shame, being repulsed by some of the people in wheelchairs. I thought I'd do Alma a favour by crossing names off the list of residents who were getting on the bus, then tell her I didn't want the job and go home. "I do," is all I say.

"After you jumped in to help, I knew you were the right person. You haven't let me down."

Someone in the hall coughs, which is followed by a shush.

I'm quiet as I wait for the 'but.'

"Not until now."

"I know," I say. "It wasn't my place to say something to Mel…."

Alma holds up her hand. "That's not what I mean." She hesitates. "It's more my fault than yours. I should have talked to Melanie a long time ago, not waited for you to speak up. I guess I thought if you didn't complain then it would be alright. I know she doesn't work hard, but I never thought it would lead to this." She looks at me with her Kewpie doll face and not for the first time do I wonder how old she is. "It's just so difficult to find employees to work here. The hours, the workload, not to mention the grumpier of the residents. I thought I'd found someone with the woman before you but she quit just one month into the job. Melanie has hung in there, so I've let things slide." She rubs her hand across her desk, pushing papers into a mishmash of a pile. "Do you know I can't name one other employee who would have taken the time to call the hospital to find out how one of the residents was doing?"

I fiddle with my wedding ring.

She picks up a pencil and begins tapping the desk. "Melanie said you left the outside door unlocked while you left the lobby."

"She said what?"

"Did you leave the lobby and allow Mrs. Brighton to walk out-side?"

"No! Of course not!"

"Melanie said Ezra called, so because you were late, she locked the front door and went upstairs, staying past her shift. Should have realized as soon as she said that, she was lying. Said she saw Fiona in the snow out Ezra's window so she ran downstairs. You weren't in the lobby, and the door was unlocked."

I grab the doorknob, which is only inches away in this small room. "High-school was a long time ago, and I'm too old for this adolescent crap. If you want to fire me, I'll be in the community room talking to Mr. McIntyre about jamming pieces into Mrs. Cunningham's one-thousand-piece jigsaw puzzle."

I open the door. Ivy, Carl, Ezra, and Beatrice press their backs to the wall. It's the first time I've seen Ezra stand that straight.

Ivy waves the backs of her hands at me, pushing me back into the room, and mouths, "Get back in there." I pull the door closed on their faces.

"I didn't talk to you about Melanie because I didn't want to get involved," I say. "Thirty-five years in a union taught me better than that." Alma doesn't interrupt. "I took this job to fill a gap, but it's turned into more than I imagined."

"What did you expect? Knitting, and bridge parties? These are people with lots of life still left in them. They are not here waiting to die."

Not having many directions I can look in this room to avoid Alma's gaze, I stare at the dead plant that's been sitting on the filing cabinet since the first day I arrived. Delivering mail is a very impersonal job. I sorted the letters, walked my route, talked to the occasional person, but for the most part, once I left the building, I was alone. I didn't have to deal with people's hurt feelings or settle arguments. I didn't have to take abuse I couldn't return, and I didn't have to call the fire department twice a day because somebody had fallen and couldn't get up. All I had to look after was myself. I could deliver mail angry at the world, and many times I did just that.

"Do you know how many people have come and talked to me about you, John? Never in all the years I've run this place have so many residents complimented me on my choice in hiring someone," Alma says. "Even the crusty ones."

I say nothing.

"Did Melanie find Fiona?"

I shake my head.

"What then?"

I pull my hands down my face and notice I forgot to shave this morning. "I arrived about ten to eleven. Melanie wasn't in the lobby and the front door was unlocked. There was a dog...."

"A dog?"

"Standing in the lobby. I waited a couple of minutes for Melanie to return but she never came back. The dog wouldn't stop whining for me to follow him outside, so thinking maybe Melanie was in trouble, I took the emergency phone with me, locked the door behind us and we left together."

"You and .... the dog?" she looks like she doesn't believe me.

"He led me through the backyard to the alley. I found Fiona unconscious on the ground. I carried her in and told Melanie to call the ambulance."

"What kind of dog?"

"Border collie."

"So, a border collie took you to Fiona."

I nod.

"Melanie said she saw Fiona out Ezra's window. That's at the front of the building. You're saying Melanie is lying?"

"I've no idea what Melanie's saying. I just know where I found Fiona."

She sticks the pencil into the jar and puts her hands on the arms of her chair. "Get your coat. We're going outside."

By the time Alma and I enter the lobby, Ivy, Beatrice, Carl, and Ezra are seated on the couch. Ivy is talking with her hands to Beatrice and Ezra has a confused look on his face as Carl says something. All four appear flushed. Ezra is rubbing the small of his back.

Alma pushes the front door open and we leave. Four noses press to the glass.

It's colder than it was last night and I pull up the hood of my coat.

Alma looks up at Ezra's window then to the front-yard where the snow lies unbroken. "No footprints," she says.

We walk to the side of the building. The window squeaks as the four greeters follow us with eyes that look bigger than they should through the moisture smeared glass.

The snow leading to the backyard is littered with paw prints and footprints. Alma lifts the hem of her skirt past her boots and together we follow the trail. I find the wig and pull it out of the snow.

"That's Fiona's," Alma says.

We follow the trail through the backyard to the alley. One of Fiona's shoes lies on the ground, surrounded by the broken string of pearls.

"Well, John," she says. "It appears Melanie is full of shit."

For a small woman, Alma has a big voice. I'm in the lobby, along with the usual suspects, beginning a tour for a potential resident and her family, when her voice carries down the hall. I continue to speak over hers, but soon concede to Alma.

"You lied to me, Melanie."

"I did not."

"You did not find Mrs. Brighton in the front-yard and you did not go to Mr. Adelman's room. What you did do was leave the front door unlocked while you left the lobby. The evidence is irrefutable so don't insult me by continuing to lie."

The family I'm giving the tour to glance at each other. I attempt to point out the features of the lobby – the spaciousness, the music, the large windows — but again Alma's voice drowns me out.

"Mrs. Brighton has agreed to not file a law-suit against you…."

"A law-suit? For what?"

"Neglecting your duties causing her grievous bodily harm."

"Grievous bodily harm my ass! She froze a finger and got frost-bite on her cheek is all I heard. And if she wasn't sprawled out drunk on the road, that wouldn't have happened. It's her fault, not mine. I didn't pour the liquor down her throat."

"She's a lawyer, Melanie. If she filed a law-suit against you, she would win. But at my behest, she has decided to forget the whole thing. I told her you've never forgotten before."

"Of course I never did it before! I know my job. I've worked here two years!"

"She mentioned she caught you stealing from her."

"Stealing from her?"

"Said you attempted to take her watch."

It crosses my mind that I should try again to move my guests along but we seem to be riveted to the spot by these voices.

"It fell on the floor and I picked it up because I figured she was too drunk to notice," she yells. "Thought she might trip on it. Sometimes she staggers…."

"Melanie."

"Well, she does. When she saw me with the watch in my hand she began to scream. I tried to explain what I was doing but she's crazy when she's drunk. Last time I do a favour for any one of them."

"She wants you to stay clear of her. If she needs anything, John or I will look after her."

We hear a snort which I assume comes from Melanie.

"If you bother her in any way, she will file that law-suit. And

I want no doing of your nails or reading magazines while you're working. And no making phone calls or playing games on your phone while you're supposed to be paying attention to residents. And I can't believe I have to mention this, no making comments about residents dying."

I look at Ivy. She shrugs her shoulders.

"Did he tell you I said that?" Melanie says. "He's lying. I was just…."

"Where were you when Mrs. Brighton left the building?"

"I told you. I was upstairs."

"We've established it wasn't with Mr. Adelman."

"Ok, so I wasn't with Adelman."

"You mean, Mr. Adelman."

Her voice is shrill. "How am I supposed to remember who called? Sometimes I get four or five calls a night. These people always want something."

"That's your job, Melanie. To look after the residents."

"And fold the napkins. And fill the coffee pots. And answer the phone, call bingo, run errands, unplug toilets. Not to mention looking after the residents who are losing their marbles."

Alma cuts her off. "I came into work today to let you go."

"Let me go? I need this job. I'm helping my mom with the bills."

"I realize that, and that's why I've decided to give you another chance. Do not leave the lobby at night without locking the front door. Do you understand? One more mistake and I'll have to let you go."

I decide we've heard enough of this conversation and begin to usher the potential resident and her son and daughter towards the dining room. Before I can move them out of earshot of the Walmart greeters, the daughter asks if drinking is allowed on the premises and if that would be a problem for her mother who does not drink. Ivy attempts to allay their fears.

"No, no, not to worry. Fiona has a few too many sometimes, but she's harmless. Anti-social anyhow so you'll be ok. And Marigold drinks mostly wine. Gentle as a lamb when she's had too much.

Ernestine puts amaretto in her tea, which I love. Never turn down an invitation to her place if you can help it. Anyhow, amaretto's a teetotalers' drink if you ask me. Just ignore all the pictures with eyes that follow you around the room." She taps her chin. "And there's Darlene who likes a glass of port at night. She enjoys telling people things. Always asking if you know about this or that, like we know nothing and she's an encyclopedia. Has a slight fainting problem and she's a large woman, so don't want to be near her when she goes down. And Allan, of course, drinks whiskey; he is a man. Good looking, but he's spoken for so don't get your hopes up. And Rachel, even though she pretends she doesn't drink, likes something called Raspberry Sourpuss. Hard to have only one. And…."

I've been standing behind the family, trying to get Ivy's attention, but she's too busy talking to notice me. As the woman and her son and daughter listen, Alma's office door stutters open. Melanie rushes past us, and the would-be resident and her son and daughter follow her out the door like they're being chased with an axe.

Two days after Alma's lecture to Melanie, which Ivy and Beatrice have memorized word for word, it has been repeated by them to anyone who would listen. At one point Ivy even began telling me until she realized I'd been there.

Melanie and I haven't spoken. Neither have I spoken to Fiona, nor she to me. I'm quite sure she would never initiate a law-suit – she wouldn't want the world to know how much she drinks. Alma's threat was a way to scare Melanie into actually doing her job. So much for this generation knowing more than us. Fiona's cheek is red, and she still has her right hand bandaged, but other than that she doesn't seem to be too bad. I'm sure alcohol makes a perfect pain-killer.

But the residents, oh, the residents, I've never had so much attention. My actions are the highlight of the year. Before I found Fiona in the alley, most of the residents only knew her as *that drunk*, now her name is on everyone's lips. Some are sympathetic, some are not.

"Poor Fiona, she certainly struggles with the bottle. She's lucky you found her, John."

"Silly woman. If she didn't drink so much, this never would have happened. It's a good thing you're a strong young man."

"Fiona would have died if you hadn't found her and it would have been no one's fault but her own."

No wonder Fiona won't speak to me.

Chapter nineteen

Clem bounds down the hall behind Marigold. I arrive in her kitchen at a slower pace, wondering what this woman's motives are and feeling my defenses rise.

Marigold places a bowl of water on the floor which Clem begins to lap up, then holds a cup of coffee laced with Irish whiskey and smothered in whipped cream out to me. I haven't had Irish coffee since Elaine and I went out for a fancy supper and we ended it with a cup. We sat in that restaurant until it closed, reminiscing about the kids, about our life together. The following month she got sick. It's like she had a premonition.

Unable to resist the warm, rich smell, I accept the cup and take a loud sip, getting whipped cream on my upper lip and nose. Marigold hands me a napkin.

"My husband swore by this stuff," she licks cream off her fingers. "Said it saved our marriage. A cup of this mellowed many a fight, and we had a few of those, especially in the beginning. But I suppose most marriages have bad days."

From the outside, Elaine and I were the golden couple. Many times we were asked how, in this day and age when so many were divorcing, we managed to stay together. I would repeat something I overhead at a sleepover when I was a kid. My friend's parents were having a party on the patio and I stayed awake and listened to them talk through the open bedroom window. When his parents were asked how they remained so happy after all these years, his mom said, never totally blame the other for poverty, nor totally take the credit for fortune. Those words stayed with me and years later, even though it felt like a lie, they became my refrain whenever anyone asked us the same question. I'd see Elaine glance at me each time I repeated it, but she never argued.

The bottle of whiskey is sitting on a table by the china cabinet and I notice the brand; it's top notch. I bought it once, many years ago, for a getaway I had with some buddies, all working fathers like myself. I never told Elaine I'd purchased such expensive hootch; she'd have killed me. We rented a cabin at Waskesiu lake and drank the weekend away, telling ourselves what we were doing was owed to us.

When we finish our coffee, Marigold opens her fridge and pulls out a bottle of very good white wine.

"I see you like the good stuff," I say.

"Never been one to deprive myself," she searches through her china cabinet clinking glasses together, then takes out two wine glasses and sets them in front of me. "How are you doing?"

"I'm ok. How are you?"

"I mean, John, after the whole Fiona, Melanie thing."

"Oh, that. I'm good."

"Thought maybe it was on your mind."

"Trying to forget it happened, actually."

She pours us each a glass. "Seems you've ingratiated yourself with everyone, even if that wasn't your intention."

I look around the apartment that I haven't been in since Christmas. "You have the best suite in the building," I say, in an attempt to change the subject.

"I've been here a long time, got first dibs when the place opened," she turns the conversation back onto me. "You don't think you're a hero?"

I dismiss her idea with a shrug.

"I think, John, you underestimate yourself." She lifts her glass, "Salute."

I lift my glass and we both drink.

"I know you're a private man and don't like to get close to people."

I remember my mother accusing me of the same thing. She said I was cold and standoffish like my dad. As a kid, I was never sure if it was a compliment or a criticism.

"But there are times it's good to talk to others, tell them what's on your mind and hear what they have to say. I know it's an old truism, but believe it or not, age and experience really do bring wisdom."

And some secrets are meant to be taken to your grave, I think to myself.

"I learned a lesson a long time ago. Want to know what it is?"

"I'm sure you'll tell me even if I say no."

She frowns at me. "You're a bit of a smart ass, aren't you, John? You keep that part of your personality well hidden." She taps her glass with her fingernail. "There's no quick way to grieve. You have to embrace it and allow it to take you wherever it takes you, even if that place is uncomfortable. And sometimes you have to allow others to help you along the way."

"I'm here to get a lecture?"

"Not a lecture, just a bit of advice."

I put my hands on the arms of the chair to stand.

Marigold presses me back down. "For heaven's sake, sit down. Allow an old lady an indulgence. What is it about men that they have to always be tough?"

I decide to stay, at least till I've finished my glass of expensive wine.

She rubs her finger around the rim of her glass. "It's the cost of living."

"The cost of living?"

"Loving and losing. Without love we wouldn't lose, but without love, we wouldn't live."

I don't respond.

"You're a man of few words."

I finish the wine too fast and my head begins to swim. Marigold pours me another.

"I don't mind a man of few words, gives me more of a chance to talk. Have I ever told you my life story?"

"Won't that take a long time?"

"Ah, you can crack a joke. Not my entire life story, but an excerpt."

"You've barely told me anything about yourself."

"I was born into wealth, lived a childhood of privilege and money."

It is surprising that this grounded woman was raised in that manner, though with the cost of this place, the fact she's wealthy isn't unexpected. Living here, on my pension, is something I'd never be able to afford.

"When I was twenty-three, Dad wanted me to marry a man who came from a well-off family. Nice enough, but not my type. I was in love with someone my parents didn't approve of. Dad thought it was rebellion and I would out-grow that phase. But I didn't. He became quite famous."

"Your husband became quite famous?" I say.

"No, John. The man I didn't marry. Dad was angry." She looks at the ceiling, "He's still alive, I believe."

"Your father's still alive?"

She pulls her wine glass away from her mouth and scowls at me. "Are you purposefully trying to be argumentative? Of course my father's not still alive. That would make him close to one-hundred and ten. The man they wanted me to marry, he's still alive. Started a fast food franchise. Now there's one on every corner. Surprising he is still alive with all that grease he must have eaten in the past fifty years."

"You turned down a marriage proposal from...."

She puts her finger to her lips. "No names. Besides, he wasn't big then. Didn't open the first franchise until the sixties. Not that it would have made any difference. I didn't love him." She twirls her glass by the stem sending shafts of light bouncing off the walls. "I was a romantic."

"You let a big fish go there, Marigold."

"The day I left, my father told me I'd never amount to anything.

Said I'd ruined my life. It was the fifties. Certain things were looked down on. Races didn't mix."

I'm quiet.

"Tried to re-connect when my first child was born, but it ended in a shouting match, so I quit trying."

"I'm sorry, Marigold."

"Worked out for the best. Didn't have my life handed to me." She takes a drink.

"What did your husband do for a living?"

"This and that in the beginning. Found our niche in real-estate."

"He sold houses?"

"No. We bought them. Hotels typically. Paul and I were a team. At one time, we owned fifteen buildings around the country. We made our own fortune. Didn't need my father's money."

"That kind of thing doesn't lose its value."

"Dad was right about some of the things he said. Paul didn't always get the respect he was due. There were people who hated us, called my kids half-breeds. Back then, races mixing was frowned upon far more than it is today. But I told my kids, people like that aren't worth getting to know. Made them stronger. I think you and I are much alike. You're a man of conviction too, even if you believe yourself to be a fence-sitter."

I think about all the times as a child I wished to be taken away from that life. All the times I allowed Elaine to take the lead. I straighten my bobbing head. "I don't know about that, Marigold."

"You went outside to save Fiona. Lots of people would have chased that dog out into the cold, wouldn't have bothered themselves to see what it wanted. You followed your gut. That's a man of conviction as far as I know the definition."

"Do you have any pictures of your family?" I say, wanting to talk about something else besides me.

"I do," she takes a picture from the top of the china cabinet. "That's all of us on New Year's Eve the year before Paul died. Hired a photographer to take a few pictures."

Marigold and Paul are sitting in front, each with a baby on their laps.

She points. "That's me, of course, and Paul. The two babies were born within weeks of each other; they're now twenty-six." She points to another child, "Jenny was six at the time. That makes her thirty-two I guess. Alex was four, and Harry was three. Jason was nine, he was my first. Can't believe I have a grandchild who's thirty-five." She continues to point, "That's my son Theo and his wife, and my daughter Pam and her husband and my other son Albert and his wife. Albert isn't married anymore, divorced. The others are still hanging in there."

"I met Albert at your Christmas party."

"Only one living in town." She takes the picture from me and rubs her hand across the surface. "I have no regrets; about this anyhow." She puts the picture back. "Difficult to get through life with no regrets."

"What do you regret?" I lean back and stretch out my legs.

"Tell you sometime when we aren't drinking. Get too maudlin when I'm drinking." She tops up my glass and I don't object. "Having drinks with us, going to dances, Christmas parties, running out into the cold to save someone's life. Working here has seeped into you. I think you've even begun to forgive yourself."

"And what do I have to forgive myself for?"

"For whatever it is you wish you could do over."

"There's nothing I want to do over," I say.

"Is that right." She tips the bottle of wine into her glass; it's empty. "You're a lucky man, John. Most people have a regret or two in their lives." She opens the fridge. "Did you know that Ed Brown, the man who died a few months back, owned a border collie before he moved here?"

"Really? That's the kind of dog that was in the lobby the night I found Fiona outside."

"Smartest dog he ever had. Person in a dog suit is how he worded it. Broke his heart when it died. Looked into his eyes and said he could see that dog's soul."

I pat Clementine's head. She looks up and I know what Ed

Brown meant about seeing the dog's soul; it is in their eyes. Only it's not Clem's soul I see in her eyes, it's Elaine's. "Fiona told me Ed Brown killed himself."

"Yeah, well, not to speak ill of Ed, but some people think it takes courage to take your life. I think it takes more courage to grow old."

Chapter twenty

1983

"What's this, Elaine?"

Barbie is playing on the floor, pretending to feed her baby doll with a toy bottle. She looks up as I hang my coat on the back of the kitchen chair. I enter the dining room.

"Antique china cabinet," Elaine says.

"Look, Daddy." Barbie holds her doll out to me.

"Yes, Barbie, I see." I push the doll away. "What are we doing with an antique china cabinet?" Mark is standing in the playpen batting at a toy with his chubby fist. It makes a loud squeak every time he hits it.

Elaine turns to me with a puzzled expression. "I'm putting things in it, of course. What else would I be doing with it?"

"But, I thought we agreed they're too expensive?"

She doesn't respond.

"Elaine, you bought this without my consent?"

Our neighbours are constructing a new deck and the noise of hammering and sawing echoes through the open window. I slam the window shut.

"I did," she says.

"What the fuck?"

Her look is swift and angry.

"How much did it cost?" I say, managing not to swear.

"Thirteen hundred."

"Thirteen hundred! For Chris…. heaven's sake, Elaine!"

Barbie looks up and holds her doll out to me. "Daddy, don't yell." Tears fill her blue eyes.

I ignore her. "Elaine, what are you thinking?"

"I've always wanted an antique china cabinet so I bought one."

I shout, "Why are you playing games with me?"

"Daddy!" Barbie tugs at my hand, I shake her off.

Elaine kneels in front of Barbie and wipes the tears off her cheeks. "I don't think I'm the one playing games, John."

"You're saying I'm playing games?"

"You're saying you're not?"

"Elaine, I don't have a clue what…."

"Brenda, I'm talking about Brenda." She looks up at me.

The house is silent, even the children have stopped moving.

"Being as how you seem to have been treating yourself these past five months, I thought I'd treat myself to something."

Not wanting to incriminate myself, I'm quiet.

Elaine places her hands on our daughter's shoulders. "Barbie, would you like to do Mommy a favour? Go to the fridge and get your brother a bottle. You can give it to him if you like."

Barbie snuffs her nose. "Ok, Mommy."

Elaine stands, and I step towards her. With my face inches from hers, I hiss, "You haven't a clue what you're talking about. There's nothing going on between Brenda and me, nothing at all. And if someone has told you different, then they're lying." I step back, almost believing what I'm saying.

Elaine closes the gap between us and talks quietly. "Just so you know, John, I don't want a divorce nor do I want a separation. I don't even need a confession. You can deny it till the cows come home for all I care. But know this, I know it's true. All I want from you is to stop seeing her. It's not love; you've been sidetracked. Why, I'm not sure. Maybe you feel used, maybe you feel jealous of the kids. I don't know and right now, I don't care. Just figure it out or I will leave and take the kids with me." She turns back to wiping off the shelves. "Whether you believe it or not, we have something worth saving and I'll be damned if I'm going to let you ruin it."

She places some wine glasses that have been at the back of a high cupboard onto the glass shelf. "I have some news I was going to tell you over dinner tonight but I've decided I'm going out with my girlfriends for supper, so I'll tell you now instead. I'm two months pregnant. And I'm keeping the cabinet."

Chapter twenty-one

I stop on my driveway and watch the girls through the window. Janet and Barb don't notice, they are so involved in their conversation. They stand in the living room, hands volleying actions like words the same way their mother used to. After forty years of marriage, there wasn't much left to say I didn't already know or intuit. One shrug of her shoulder and I'd know she was upset, one sideways grin and I'd know she was amused.

My daughters are beautiful but as different from each other as dogs and cats. Barb is tall, like me. In her third decade and after two kids, still lean, muscular, her hair cut short. Janet is smaller, rounder, more petite. Elaine's twin.

As unalike as they are, they have tenacity in common, though Janet is more willing to see the other side than Barb.

The standoff is being mediated by Clementine who sits between them looking back and forth as each speaks. I stay outside, hesitant to get in the middle of their argument. Eventually they notice me watching and I'm forced to enter the house.

"Hey, girls," I say. "What's happening?"

They drop their eyes to the carpet.

"Nothing," Janet says.

"Don't worry about it," Barb says as she escapes to the kitchen.

Janet hugs me and squeezes tighter when I don't fight back. "How was work?" she asks.

"Fine." I'm about to tell her an anecdote from today — Mr. Galbraith's toupee fell in his soup. I fished it out, rinsed it in the sink and he plopped it back on his head, then finished his bowl of soup — but change my mind, still awkward sharing my world with them. Elaine was the one who regaled them with the minutia of our lives after they left home.

"Came to bring Clem a new toy," Janet says. "Barb was already here."

"Where's your toy, girl?" I say to Clem in an animated voice. "Go find your toy."

She trots off, nose to the floor looking in this corner and that before coming back with a blue stuffed cat. I try to tug it from her, she holds on tight.

"Hadn't seen any new toys in the house for a while. Mom used to buy her one every month," Janet says. "Thought I'd – Sorry, Dad."

"Is that what you and your sister are arguing about? My not looking after Clem?"

"Barb said she had to pee pretty badly when she got here, but she looks good."

We both look down at Clem; she's matted and scruffy. Elaine used to bathe her three times a year. I haven't done it since Elaine died.

"Guess she could use a bath," I say. "But I walk her every day and she never misses a meal."

Clem is looking at us with her toy in her mouth, knowing we're talking about her and hoping it means a walk. Until Barb opens the fridge. The moment she hears that sound, she drops the toy and begins to whine, a habit she's had since the first time she begged for food and got what she wanted. She clicks her way to the kitchen with the expectation Barb will give her a morsel. She always was a food dog, Elaine said it made her easy to train. She can hear a cheese slice being peeled opened from the backyard.

Barb appears in the kitchen doorway with a mouldy orange in her hand and Clem on her heels. "Why do you have to work any-how? Do you need the money? Rob and I can give you a loan if you...."

"I don't need money, Barb. My pension is plenty for one person."

"Then why, Dad?" She throws her hand in the air. "This is silly."

"It's not silly, Barbie. Please don't say that about my job."

She mocks. "Your job. You should be staying at home, looking after your dog, not gallivanting off to some old-folks home looking after people who probably can't remember you from one day to the next. What would Mom say if she knew what you were doing?"

"Barb," I say, "That was uncalled for. And you'd be surprised to know this was Mom's idea."

"Mom's idea? How the hell did that happen? Immaculate communication?"

"She suggested I look into other work even before I quit the post office. Told me I'd be bored sitting around the house."

"I don't believe you." She shakes her head, her short hair bounces. "She always wanted you to be more involved with your family. She wouldn't have wanted work to be your excuse anymore. She was glad when you retired."

"She was glad when I retired from a job that was difficult for me to physically keep up to, but that's all. She wanted me to do something, not sleep the days away. Are you upset about Clem," I say, "or is this about me not paying enough attention to my family? You think I'm purposely avoiding you?" I attempt to touch Barb's arm, she pulls it back. "I'm sorry you feel that way, but that's not what this is."

Barb marches to the kitchen. I hear the garbage open as she drops the rotten orange in.

Janet is sitting on the arm of the couch watching me. "You look different, Dad."

"I look different?"

"Happier maybe? More relaxed. And if it's the job making this change in you, then for God's sake," she puts her hand to the side of her mouth and whispers, "don't listen to Barb and quit."

Barb returns and looks me in the face. Her eyes never changed to brown as Elaine said they would, but remained blue, the only one of the three kids with Elaine's eye colour. She catches me off guard and gives me a kiss on the cheek. "Your fridge is filthy," she says. "I have to go home. Just stopped to bring you a casserole and let Clem out."

I touch my cheek. "Thank-you."

The girls leave and I sag to the couch. Clem lies at my feet, her chin resting on her new toy.

1997

"It's Friday at two, in the auditorium, Dad. You'll be there, right?"

My shoulder is burning and my knees are throbbing. "I'll try, Barb, but I can't promise anything. The post office is…."

Barb rolls her eyes. She's grown this year and now stands just a few inches shorter than I do. Volleyball is her sport and she's had many games around the city and the province during her senior year, of which I've managed to attend one.

"I know," she says. "You've told us a hundred times; the post office is restructuring; the routes are longer. But this is my graduation, you can't miss. You already missed a bunch of stuff this year."

"Barb, I said I'll try, that's all I can do."

***

"What do you think about me bringing Clementine to work?" I've cornered Alma in the elevator. She has no choice but to listen as we ride up together.

"Clementine?"

"She could be a therapy dog."

"Perhaps," Alma says. She's carrying a stack of papers and removes one hand from the pile to reach for her phone. She taps the screen and answers me at the same time. "Place could use some cheering up. And they say dogs do wonders for the elderly." She lifts her face to mine. "She's gentle?"

"Never had any trouble with her."

"Bring her. We'll have trial week. Maybe she'll catch the thief."

In the past month Rachel has lost a statue of Saint Francis, and Carl, a pair of cufflinks his grandfather gave him. Darlene Carillion lost a figurine of Ganesh and a set of prayer flags, both of which she bought in Nepal. Not valuable, but keepsakes that reminded her of her trip. A ring that belonged to Allan's wife has disappeared from her jewellery box, and Jack Belgrade has lost a crystal candy dish that belonged to his mother.

"If all goes well, she can have a job," Alma says. "Might even help Melanie's disposition. Girl's as sombre as a hanging judge since I read her the riot act."

Clem is not a dog that likes baths. After coaxing and getting nowhere, I toss a leftover meatball from the casserole Barbie brought, into the tub. She jumps in.

"Guess I am a bit smarter than you," I give her a kiss on the nose. "But not by much."

She hangs her head over the edge, her way of thinking she's not obeying, and I manage to soak her, suds her, and rinse her, before she jumps out.

"Sorry, girl, I'm not as quick as Mom. I should have been looking after you better. Sort of lost track of time."

She shakes water all over the bathroom which now looks like I bathed a herd of wild swine, not one sixty-pound dog. Clem stands in the middle of this mess, her tongue hanging out, tail wagging, and a smile on her face. I never knew dogs could smile until Elaine came home with Clem.

By the time I've dried her and wiped down the bathroom, I'm exhausted. "Well, Clem, this is the best I can do. Time for bed."

I toss and turn all night long, dreaming about what Elaine would say if she knew I was taking Clem to work. Clem twitches in her sleep, chasing the same rabbit she's dreamt about since she was a puppy.

The first incident happens the second day into Clem's job when Ernestine phones claiming, yet again, that someone is in her room.

"Come on Clem," I say. "Let's go and scare that ghost out of there once and for all."

Clementine braces her four legs in a wide stance as we ride the fast-moving elevator up then bounds off and runs towards Mrs. Hawkins who is standing in the hall, hunched over her cane like a grey-haired Yoda. I zig zag my way towards them both, my legs unstable from the dizzying ride.

"He was right here, I tell you." The three of us have entered her bedroom. "Standing beside my closet rooting through the top shelf."

"Looking through your closet?" I say. "What would the grim reaper want with," I glance at the shelf, "scarves, and purses?"

"How the hell should I know?"

"What did he look like?"

"Like the grim reaper. Hood, scythe."

"He had a scythe?"

"Are you questioning my eyesight, John? I'll have you know I have twenty-twenty vision."

"What did you do?"

"I screamed, *what do you want*, and he disappeared."

"He disappeared?"

She throws her hands in the air. "Poof, and he was gone."

I step into the hall. "Maybe he ran to the door without you seeing."

"He did not."

"Then rode down on the elevator."

"Not a chance."

"He could have run around the corner and taken the stairs."

"Did you see him on the elevator? And he would have had to run past you to get to the stairs."

I notice the phone on her nightstand. "Perhaps by the time you got off the phone, he'd have had time to leave, don't you think? He may have already been on the stairs when Clem and I were in the elevator."

Clem's sniffing around the bedroom. When she nears the closet, she stops in the spot Ernestine claimed she saw the grim reaper and begins to whine.

"What's the matter with her?" Ernestine asks.

"I've no idea."

"Smells him, that's what's wrong."

"Clem smells something, but I doubt it's the grim reaper."

Clem has started pawing the floor in the closet.

"Stop that," I say.

She sits and continues to whine, her begging posture.

"Smells death, I tell you."

I grip the dog's collar and drag her hind end across the polished hardwood floor and out of the bedroom. "Mrs. Hawkins, Ernestine, I guarantee you Clem is not smelling death. She smells something; meat, gravy, the aroma of food, anything edible. She is not smelling the grim reaper."

The second incident happens five days later on Clem's last day of probation. She and I have arrived at work for the night shift and the door has just closed behind Melanie. When I turn around, I spot a mouse nosing its way across the lobby. Before I know what's happening, Clem's jerked me inside then begins to drag me past the coat rack with my boots still on. I have no choice but to let go of the leash. Clem takes off, weaving and pouncing across the tile floor, mimicking the movements of the much more agile rodent all the while barking loud enough to wake Mrs. Hawkins. I run after both, leaving muddy boot prints behind me, but somehow have the wherewithal to grab the waste basket as I pass. Clem gallops towards the kitchen in pursuit, not stopping at the doorway as she usually does.

The day Clem met Dave, she trotted up to him and began to sniff his pant legs, probably smelling the roast beef he'd made for supper. She began to whine, hoping for a morsel of meat to be thrown her way. But Dave pushed her away and insisted this animal is never, under any circumstances allowed in his kitchen. Clem now makes a wide berth around him or hides behind the desk whenever he approaches. But tonight, in the excitement of the chase, she's run right in without stopping at the doorway. By the time I arrive, she's sniffing the floor either looking for the mouse or licking crumbs that haven't been swept up; most likely the latter. I grab her leash and pull her back.

"Sit," I say. She sits. "What the hell, Clem?" She cocks her head at me.

The office door stutters open and I hear Alma cross the lobby. "Everything alright?" she says when she sees us.

"Clem chased a mouse into the kitchen."

She pats Clem's head. "Good girl, Clementine. Who needs a cat when we have you?"

Alma always addresses Clem as Clementine. Says Clem is no name for a girl dog. She's never seen her after she's dug a hole as big as a grave then rolled around in the mud.

"It got away," I say.

"There should be some traps in that drawer," she nods at the garbage can still in my hand. "Might be more effective than the waste basket. If it squeezes under the basement door, go down and set a few, please. I'm going home."

"You want me to go to the basement? Tonight?"

"Dave's already ornery and if he finds a mouse creeping across the kitchen floor in the morning, he'll quit before breakfast. I don't have time to begin interviewing potential cooks. So yes, John, I want you to go to the basement and set some traps. Is that a problem?"

"No problem. Have a good night," I say with my head under the sink as I pretend to look for the mouse. Anything to avoid Alma seeing the fear on my face.

"By the way," she adds. "Have you noticed Ezra seems to have sparked up? I haven't found him in the dining room at night looking for his breakfast for weeks now."

"He does seem happier."

"Must have got something off his chest," she says.

I sit on Dave's stool and remove Clem's leash. Suddenly the tip of the mouse's tail disappears under the basement door and Clem flies across the room in three bounds, skidding to a stop in the freshly waxed floor.

"Shit," I mutter.

1992

"It's only a hamster, John. Quit making such a fuss." Elaine stands in front of me, her hands on her hips, mocking my aversion to rodents.

"I won't have it under the same roof as me, scratching while I'm trying to sleep." I shiver at the sight of the creature poking its pink nose between the bars of the tiny cage. "They're nocturnal, you know. And the thing can't live on table scraps."

Mark is watching us, looking embarrassed, then skulks up the stairs.

"Good God, John. Barbie's going to use her babysitting money to buy the supplies. You can't control everything in this family. The kids and I have as much right to make decisions as you."

By this time Barbie is running upstairs, tears streaming down cheeks which, as she leaves childhood and becomes a teenager, have lost that baby chubbiness. She's yelling something about how she loves Hammy and it will be over her dead body I'll take him away — she's already named the damn thing. I sink onto the couch and wonder why it's getting harder to have people listen to me, cursing teenagers, and thanking God I was never allowed to be so melodramatic when I was one.

After supper, Elaine and the kids clamber up to Barbie's bedroom to clear a spot in her closet for the hamster cage. I sit stubbornly on the couch and listen as Elaine tells them about a rabbit named Butterscotch she had when she was a girl. It slept outside in a hutch and the kids in the neighbourhood would come around and feed it carrots and lettuce. Butterscotch got so fat she had to leash him then hop him around the backyard to keep him trim.

I don't go upstairs until everyone is asleep, wanting Barbie to know I'm not happy with her decision to buy a pet. Even with my pillow pulled over my head, I hear the creature spinning round and round on its wheel and the urge to take it from its cage becomes so vivid I can practically feel it squirming in my hand. I begin to think of ways to get rid of it. I could give it some of the Rodent Doom I used on the gopher we had in our yard a couple of years ago. Or

I could let it go out the back door and a cat would eat it. No one would be the wiser. Barbie would think she forgot to latch the cage door properly.

I wait for half an hour then steal down the hall towards my daughter's room. I peek through the crack of her partially closed bedroom door. Her room is a contradiction of childish things and teenage necessities. Kurt Cobain posters on the wall and the Barbie nightlight plugged into the corner of the room seem to challenge each other in their extremes. She's taken the cage from the closet and placed it close to her. Her arm is draped over the edge of the bed and her hand is blindly resting on the cage. I stare at my eldest daughter's face. Her cheeks are rosy with sleep, her lips puckered, and her eyelashes long as they rest on a face that, in the dim light offered by the Barbie nightlight, doesn't look as old as it did this afternoon. A floorboard creaks behind me and I turn to look down the hall. Mark's bedroom door is closing to a crack and a shadow moves away from the gap. Springs squeak as he climbs back in to bed. I abandon my mission and tip-toe to my bedroom, my legs weak with guilt.

A few days later I find Mark in the backyard with the tiny animal in a plastic ball rolling itself around the lawn. He says he feels sorry for it stuck in its cage and every living thing on the planet deserves some measure of freedom. He only does it when Barb is at her soccer games and begs me not to tell her as she'd get mad at him for going in her room. Since he's begun doing this Hammy doesn't claw and scamper around its cage as much at night so it won't disturb my sleep. I pat him on the back then leave him to his chore without admitting anything.

***

"John, what are you doing?"

I feel my heart jump in my chest and turn to face Marigold standing in the doorway in a pink flowered housecoat. She has cream on her face and pink rabbit slippers on her feet. I don't know what scares me more, the sight of her or the fact I now have to go to the basement in the middle of the night in search of a mouse.

"What the hell, Marigold. Don't sneak up on an old guy like that."

"What's with all the barking?"

I place my hand on my chest. "Really, Marigold, you just about gave me a heart attack." I pull a piece of paper towel off the roll to mop my forehead. "Clem chased a mouse into the kitchen but it ran under the basement door. Alma wants me to set traps down there."

"What are we waiting for?"

"You want to go to the basement?"

"You're not afraid, are you, John?"

Her attempt at coercion doesn't sway me. "Thought I'd wait till tomorrow."

"Nonsense. Two sets of eyes are better than one."

"It's ok, Marigold. I'll do it alone. You'd better get back to bed."

She glowers at me. "I am not a child, and have not been a child for over seventy years. Quit speaking to me as if I am." She whips a can out of her housecoat pocket. "Besides, I have this."

I squint at the label. "What's that?"

"Bear spray."

I'm alarmed she owns such a thing. "Why do you think we need bear spray? And what in God's name are you doing with it in the first place?"

"When I heard all the barking I thought it might be a good idea to bring it along. Good thing too, you never know what you'll find in a dusty old basement. Could be more than a little old mouse down there. And in answer to your second question: I bought it when I used to walk at night." She pulls open the basement door. "Still want me to go back to bed?"

Two minutes later I've unlocked the basement door, reattached Clem's leash and grabbed the phones. Marigold has stuffed a few mouse traps and cheese slices into her housecoat pocket. As much as we coaxed her, Clem wouldn't take the lead. I'm not sure if this is out of fear of the basement or love of the cheese slices in Marigold's pocket. Whatever the reason, I'm in front holding my phone with the flashlight app on and Clem's behind me with Marigold in the rear hanging onto the leash. I curse myself for forgetting to replace the burnt-out bulb on the landing; without daylight from the kitchen, we're walking very slowly. Marigold sees it as a time to talk.

"Did I ever tell you my regret, John?"

"Your regret?" I put my fingertips on the wall to steady myself and feel something brush my knuckles. I jerk my hand back.

"When we were sharing that bottle of wine, I said I'd tell you some time."

I shake my hand hoping to dislodge whatever is on it. "First of all, we both had quite a bit to drink that day; I can't remember what was said, I'm surprised you can. And secondly, you think this is a good time?"

"Don't be a smart ass."

I hear something scuttle below me and shine my light down the stairs. I see nothing but a concrete floor.

"I should have forgiven him," Marigold says. "But I let my anger at him stop me."

"What?" The furnace has cut in and I'm having trouble hearing her words.

"My father, I should have forgiven him, that's my regret. He said he wanted to get to know my family, said he missed me. But I told him no. Told him if he was able to kick me out all those years ago with no regret, he didn't deserve to meet my family. I hung up the phone that day without so much as a *how are you doing*. He died a month later in a car accident."

I hear the sound of something from below that doesn't belong in an empty basement and keep my feet planted on the bottom step while I slide my hand across the wall in search of the light switch. When I flip it up, Marigold and I stand motionless, blinded by the light.

"Did you hear that?" I ask. I turn around, Marigold is rubbing her eyes. "You ok?"

"I'm fine. Just bright," she wipes her cheeks with the sleeve of her housecoat. "What did you hear?"

"I'm not sure. Footsteps?"

"I didn't hear a thing, John. Probably just the mouse, unless it's already found a way out of here."

I tour around the furnace, the can of bear spray extended in front of me like I'm some ill-equipped exterminator but find nothing. I place a mousetrap loaded with cheese in the furthest corner away from the stairs.

"It probably went under one of those doors." Marigold points towards the trio of doors I opened last Christmas. When I don't make a move, she steps forward and flings open the door which leads to the room I was stuck in. Marigold steps inside and flips the light switch while I wedge a bin of God knows what against the door. Marigold raises an eyebrow.

"Don't want to be locked inside," I say.

The three of us stand looking around the room. The decoration bins are still sitting here, pushed against tables leaning against the tower of junk. I kick some garbage out of the way then duck a chair that's hanging from the rafters. Perhaps my mind was playing tricks on me that day. I was spooked at the time from all the talk about crossing over. But I do remember the knob not turning, as if someone was holding it from the other side. Unless my hand was sweaty, as tends to happen when I'm nervous.

"Look at this mess," Marigold says. "I should have had it cleared out ages ago."

It's my turn to raise an eyebrow. "Wouldn't that be up to Alma or whoever owns this place? Who does own this place anyhow?"

"I thought we were here to find a mouse," she strides into the room. Suddenly the mouse scampers out of a corner and disappears into a pile of junk on the side wall. Marigold begins pulling things away. A chair tumbles to the floor, then a suitcase, followed by a crokinole board.

"Careful, Marigold. If that piles gives way, it could bury the both of us."

"There's a doorway back here, John. Connects to the kitchen next door."

She pulls out a box and an avalanche of junk teeters. I put my hand on her arm and yank her out of the way just before it tumbles down. We peer through the opening that now connects this room to the kitchen.

"We should use the door, Marigold," I say as she begins to climb over the rubble.

"Do you know this building was a hotel back at the turn of the twentieth century?" she says as she follows me to the kitchen.

"Ernestine mentioned something about it."

"Fancy place, lots of muckity-mucks came here to party. After the kitchen closed, the staff would eat in that room we were just in. Things were done differently a hundred years ago. More civilized. The staff would get together and talk about their day, learn about the lives of their co-workers. Now everyone is in such a hurry to get their jobs done and go home to talk to their virtual friends that they barely know one another. As if someone you've never met is your friend!" She reaches up and taps one of the copper pots hanging above the butcher block. A large spider crawls out and drops to the floor. He scuttles out of sight and I secretly hope that mice eat spiders.

Clem lifts her head and looks across the room. We follow her gaze and spot a mouse inching along the baseboard. I hand Clem's leash to Marigold and gingerly step across the kitchen, keeping an eye out for spiders.

Last time I was down here, I didn't enter this room, but looked at it from the periphery of the doorway. As I examine it more close-ly, I see everything from tarnished silver-wear to jewellery boxes opened wide with dancing ballerinas frozen in their poses. A par-tially deflated basketball sits peeling inside a rusty hoop and a ce-ramic bread box, its door open, has a set of salt and pepper shakers shaped like a Dutch girl and boy inside. One pile catches my eye. It's a collection of photographs and I stop to take a look.

"What are you looking at, John?" Marigold calls from the fur-nace room.

I glance at her from between the copper pots. "Pictures. There's a bunch of old pictures here."

"Just a minute, I'm coming across." She begins to weave her way around the butcher block with Clem by her side. She stops beside me and pulls a silver frame from the pile. "That's Beverly Hawkins."

I look at what she's holding. "You're right. Ernestine showed it to me last time I had tea with her. What the hell is this doing down here?" I thumb through the rest of the pile but recognize no one.

"Someone must have swiped it from her room, though why they'd steal a picture of this man, I've no idea. Either that or Ernestine is walking in her sleep." She kicks at a pile of trash that Clementine is sniffing on the floor. "Someone's been sleeping down here. This looks like a makeshift bed to me."

An old stained mattress and rumpled quilt lie by our feet. As we're staring at the pile, the mouse burrows out from the blanket and runs between Marigold's legs and into the freezer.

I move across the kitchen with the mouse-traps in my hand. "Gotcha," I say to the mouse.

Marigold slides the picture into her housecoat pocket and all three of us enter the freezer. A little brown mouse is standing in a corner blinking at us. Just as I pull the string on the light, it disappears into the wall of the freezer.

"Did you see that?" I ask Marigold.

"It's dark in here, John. An elephant could have run past and I wouldn't have seen."

"The mouse, it just disappeared into the wall. Poof and it was gone," I paw my face. "I'm beginning to sound like Ernestine."

"Mice can squeeze in the smallest of cracks. Place has been renovated so many times over the past hundred years, there'd be all kinds of spaces behind these walls, some probably even big enough for a man to squeeze through."

Chapter twenty-two

I have never reached to the top shelf of Elaine's closet. I asked her once to tidy it, but she said this was her space where she kept the objects she treasured: artwork from the kids when they were young, corks from a bottle of champagne that marked a special occasion. *As long as it didn't spill into my space,* I told her.

When she died, I didn't have the courage to sort through the pictures, to smell her scarves, to dig through old purses, finding lipstick, grocery lists. So now, two years after her death, the boxes still sit on the shelf, melting into each other from disuse. Today I push past my fear and pull a stack of photo albums down and blow the dust off. Clementine sneezes and wags her tail. Perhaps she hopes we'll find Mom within the pages.

I lug the albums to the dining room and dump them on the table where the pile tips and scatters across the surface. I get a beer from the fridge then sit in the living room to drink, stalling the task. When the bottle is empty, I amble to the dining room. Clementine clicks her way behind me.

The albums take up a good portion of the table which can easily seat twelve, not that it has in recent months. The last time everyone gathered here for a meal was before Elaine died.

After standing and staring at them for another couple of minutes, I pull an album from the middle of the pile. Nineteen-ninety is printed on the spine. The first page is a picture of Barb. In Elaine's handwriting on a piece of paper stuck under the plastic at the top of the page, it says, *eleven years old, grade five.* Barb has braces on her teeth and is wearing glasses. I forgot about that, she wears contacts all the time now and has perfect straight smile. A Chiclet smile, she liked to call it. When the braces came off, she'd race around the house saying, *see, see,* as she pressed her tongue behind the perfect whiteness of her teeth. All I could think of was what that five-thousand dollars could have bought us.

I turn the page to find a picture of Mark. Elaine has written, *nine years old, grade three,* underneath. He looks scared. I wish I'd told him everything would be fine. I should have been more empathetic to the fact he was a little bit shy. Instead of helping him through it, I held it against him, thought he should be stronger. *When you become an adult there's a lot worse crap than school,* is all I could say to him. And with eyes wide, he'd nod his head, hanging onto every word I said.

The picture on the opposite page is Jan. *Age six, grade one.* She was so eye-catching with her red hair, and big brown eyes, people would stop us on the street and tell us how cute she was. I wonder if Mark and Barb were jealous of the attention paid to her, the baby of the family?

I browse through the pages, stopping to peer at this and that: Elaine laughing with that uninhibited exuberance she had as she slides down a playground slide, Janet on her lap. Elaine running alongside Mark as he learns to ride his bike, or Mark, so engrossed in one of his sketches he didn't know he was having his picture taken. I used to be disappointed he seemed to be interested in art more than sports, but I didn't know then that he'd grow up to be an architect. There's a picture of Elaine, her arm around Barb's shoulders as they stand in front of Barb's first car, a seven-year-old Ford Festiva. I criticized her for buying it, told her it would probably break down the first time she drove it. I wouldn't even come outside to help her attach the licence plate; Elaine had to do that. I wish I could tell her I regret being angry at everything. I browse through a few more pages and find the occasional picture with me in it, mostly in the background, lighting the barbeque, or washing the car, cutting the lawn, or cleaning out the eaves while the kids splashed in the pool.

Elaine and the kids must have been the photographers. It sure as hell wasn't me.

I pick up another album. On the spine it says, *My year of cancer treatments, 2014.* This surprises me. I didn't know Elaine was taking pictures while she was undergoing chemo. She must have known I wouldn't want to see them or she wouldn't have labelled it in such a bold fashion. I put it back down. Looking at my wife as she progressed through her illness is not something I ever want to face again.

I choose a different album. Nineteen seventy-four, our wedding pictures. The page is stiff as I pull it open, the plastic covering the pictures, crinkly and yellowing at the edges. A picture of Elaine and I posing at the photographers greets me. Elaine looks content, mature, confident. I look pensive, worried and perhaps a little blinded by what was happening. Despite what Marigold said about me being a man of conviction, I know I've always had a hard time following my gut; deciding what is the right direction to take. Like the job at The Wheaton. I knew I had to do something, but even to this day, even though I know I'd be depressed had I remained on the couch, I continually second guess myself, relying on others to reassure me.

I rub my thumb over Elaine's face. She was never a woman to critique herself in a negative way. I'd hear other woman complain about their bodies, their faces, their hair, but Elaine never did. Not that she thought she was perfect. Her figure thickened as she aged, which she didn't like, and she always said she had her dad's chin; just a tad too long. But she'd say things like, "It is what it is. Nothing I can do about it." I loved her for that. I turn the page to a picture of my mom and me dancing. I was so scared of tripping, I looked at my feet the whole time. If Elaine could have seen me at the Valentine's dance this year, she'd have been jealous.

Elaine is turned sideways where she's giving her dad a kiss and I look at her tummy and wonder what that child would have grown up to be. While she was pregnant, I was so worried about being able to support a family I never thought about the reality of raising a child. After the miscarriage, we didn't talk about it; my fault, not

Elaine's.

I turn the page and see a picture of my sister dancing. "Wow, she's just a kid."

"Who's just a kid?" a voice says behind me and I jump.

"Jan, I didn't hear you come in. What are you doing here?" Clem is standing beside her, tongue hanging out, wagging her tail, proud she allowed Jan in the house without barking.

"I knocked but you didn't answer so I walked in. Guess I don't live here anymore, I really shouldn't do that. Date fell through. Thought I'd come and visit you for a bit of moral support."

My gut clenches. "Uh, well," I shove my hands in my pockets. "I'm not very good at that sort of thing, Jan."

She slides her hand down my arm, a habit her mother had as well. "It's ok, Dad. Just coming home for a few minutes makes me feel better." She looks at the albums scattered in front of me. "What are you looking at that's so engrossing?"

"Pictures. Wedding pictures. Haven't looked at them for years. And this is still your house too, Jan. You can walk in unannounced anytime."

She pulls the album from me. "I don't remember ever seeing this album. Where did you find it?"

"Mom's closet. Never cleaned it out."

She examines the picture I was looking at. "Hey, that's Aunt Grace, isn't it? She's so young."

"Only fifteen when your mom and I married."

"Who's that she's dancing with?"

"Not sure."

"Huh." She peers closer at the page. "It could be you, Dad, I mean there's a faint resemblance."

I look more closely. "Maybe," I say. "Probably a relative I never met."

"Whatcha lookin' at?" We turn to see Mark behind us, Clementine, at his side. "Sorry," he says. "Didn't mean to scare you. I knocked but only Clem answered the door so I came in." He scratches behind Clem's ear, who licks his hand.

"Pictures of Mom and Dad's wedding. Come, see."

Mark steps forward. "I remember these. Mom used to give them to Barb and me to look at when she was busy with Jan." He punches his sister in the shoulder then leans over an album and begins to turn the pages. "Don't know how quiet it kept us, though. We were always running up to her to ask who so-and-so was."

Janet turns back a page then points to the picture of the man she thought looked like me. "Who's this, do you know?" she asks.

Mark adjusts his glasses. "Either Mom never told us, or I don't remember. Do you remember who it is, Dad?"

"I've no idea," I say.

"Maybe Barb would know." He studies the picture again. "Looks a bit like Dad."

"That's exactly what I said." Jan turns the page and finds another picture of Elaine and I. "You both look so young, but you lasted a long time," she says.

I remember this picture. We couldn't afford a honeymoon at some far-off destination, so we booked a cabin at Emma lake. It was the off season, being so early in the spring, and the local grocer, with not many other customers, took a liking to us. Over the course of our stay, he invited us for dinner with he and his wife of forty-five years. Lots of food, kids, grandchildren, laughter and wine. After the meal he took our picture in his backyard under an apple tree. I remember Elaine saying, *if we turn out like George and Adele, it would be a marriage made in heaven.*

"Wish there could have been a few more years." I pause. "Worked at it, I suppose. No marriage lasts forty years without some things happening."

"Whoa! I remember these," another voice says.

The three of us turn to see Barb, Colin and Clem walking across the living room. Either we're all going deaf or Clem is the worst guard dog in the world.

"Oh, hi Barb, hi Colin," Mark says.

"We were driving by to see if your car was home. Thought maybe Clem might have to pee. Saw everyone else's car in the driveway,"

Barb says, a quizzical expression on her face.

"I talked Mom into stopping," Colin finishes.

"Just a coincidence, Barb," Janet says. "We didn't plan it."

"You're looking at the albums," Colin says as he runs up to the table. "Grandma showed me these when I was a kid." He blushes. "When I was a younger kid, I mean. Before she died." He grabs his mom's hand. "Come, Mom, look at them with me."

Barb allows herself to be pulled forward. I go to the kitchen and when I turn back with beers and a Coke in my hands I watch as my three children and one grandson bend over an album and a feeling of contentment washes over me. Barb breaks the spell when she lifts her head. I step forward to pass out the drinks.

"Barb," Mark says as he takes a gulp of his beer. "Do you know who this is?" He taps the page. "We thought it looked like Dad, but it's not him."

Barb bends to the album along with her siblings. "That, if I remember right, is Grandpa Davies. Your Great-Grandpa, Colin."

There's silence all around until Colin speaks.

"You mean, Grandpa's Dad?" Colin says.

"I guess." Barb takes a swig of beer but doesn't meet my eyes.

"Did you know he was at your wedding, Dad?" Janet asks.

I shake my head.

"Are you sure, Barb?" Mark asks. "I mean, why would he be there? And how did Mom know it was him? And why didn't she tell Dad?"

"You're asking me questions I don't have the answer to. I only remember Mom said it was Grandpa Davies, but that's all. I was too young to ask any questions. Forgot all about it until just now."

"Well, mystery solved," Janet says as she looks quickly at me then away again.

For a few moments, no one speaks.

"Perhaps he showed up uninvited and my mom didn't want to upset me by telling me," I say, in an effort to get mine and everyone's mind off the obvious: that my father didn't want to make a connection, even at my wedding. "Your Grandma Davies put an announcement in the paper about me and your mom getting married, I suppose he could have seen it. No sense worrying about it after all these years,"

"You're probably right, Dad," Mark says. "That must be what happened."

I don't mention that my mother probably wouldn't tell me because she still held a lot of resentment against her husband.

"You ok, Dad?" Janet asks.

"I'm ok," I say. "Like I said, ancient history. Enough to think about without worrying about something that happened over forty years ago."

"What made you get the albums out today, after all this time?" Jan asks.

I force myself back to the present. "Ernestine was showing me her pictures the other day. And Marigold too. Actually, most of the residents have pictures sitting around, except for Fiona."

Barb interrupts, "You seem to know quite of few of these residents by their first names."

"I work with them everyday, Barb. Hard not to know their names."

She looks away.

"Marigold and I found a pile of old pictures on a table in the basement while we were trying to find a mouse in the middle of the night. Jogged my memory for these."

"You found some old pictures in the basement?" Colin asks. "In the middle of the night?"

"Kind of peculiar. There was a picture of Ernestine's husband there." I look at Barb, expecting her to criticize me again, but she says nothing. "Don't know how or why it got all the way down there. Don't think Ernestine is able to navigate the basement stairs. Even Marigold, who's quite spry for her age, has trouble."

"Maybe someone took it from her room and put it down there?" Colin says.

"We did find a mattress as if someone has been using the basement as a place to sleep. Though I can't imagine who would want to.

Nothing but old junk, mice, and cobwebs. And how they'd even get down there without anyone noticing, I haven't a clue."

"Probably a separate basement entry," Mark says. "Lots of old buildings have entrances on the outside. Last year, when our company remodelled city hall, we found quite a few boarded-up entrances leading out of the basement. Didn't you say The Wheaton was a hotel at the turn of the twentieth century?"

"It was."

"Then the original kitchen was most likely in the basement. All the deliveries would have been made at the kitchen door. Wouldn't have wanted the help to be seen by the guests. Probably got yourself a vagrant looking for a warm place to sleep. Maybe been sleeping there for months, years even if no one uses the basement for anything but storage of junk."

"There is an old kitchen down there. And last Christmas when I was in the basement looking for decorations, I thought someone pushed me to the floor."

"Someone pushed you?" Colin's eyes are big.

"Well, it could have been my imagination. You should see the crap down there. Piled everywhere. Very precarious. Something could have fallen."

"Can I come and see, Grandpa?"

"No," Barb says. "Grandpa does not need you bugging him at work."

"I don't mind, Barb."

"No, absolutely not."

"Aw, Mom," Colin says. "Grandpa said it was ok. I promise I won't get in his way."

"Please, Barb," I say. "It's perfectly alright. I don't mind at all."

She walks to the kitchen and puts her empty bottle on the counter. "Well, I guess if Grandpa says it's ok, then that's the final word. No time like the present to start parenting."

"Barb, please don't be like this," Mark says. "Dad's trying, surely you can see that. Quit making it difficult."

"And you think I'm being a bitch," Barb says.

"Hey, hey," I say. "No need for that."

Everyone's quiet as heads turn away.

"I'm not the one making this difficult." Barb puts her hand on her son's shoulder. "Colin, we're going home."

They're halfway to the front door, Barb pushing Colin ahead of her, when, for better or for worse, the words come out of my mouth. "This has nothing to do with Colin bothering me at work and you know it," I say to her back. "It's entirely about you thinking my job is a way to get out of family responsibilities and you're mad."

She turns, her face is full of anger. "Well, that's right, isn't it? You used work as your excuse then and you're still doing it. You ignored me my entire childhood. Why should things change now just because Mom's dead? You're more concerned about this old lady, about all of them," she waves towards the front door, "than you are your own family."

"I'm sorry you think you had a bad childhood." I look at Mark and Janet standing beside the table, then back at Barb. "I'm sorry all of you think I wasn't a good parent."

Mark objects. "I didn't have a bad…."

Barb cuts her brother off. "I suppose that makes me wrong, just because I'm the complainer. I called last week to invite you for supper and you weren't home," she says to me.

"You did? I didn't get the message."

"Didn't leave one. You probably would have made an excuse anyhow so why should I bother?"

"You should have left a message. I'd have called you back."

"Would you have? I don't know, Dad, I just don't know." She turns her back to us and puts her hands to her face.

Colin puts his arms around his mom. "It's ok, Mom. I don't need to go to Grandpa's work."

She says through her fingers, "No, you go, that's fine."

I step in front of her. "Barb, if you don't want Colin to come to The Wheaton, then he doesn't have to. You're his parent, not me." I attempt to give her a hug.

Suddenly she's punching me in the shoulders. "Why did you ignore me so much, Dad? Why wasn't I as important to you as your job seemed to be? Why aren't I as important as Ernestine and Marigold, and Alma and Fiona?"

I don't move out of the way. Nor do I deflect the punches. "You were important to me," I say. "Why do you think I worked so hard at the post-office? Being the breadwinner was what I was supposed to do. I thought you understood that. I was taking care of my family." I stop short of apologizing.

Clem has become agitated and begins to whine and paw my legs. Barb stops pummelling my shoulders and grabs onto me like she's going to fall to the floor. "I miss Mom so much. I'm sorry. I miss her so much."

"I know," I say.

"I was sure after two years I'd be fine, everything would be fine. But you're not here for me, you're busy with everyone else, just like you always were. I'm still in the way."

"You're not in the way, you never were."

She steps back and wipes her eyes. "You can take Colin to work. I have to go home now."

I reach for her. "Don't leave."

"Text me and set up a date. It's fine." She opens the door and she and Colin disappear into the twilight.

Chapter twenty-three

Late spring

Winter has been hard on the older headstones in this cemetery and some have tipped sideways into holes that formed as the ground began to thaw. I step around pieces of broken concrete as I wind my way towards Elaine's grave. The day I buried her was much like this; cold and grey. Clem and I stop beside her plot.

"Winter just doesn't want to let go this year, sweetie. You'd be itching to get at the garden right about now, but it's still nothing but mud. Every time Clem comes in I have to wipe her paws. Don't know what I'll do with the yard. Maybe Jan will want to plant something, if she's not too busy writing her thesis. She's getting close to being done. Don't understand most of what she tells me. She certainly didn't get her brains from me.

"Mark and Deanna are great. Busy raising that family of theirs; you'd be in there like a dirty shirt helping. Wish you could have met Amanda. Sweetest baby in the world. Red hair like you and Jan. She'll be one this summer."

Clem barks at a magpie defending his territory.

"I don't know how you managed to fit everything in, all those years you were raising a family. Working, housework, meals. I wasn't much help. Guess I should have figured that out years ago.

"Barbie's ok. She'd rather I wasn't working, thinks I'm doing it to avoid family obligations. I suppose when I first began that was something that motivated me, but now, it's more than that. I need this job, it's what's keeping me sane. I feel like I'm doing something worthwhile. Just as you did all those years looking after us. Just like you did when you got the job at the library. I feel useful."

Another car pulls up to the gate and a family clamours out of their SUV. The children race between the headstones, stopping for a moment to stare at me before they resume their game of tag.

I wait for them to pay their respects. When they drive away, I decide, what better place to get this off my chest than here, talking to someone who can't tell me I'm making something out of nothing.

"Why didn't you tell me my dad was at our wedding? I don't understand why you didn't say anything." I stare at her headstone. "It just seems so odd that you, and I assume, Mom knew, but not me, his son. I called Grace to ask her if she knew, but she said no, she can't remember being told he was there. But she was pretty young at the time and it was forty years ago. I sent her a picture of her and Dad dancing, perhaps it will jog her memory. Did you think I'd get angry if I knew? Did you think I'd make a scene?" I say softly, "I suppose back then I was a bit of a hot-head, but I like to think I wouldn't have gotten mad at our wedding. I like to think I wouldn't have done that to you. Did he tell you why he didn't want me to know he was there? Was it because he still didn't want to get to know me, his grown-up son? Was he afraid I'd ask for money, for help?" A noise makes me crane my head back. Thousands of geese are flying overhead, their bodies black dots in the sky. "You'll probably see all the kids this week at some time or another. Two years feels like just a moment ago and forever at the same time." I rub her name. "Sorry to bring up something that happened so long ago. I'm sure whatever your reason for not telling me was done out of love, not animosity. I know you loved me. I always knew that. I hope you didn't feel you loved me more than I loved you. Because I did, you know. I did love you just as much. I still do."

Clem and I drive away and as I pick up speed, I pass Mark and Barb going the other direction. In my rear-view mirror, I see their tires kicking up dust as they turn into the cemetery.

Melanie is standing beside the desk. She already has her jacket on and is tapping her toes on the tile. She crosses her arms and looks pointedly at the clock. "You're late, Davies." It's the first time she's spoken to me since the night she left the front door unlocked.

"Had to take Clem for a walk before my shift so she could do her business, and…."

"I don't care about your GD excuses, I only care about you being here on time. I will not work one minute of your shift ever again, not one minute. And this is the last time I write down any of your messages. You need to tell your friends," she shakes the pieces of paper she's made notes on, then drops them on the desk, "to call while you're working or don't call at all. If you can't get your shit together, then quit."

I grip the leash. Clem wags her tail and lifts her head, always hopeful for a pet, but Melanie stomps past without a glance. I hang up my coat and look at the notes she's left, scrawled in her childlike handwriting and stuck to something she's spilled on the desk. I peel one away. Fiona Brighton wants me to come to her room.

Alma's in her office doing paperwork. "Where is everyone?" I ask. "The regulars aren't in the lobby."

"Upstairs, Marigold's room. Some clandestine meeting, think I don't know." She pats Clem on the head. "My guess is it's about things going missing." She looks Clem in the eyes. "Need to have you here more often, girl, catch the culprit in action." She kisses Clem on the nose. "I haven't had any reports of theft for at least two weeks now. I'm hoping it's like last time and it's over. Trouble is, the elderly won't always speak up the moment something is missing thinking they've misplaced it and don't want to be embarrassed. As a consequence, things that should have been reported, get delayed. I've been thinking it's time for a meeting."

I wave Melanie's note. "Fiona wants me to come upstairs. I've got the phones in my pockets."

"Fiona?"

"Probably just needs a light bulb changed."

I leave Clem at the desk. Fiona's door is ajar and I push it open.

"Fiona, you wanted to see me about something?"

"Come in, John," she says.

I walk down the short hall and she points to the other chair, the one I've used to stand on to change light bulbs. "Sit down for a minute. Have a cup of coffee with me."

I look at my watch. "I really can't stay today," I say tapping my watch. "Melanie's already left."

She looks out the window. "I'll make this short then. I want to report a theft. My pearl necklace is missing."

"Oh, Fiona, I'm sorry. I guess no one told you. It was in the alley the night I found you. Beads were scattered everywhere. Should have gone back to pick them up, but I didn't think...."

Her face turns red. "Didn't know that." She glances at her dresser, "There's an emerald ring my husband gave me missing as well."

"Did you have it on that night?" I ask. "I could go and scour the alley, though I suppose by now someone's scavenged it."

She shakes her head. "I never wear it. Keep it right here in my jewellery box." She points to the dresser beside her bed.

There's no empty liquor bottles on the coffee table. I scan the room. There's none sitting around either.

"I'm not imagining things, if that's what you think."

"When did you lose it?"

"I didn't lose it, John, it went missing. I keep it in my jewellery box at all times. Shortly after my–" she swallows, "–episode, I noticed it gone. Can't say how for long."

"Have you told Alma?"

"You're the first I've told."

I point down the hall. "Have you been keeping your door open?"

"No."

"It wasn't locked today and as far as I can recall, any other times I've been here, it's been open."

"I only just opened it because I was expecting you. But as you and I both know, on previous occasions, I probably forgot to close it. That doesn't happen now."

"Oh?"

"I've quit."

"You've quit?"

"Drinking, John. I've quit drinking."

"Just like that, you've quit?"

Her retort is immediate and sharp. "I may be an alcoholic but I'm still able to recognize condescension when I hear it." She says less sharply, "I've joined AA. Been going to meetings. Thirty-one days sober."

I push my hand through my hair. "Oh, well, Fiona, that's great."

"You sound like you don't believe me."

I'm reminded of our first conversation when she said the same thing about not being a drunk. "Sure, sure I do." I scratch my head, "Thirty-one days. That's great Fiona. What is it you want me to do about the missing ring? I could tell Alma if you like?"

"Fine," her voice has become detached.

I remember the meeting. "There's a meeting in Marigold's room right now about this very thing, if you're interested. A few residents have noticed things missing as well. You should talk to them, tell them you've been robbed."

"I think not, John."

"No one goes through life untouched by something embarrassing. They'll understand."

She lifts her face to mine, her eyes wide with hope. "Would you accompany me?"

"I'm sorry, Fiona." I begin to make excuses. "I have a lot to do tonight. Fill the coffee urns, bingo, set the table for breakfast. Plus, sometimes Mrs. Crawford comes downstairs and I have to help her back up. I heard they finally found her a bed in a nursing home. She leaves…."

"Alright then," she says, once again becoming cool. "You'd better get back."

Two steps and I'm past her kitchen.

"John, just a second, don't leave. That's not all I have to say." She turns to her window. "I meant to invite you up sooner, but I've been avoiding it." Her posture, which is always straight, rounds as she sags her shoulders. "Feeling uncomfortable about everything, about what you had to do that night. What kind of a fool wanders out in that kind of weather without proper clothing? You saved my life."

I detest explanations. I'll skip pages in a book to avoid them. "Accidents happen. Glad I was there to help."

"No," she shakes her head, "that's wrong." She presses her fists to her hips. "I need to do this right if I want to set things straight between us. I need to be honest with myself and with you. I didn't just wander outside that night. It was no accident."

That thought had crossed my mind.

"It's not what you think. I didn't go outside to kill myself. I was thinking clear enough to know I needed a coat and gloves, but I misjudged the temperature and how much I'd already had to drink that day. I was simply trying to leave, to run away from my troubles. Thought if I got away from here I could start over, make some friends, stop drinking. I chose a time you weren't here," she wipes away a tear. "I had enough sense to realize I'd have trouble getting past you. Figured I could get past without Melanie seeing. Not that she'd care if she did see me go outside. I've seen her walk past people struggling to get up from a fall. Forgot about the door being locked at night if there's no one at the desk. Just by chance it was open. Sat here all that day and drank myself into a stupor. I have no friends here anymore, except you."

The muscle under my right eye begins to twitch.

"You look surprised," she says, "that I consider you a friend?"

"Oh, sure, I mean, no. I consider you a friend too, Fiona." I rub my eye then shove my hands in my pockets.

"I've contacted my kids. Part of the AA program is to set things straight, acknowledge your mistakes. I told them about you, about how you've helped me. They're grateful."

I look at my watch and shuffle my feet. "I really have to get back to work. Think about going to Marigold's. I'll let Alma know you'd like to speak to her."

She turns back to the window. "Fine, John, fine. Thanks for coming up."

Chapter twenty-four

A week later I've drawn the overnight shift. Alma is behind her desk when I enter her office.

"You should have a quiet night. No deliveries until morning so no one should be at the door until Dave gets here," she says. "I've locked the kitchen and basement doors already."

I straighten up the reception desk, then go to the dining room to set the table for breakfast, a job Melanie was already supposed to have done. For the next couple of hours, I busy myself with chores and enjoy the peace and quiet; one of the few perks the night shift offers. No one asking anything of me, or regaling me with stories of days gone by.

Even as a kid I liked the nighttime better than the day. Sometimes, after Mom had gone to bed, I'd sneak out of my bedroom window on a warm summer's night to sit on the step, or walk around the block, enjoying the solitude. I suppose I've been a lone wolf most of my life.

I'm wheeling the coffee cart into the dining room after filling the urns with water for the morning, when I hear a noise that sounds like Alma's office door stuttering closed. I step into the lobby with Clem by my side and see the shape of a man running into the kitchen. Clem takes off after the intruder, I follow as fast as I can. By the time I get there, Clem's standing by the kitchen door as it closes on her face. I open the door and peer down the length of the yard but see no one.

First, I call the police, then I call Alma. She arrives before the police, wearing her winter coat thrown on over a nightgown. She's scrubbed some cream off her face but traces of it still linger in the corners of her nose and eyes. Her hair, instead of being in the usual tight bun on top of her head, falls in gentle waves to the middle of her back. She smells of sleep.

Alma and I, along with a police officer, go from apartment to apartment informing residents what has happened and making sure everyone is alright and accounted for. The police search the rest of the place while Alma, Clem, and I wait in the lobby, but they find nothing. They ask me a few questions but all I can tell them is Clem and I chased someone out the kitchen door which was locked. That means it is either a staff member or someone a staff member gave a key to. They tell Alma to get the locks on all outside doors changed and suggest we hold a meeting to inform residents to keep their apartment doors locked at all times.

Some of the residents have computers, but not all, so emailing is never used to send out a group message, much to the complaints of the computer-users. They whine that in this day and age everyone needs a computer and life would be much easier if they could simply read announcements in the convenience of their homes. Keep up with the times, they say to these non-computer users. Are you still riding a horse to town, or using an ice box? Do you wash your clothes with a wringer washer, or use a rotary phone? No! Life's too short to be fearful of modernization. Just never, they continue to say, push the wrong button or you'll have to phone a computer technician then try to explain to the person on the other end of the line, who's an expert and probably thinks you are somewhat stupid, what button you pushed to get into this predicament.

But much to their chagrin, the non-users stubbornly remain, as the computer users call them, in the dark ages.

So, because of those residents without computers, we use a bulletin board for all announcements. It's located conveniently just outside the entrance to the dining room and is a source of continual entertainment. That's where we post the notices of pot-luck suppers, dances, birthday parties, and inform residents of the community room being rented for such-and-such a date. Sometimes we even post the time and place of funerals of residents, if the family allows.

Residents can also post their own notices.

Tea party - E. Hawkins - 2PM Friday, or *Wine and Cheese - Marigold's 7PM Sunday. To give away - never used – padded - elongated toilet seat for men. P. Humphrey, suite 271,* or, *For sale - set of bone china dishes. Heirloom from Grandmother. After last year's fiasco, never hosting another family reunion in the community room, again. G. Harrington, suite 302.*

Occasionally, people not living here can drop off posters to hang if we deem them appropriate, and every day someone comes with a fold-up massage table to knead a residents' flesh back into compliance.

Businesses advertising wine making are also popular. *Make your own wine for just five dollars a bottle without the hassle of having the equipment in your own home,* the posters say. I know of many residents who share kits and have rack upon rack of wine stacked in their closets.

This spring, garage-sale posters have dominated the board, with residents crowding around, then heading out bright and early Saturday morning to get the best deals on ceramic cats, bread baskets, and balls of wool, 'never been opened!'

The rest of the year, at any given time of day, there are usually people milling around this board, writing down information, or simply shooting the breeze with a cup of coffee in their hands. It's our version of the water cooler.

After the police left, Alma posted a notice on the bulletin board calling for a discussion to be held in the dining room the next day at 7PM. Usually, Alma told me, there is only one meeting a year, the AGM held in the Fall. This is going to cause a stir, she said. And she's right. I get inundated with questions all day long.

"John, John," Ivy comes running towards me. "Is this about firing Melanie? I bet it is."

"No, Ivy. As far as I know, Melanie's not being fired."

"Well, if she's not she should be. I've a mind to come downstairs every night to make sure the door is locked myself. Imagine, leaving it unlocked so anyone could come in and murder us in our beds!"

Mr. Belgrade cuts in. "It's about that damned road construction that's going to happen this summer, isn't it? When I think of all the taxes I've paid to this city, you'd think they could get it done right the first time. Was fixed only a couple of years ago."

I guess for all Mr. Belgrade's talk of becoming a better person after he went to the other side, he still needs a bit of fine tuning. "I don't think….," I begin to say.

"Are we being evicted, John? Is the place losing money?" Beatrice bends close and says behind her hand, "I'm willing to pitch in, let Alma know, would you? I'm not, how shall I put it, scraping the bottom of the barrel as far as money goes. I have enough selfish relatives to give it to, and still have some left over." She gives a discreet wink and pats my hand.

By this time, I have a crowd of twenty people standing in front of me, all talking at once.

"Just come to the meeting. That's all I can say."

As people take their seats around the dining room, they talk quietly to each other, waiting for Alma to stand at the dais. Word seems to have gotten around about my so-called heroics because I hear whispers of, "Chased him right out the door," and, "Wish I'd been there. John wrestled the thief to the ground. I'm sure he scared the bejeezus outta him."

There are, however, some left out of the loop.

"What's all the whispering about?" Mabel asks. "Is it my birthday? Am I having a surprise party?" She swivels her wrinkled face around the room, tittering and waving her hand like the Queen, then turns back to her friend and puts her fingers to her lips, shushing herself. "I'll pretend I don't know, Ester. I was always good at keeping secrets. Once Earl tried to surprise me but I…."

"No, Mabel, hush now. It's not a surprise party for you. You had your birthday last month, remember? Your family came and took you out for supper."

"They did?" her watery blue eyes become wide as she remembers. "That was nice of them. I have good kids, don't I, Ester?"

"You do, Mabel. You're a lucky woman."

Mr. Granger says, "Did I leave my hearing aid in my suite? Everyone's talkin' but I can't hear a damned thing."

"Nope, it's there," Arnold says as he peers in Mr. Granger's ear. "Perhaps your battery is dead?"

"Order, order," Alma says.

It's a full house so it takes a while for silence to reign, but gradually the whispering stops as heads turn towards Alma, with the last holdouts standing at the back of the room.

Alma continues. "As some of you already know, John chased an intruder out of the building last night."

The room erupts with voices as every rheumy eye looks for me in the crowd. Alma pounds her gavel.

"I'm holding this meeting to tell you what the police advised me. Keep your doors locked at all times, even when you're at home. Don't let anyone in unless you're confident you want them to come inside. If you see someone you think doesn't belong, or is acting suspicious, please tell John, Melanie or me. Do not, and I repeat, do not approach them yourselves."

Heads nod. A hand is raised.

"Yes, Irma?" Alma says.

"We could have teams. I'd be willing to organize them. Like the neighbourhood watch programs, only ours would be for each floor."

"I don't think that's really necessary. I don't want the residents to be putting themselves into any kind of dangerous situation. The police simply said to be on the lookout for people that don't belong and I was to inform the residents to keep their doors locked. I think that's all that's necessary at this time."

Irma looks disappointed.

"It's also come to my attention that the residents don't always let us know when they believe something has been stolen. Please, if you believe something has been taken from your apartment, let one of us know."

Beatrice raises her hand.

"Beatrice has the floor," Alma says.

"Do the police have any suspects, Alma?"

"They don't. The person John saw may not even have had anything to do with the thefts, though it seems suspicious. We do know it was someone with a key as the door was locked earlier in the evening."

Like a bee in the wind, Melanie's name buzzes through the air.

"John said he thought it was a man," Alma says. "Which rules out Melanie."

"I think it's that boyfriend of hers," Carl says. "She's given him a key. There are disreputable places that will duplicate keys even though they say no duplications right on them."

Again, Irma raises her hand. "When Melanie puts on that coat of hers, she could be mistaken for a man."

Many people nod in agreement as murmurs circulate the room.

"We will not be accusing anyone," Alma says. "Not without proof." She looks pointedly at a few of the faces. Not one of them breaks Alma's gaze.

Chapter twenty-five

Even with Alma's cautionary words, the air is electric with suspicion. Alma can feel it, Dave can feel it, I can feel it, and even Clem can feel something as she spends much of her time in an overly excited state. Apparently the only one who can't feel it is the one the suspicion is directed at: Melanie. She seems oblivious to the fact that many of the residents think she's the one doing the stealing. Alma hasn't questioned her because there is no proof. That, combined with the fact she doesn't suspect people think it's her, leads me to believe it can't be her. Not to talk disrespectfully of Melanie, but I'm of the mind she's not smart enough to be able to complete the thefts without getting caught, though I don't share my thoughts.

There are a few, however, who are of the same mind as me and these people don't hesitate to let the others know what they think.

"Of course it isn't her. She doesn't have the brains to pull off any kind of heist. She'd be caught before she had the stolen goods out the door." And, "She wouldn't have the opportunity to take anything, she's never in a residents' suite long enough. Only comes inside mine when she has a chore to do and then she holds her nose the entire time, as if I have some kind of old age disease or something."

The ones who believe it's Melanie don't hold back either.

"Who else could it be? She's the only one here that would do something as brazen as that. Thinks we're all a bunch of numbskulls just because we're old. And that boyfriend of hers, he's a bad apple if ever I saw one. Drives that muscle car like he owns the road.

Squealed past Herb and me just the other day. Near about ran us into the ditch."

Even without proof they're adamant it's Melanie and take every opportunity to stare her down, trying to let her know they're on to her.

1998

I open the front door. A police officer is standing on my step.

"Does Mark Davies live here, Sir?" the cop asks.

"He does," I say.

"Is he home?"

"Is Mark home?" I repeat.

"Yes Sir."

"What's this about?"

"I have some questions. Could you get him for me please, Sir?"

"He's my son and he's only thirteen."

"Yes sir."

I open the door and let the officer inside. He's lean, with clear skin, and very young.

"Mark," I call up the stairs. "Come down here."

His voice is muffled through his bedroom door. "Can't, Dad. Doing homework. Have to get it done before chess club tonight."

I yell louder than I should. "Now, Mark." I glance at the cop's impassive face as he waits patiently for me to get my son. "Get down here now, Mark."

His bedroom door opens and the cop and I hear the tinny sound of a song squawking from his Walkman headphones. "What is it, Dad? I told you…." He stops talking when he sees the police officer. He descends the top two steps.

"This officer has some questions for you. Have you done something you shouldn't?"

"Please, Sir," the cop says. "I'll ask him myself." He looks at my son, skinny and scared in his baggy jeans and gelled back hair. "Are you Mark Davies?"

"Yes," Mark says in a quiet voice.

"Just have a couple of questions for you, son. Come down here please."

Mark descends the rest of the way.

"Were you at," the officer consults his notes, "783 Broadway Avenue this afternoon? It's an athletic shoe store."

Mark nods.

"And were you looking at a pair of shoes that looked like this?" He pulls a picture, like a mug shot, out of his notebook and shows Mark. It's a pair of running shoes.

Mark looks at his feet.

"Mark," I say a little too loud. "Answer the man."

Mark lifts his face to the picture. "I was."

"And were you there with another young man named Reginald Macdonald?"

Mark's nod is so small it's almost imperceptible.

"What did you and that punk do?" I grab Mark's arm and pull him to face me. "I told you I don't like that kid and you're not to hang around with him."

"Did you and your friend steal the shoes?" the cop asks, stepping in front of me.

"I dunno," he shrugs. "I was lookin' at other stuff. I never saw what Reg was doin'."

"Did your friend tell you to leave in a hurry?"

Marks eyes are huge. "Maybe."

"What the hell, Mark?" This time I'm yelling. "What have you done? Did you shoplift?"

Mark says nothing. His freckles are standing out on his pale skin.

"Did you leave with a pair of shoes you didn't pay for?" the cop asks.

Mark shakes his head. "No."

"Did your friend?"

Mark's quiet.

The cop steps forward. "Look, son, I know you don't want to implicate your friend, but if it was him and not you, you're not doing yourself any favours by not telling me the truth."

Still Mark says nothing.

"My partner is at Reginald Macdonald's house right now asking him the same questions. Is he going to tell us you took the shoes? Do we have to search your room?"

For the first time, Mark looks directly at the officer.

"Are the shoes in your room, Mark?" the officer asks.

Mark looks up the stairs towards his room.

I move around the cop and grab Mark to shake him. The officer removes my hands and presses my arms to my sides. "Mr. Davies, step back. Allow me to do my job." He looks at Mark. "I'm going to have to go up to your room now. Wait here with your dad." He ascends the stairs.

Again, I grip Mark's arm as I try to keep him in front of me but he pushes me off and turns his back to me.

"I can't believe this, Mark. You shoplifted? Do you know you might have ruined any chance you have of ever getting a job? Or even getting into university?"

We can hear the cop upstairs in Mark's room. Something heavy drops to the floor, then something else slides across it. There's a knock on the front door. I glance at the window in the door and see the outline of a man through the pebbled glass. I pull the door open expecting to see the other officer. It's a neighbour.

"Hey, John. Everything ok? Saw the police car, thought you might need some help."

"Nope, Jason," I quickly look up the stairs hoping the officer doesn't pick this particular time to come down. "Everything's fine, thanks. Just, uh, Mark thought he saw someone trying to break into the house. Turns out it was just, um, an over eager door-to-door salesman. Opened the door before we had a chance to answer. Nothing to worry about."

"Oh yeah? Well, I'll be sure to look out for him. Kick him off my property. Tell Mark he did the right thing. Need to teach these guys a lesson."

"Sure. Yeah," I laugh. "Talk to you later." I close the door before he has a chance to engage me in more conversation, and stomp to the kitchen where Mark has gone.

"God almighty Mark, you've made me look like a fool. What are your mother and I going to tell the neighbours now?"

"I've made you look like a fool, what will you tell people?" Mark repeats. "Is that all this is about, how you look? Shouldn't you be asking me if everything's alright? Maybe that should be your first question, not asking me how it makes you look."

Before I can answer the cop returns with a shoe box in his hand. "You'll have to come with me now, Mark. Your dad can follow in his car."

Chapter twenty-six

I enter the lobby and a hush comes over the group. Many cast their eyes down when they meet mine while others shake their heads. Everyone's face is sombre.

Marigold steps forward. "John, Alma wants to see you," she says.

I scan the assembly to see if anyone is missing. "What's going on?"

"Just go and talk to Alma. She's in her office."

Ivy, Ezra and Carl step out of the crowd and their eyes follow me as Clem and I walk down the hall. I feel like a school kid going to the principal's office while all the other kids are glad it's me and not them.

Alma's hanging up the phone when I enter the office. "John, have a seat."

"What's happening?"

"First of all, I think I've gotten to know you these past few months and I don't want you to think this is in any way your fault. She tried once before, there's no reason to think she wouldn't attempt it again. Most do."

"What?"

"It's Fiona, John."

"Did she start drinking again?" I grip the arms of the chair, bracing myself for the worst. "I knew I should have been paying closer attention. Damn it. Last time I was in her suite she wanted to talk but I told her I was busy. Said she'd joined AA so I figured she had the right people looking after her. I should have known she was vulnerable."

"John," Alma holds up her hand. "John, Fiona's dead. Julio found her on the lawn this morning when he was pulling the bus out of the garage. I sent him home. He was quite shaken. The paramedics think she fell from her balcony. She'd been drinking so it could have been an accident, but they can't rule out suicide."

"I don't understand."

"Paramedics guessed from the rigor, that it happened sometime during the night. No one heard or saw anything."

"No," I wave my hand at Alma. "That's not right. She joined AA. She quit drinking."

"She had a relapse; it happens. No one ever recovers from being an alcoholic. It's something they have to choose not to do every day for the rest of their lives."

"But she had chosen," I insist. "She wanted to be sober. She wanted a new life for herself." I lift my head and look directly at Alma. "Have they ruled out that someone could have pushed her?"

Alma taps her pencil. "Pushed her? That seems unlikely. The police searched her suite and found empty liquor bottles. She was drinking again." She pauses. "This is no one's fault but hers. Don't go blaming yourself."

"She talked about reconciling with her kids. She talked about making some friends here. Was her door locked? She always forgot to lock it."

"John, she fell. That's what's going to be written in the report. Whether it was an accident or suicide, I don't think we'll ever know."

"She wouldn't kill herself, she told me so. Said she didn't go outside last winter to kill herself, just went out to run away, to make a new life for herself and start over. Said she'd been drinking and wasn't thinking clearly. She told me she was sad her friend, Ed Brown, took his life."

"Then she fell. She drank too much and fell."

I stand. "I'm going up to her suite. I want to see for myself."

"You can't, the police have it taped off."

I swipe at my cheeks. "She told me she considered me a friend and I barely responded. Maybe she'd still be alive if I'd not been so selfish."

"Now that's ridiculous. When people drink, they don't think straight. She could have had all the friends in the world and it would have made no difference." Alma stands and tilts her head back to meet my eyes. "You had nothing to do with her starting to drink again. You need to go home. Get some rest. I'll cover for you."

"No. I'm staying," I push open the door. "I've got lots to do today."

Two days later, Fiona's children, one son and two daughters, arrive to clean out their mother's suite and make the funeral arrangements. I remember the day Fiona told me she had kids, but I did not make an effort to ask questions. A couple of times in the last few months over a cup of coffee after gathering her recycling, she'd mention them, but I didn't probe her with questions and she wasn't one to talk about her life. I think of all the questions she asked about my family, my life, and realize how much she found out about me, and how little I learned about her. I was always in too much of a hurry to leave.

Her son, Murray, shakes my hand and tells me his mother mentioned me. Said she told him she'd made a friend. Said he knew she kept to herself most of the time and he was glad she'd found someone to talk to after Ed died. I don't tell him I let his mother down.

It takes only a couple of hours for Fiona's children to empty her apartment, and when they're done, one box marked clothes/ Salvation Army, and a box of dishes are loaded into an SUV. The furniture is being donated to a women's shelter. The funeral is to be held on the weekend and Alma tells me I can have the day off; she'll reschedule Melanie to work that shift. As much as I don't want to go, and just about decline, I say ok.

I hate death. It's just too far out of the norm. It makes me have to do things I wouldn't normally do, like wear a suit or buy a coffin. I realize how selfish that sounds; if given the choice I'd rather be the griever than the deceased, but that's the way I feel. I don't like change. And even though life is always changing, most times it's easy to handle at its meandering pace. Death changes life abruptly, not smoothly. That's what I hate. The jarring that death makes on my life.

Clem knew something was up the minute I donned the suit. The last time I wore it she came with me. That terrible day when she and I arrived at the funeral home. I took her to Elaine's coffin at the back of the chapel and allowed her to put her paws on the edge. She looked at Elaine and wagged her tail and whined, then lay on the floor, her chin resting on her paws, looking up at the coffin with her big brown eyes. I truly believe she understood that Mom was no longer with us; that this body, made up to look like Mom, was not her. And she accepted it far easier than I did. More proof that dogs really do live in the moment.

I drive to the funeral home. Parking is at a premium and an attendant directs me to the far side of the lot. This surprises me; I didn't know so many people knew Fiona. I walk into the chapel crowded with guests.

Memories of Elaine's funeral flood back and my skin prickles. The dampening of sound created by the drapery and carpet. The scent of the crowd mixed with the scent of flowers that lingers in the heavy air. The quiet music filtered through hidden speakers.

"Are you family, work associate, or a friend?" an attendant asks in a soft-spoken tone, forcing me out of my thoughts.

"I, I work at The Wheaton," I mumble.

"Right this way, Sir."

He leads me to a pew on the left and near the front. Alma is already here, as are many of the residents of The Wheaton.

"John," Alma whispers. "Weren't sure if you'd make it."

"Who are all these people?" I ask.

"Some are family, the rest, work associates. Fiona was a well-respected lawyer. Even after the case that set her to drinking. Didn't she ever mention that to you?"

I nod but don't elaborate. Fiona did mention it once, something about people not judging without knowing the entire story, but I didn't ask her what she meant.

Alma leans into me. She talks quietly. "Apparently, she defended someone in a rape charge, got him off. Turned out he was guilty and didn't get caught until he murdered the next woman he raped. She never forgave herself. Took the burden of the woman's death onto her own shoulders. She wouldn't let anyone into her life after that, even her own family. You were the only one, besides Ed Brown, she let get close to her in all the years I knew her. Guilt is a powerful emotion. Can change your life."

The minister stands by the dais and begins to speak. He says he's known Fiona for fifty-three years, ever since she was a young mother with a growing family, and knew her to be a kind, generous, and intelligent woman. A woman who knew what she wanted and was never one to back down. He talks about how things that happen in life can change a person on the outside, but on the inside those people are still the same. I look at Fiona's children nodding as he speaks. When he's done his speech, he introduces Murray, Fiona's son.

"Good afternoon friends, family, co-workers of Mom, and staff from The Wheaton."

He glances my way and I look at my hands in my lap.

"Reverend Smithers words couldn't have been truer." His eyes touch on Fiona's coffin. "Mom was a fighter. She was feisty and she always told it like it was. Many of her co-workers considered her to be pushy, but she knew that was how she would promote change. Not only for women in law, but for women everywhere. She knew she had to let men know she could do the job as well, if not better than they could. Believe me, being the only son growing up in a house with a mom like that, I heard those words more times than you can imagine."

Subdued laughter.

"Mom was one of the strongest women I knew. She would never back down, never proclaim defeat. And even though, at the end of her career, she struggled with some things, that's how I remember

her, that's how I'm always going to remember her; as a strong woman who spoke her mind. She taught me and my siblings how to be
strong, how to make our own way in this world. She told us everyone makes mistakes and that's how we learn, that's how we grow
and become responsible, mature adults. I can't imagine us being as
successful as we are, without her guidance."

1998

Mark is trying not to show fear in front of me. We're sitting in a
small square room in the police station waiting for the officer to
return with a Coke for Mark and a coffee for me. We were ushered
here through throngs of cops and criminals alike and I marvelled
at the organized chaos. I'm sure Mark didn't notice. His mouth is a
thin white line as he tries to be stoic, but every once in a while, his
bottom lip quivers.

"Mark, tell me the truth. Did you take the shoes?" Somehow, I
manage to keep the anger out of my voice.

Mark stares at his fingers, pressed hard into each other and says
nothing.

"If you did, we'll figure out what to do. If you didn't then don't
pretend you did just so your friend will still like you. He's not much
of a friend if he's willing to let you take the fall."

He keeps his eyes glued to a spot on the opposite wall.

I lose patience and slam my fist into the table. "Damn it, Mark,
quit acting like a child and look at me."

He turns his face to me; his eyes are blurry with held back tears.
"You're wrong, he's a good friend. He sticks up for me at school.
You've no idea what my life is like."

"Then tell me."

He shakes his head.

"If you're having trouble at school, I'll help you. But you need
to tell me."

"Nothing like waiting till now to help," he mumbles.

"If kids are picking on you then…."

"You don't know anything, Dad."

The officer opens the door and the sounds of a busy squad room filter in before the door closes. He places our drinks in front of us.

"Officer," I say. "This seems to me like a bit much for simply a pair of stolen shoes. I mean, dragging us down here for a boyhood prank is kind of melodramatic just to teach my son a lesson, don't you think?"

"I'll get to that in a minute, Mr. Davies." He looks at Mark. "So, Mark," he says. "Are you ready to talk to me?"

"Only if I can talk without my dad here."

"You want to talk to me without your father present? Is that what you said?" The cop throws an accusing glance my way.

Mark nods.

"It's actually the law that he be here. Unless you're eighteen and I believe you're only thirteen?"

"Yeah."

"Then, I'm sorry, son, he has to stay. Tell me, what's going on with you and this boy?"

Mark takes a shuddering breath. "Reggie helps me at school."

"With school work you mean? He helps you with your classes?"

"No, I help him with those in exchange."

"In exchange? For what."

"For keeping me safe."

"Do the other kids pick on you?"

"Yeah," he fingers the moisture running down the outside of the Coke can.

"Why?"

Mark glances at me first. "They say I'm too smart."

"They pick on you? And Reggie stops them?"

"I do his assignments for him and he keeps the bullies away."

"And you don't see him as being a bully?"

"He's not," Mark shouts. "Without him I'd be beat up every day."

I cut the cop off. "But he's blackmailing you, Mark. Why don't you go to the teacher? Why didn't you come to me?"

"Unfortunately," the cop says to Mark, "your father is correct. This boy is blackmailing you. If you didn't do his assignments for him, what would happen, do you think?"

Mark shrugs. "I dunno."

"Well, I'm not here to be your counsellor. That's up to your parents and the teachers at your school." He drums his fingers on the desk. "Did you open the shoe box, Mark?"

Mark shakes his head. "I stuffed it under my bed. I never looked inside."

"It seems your friend is more than a shoplifter. The box had five-hundred dollars in cash inside as well. Do you know how it got there?"

I interrupt. "Are you accusing my son of theft?"

"We're only trying to find out what happened." He looks at Mark. "Do you know how the money got in the box, Mark?"

Mark's eyes are wide and his skin is pale. "I thought it was just shoes."

"Are you protecting him because you're afraid?"

Mark shakes his head. "He's my friend."

"So, we should charge you? Is that what you want?"

"Charge me?" There's panic in Mark's voice.

"If you don't tell us and Reginald doesn't talk, because the stolen goods were found in your bedroom, that's what will happen. You'll be charged with theft and tried in juvenile court."

The police officer and I can see the battle going on inside my son as he wiggles in the chair. Eventually the threat of being charged wins out.

"He said he needed some new shoes. I didn't know he was going to steal them. He waited until he saw a kid about his size try on lots of pairs. When the clerk was done with that customer, Reg told me to ask to try on some shoes."

"And you did?"

"The clerk went into the back to get my size. Reggie stepped behind the counter. Then he came running out and swiped a box of shoes off the pile left on the floor from the other kid, and we ran," he says.

"You had no idea he took money as well as the shoes?" The cop waits patiently for Mark to finish his story.

"No, honest, I thought he just took the shoes. I didn't know what he was doing behind the counter." Mark's eyes are huge as tears well up behind them. "I thought maybe he was hiding from the clerk so he could swipe the shoes. When we got outside, we hid behind a car in the parking lot. That's where he handed me the box and told me to take them home, that he'd call me later. Said the clerk saw him take the shoes so no one would chase me."

In the quiet that ensues, a scuffle breaks out in the hall. A door slams and the voices abruptly stop.

Mark starts to cry. "I didn't know what else to do. I saw the clerk come outside and look for us. I had no choice. I just ran with the shoes and didn't look back. Didn't know Reg got caught."

"Thank-you, Mark."

"Am I going to be charged?" he wipes his hand across his eyes.

"That depends what your friend is telling the other officer. He is a known criminal to us, so we will do everything in our power to help you."

He leaves us alone and Mark hangs his head.

"What the hell, Mark? I told you I didn't want you to hang around with that kid."

Mark puts his head on the table.

"You should have come to me. I didn't know you were getting picked on."

"That's because you're always at work, or sleeping, or listening to your effing jazz records," he mumbles into his arms. "Last week I tried to talk to you about Reg but you just kept saying *uh-huh* to everything I told you. Didn't even listen." He sits up, "Your favourite phrase: 'Not now Mark, I'm tired.'"

I look at his face; it's full of pain and indifference.

"I'm sorry," I say.

"Whatever," he mumbles.

The officer opens the door. "You're free to go, Mark."

We stand. "Reg said he took the shoes?" Mark asks.

"He did. Said you didn't know he took the money. Said he wasn't surprised you didn't look inside the shoe box, that you're a good kid."

"Why would he do that?" I ask.

"We told him because the cash and the shoes were found in your son's room, Mark would be charged unless he confessed. Then Mark would have a record and it might affect his education when he got older." He looks at Mark; his face is softer than it was during the questioning. "Seems he thinks of you as a friend, young man. Just, next time, pick better friends, wouldja?"

A grin plays at Mark's mouth and I'm jealous of the officer's ability to give my son advice.

**

I flip the switch and descend the two steps from the house to the garage. I haven't felt like doing the things that gave me pleasure when Elaine was alive, so I've only been here a handful of times in the past two years; the last, over eight months ago, just before I began working at The Wheaton. And even then, I only stayed a couple of minutes, guilt overwhelming any pleasure I might have found in my hobby.

Twenty years ago, I moved from the basement filled with Lego and dollhouses, bike tires hanging from the rafters, and broken lamps I was always meaning to rewire, and made the back of the garage into my jazz room. I wired in electric baseboard heaters, installed wood panelling and carpet, put in an acoustic ceiling and insulated the connecting walls and doors. I bought expensive cupboards for my records, and a turntable and stand that would make a disc jockey jealous. I never did change to tape or CD, and digital is beyond me. I like the way vinyl feels in my hand, the way it looks when I place it on the turntable, and the sound it makes as the needle slides through the groove. It feels like music.

Elaine used to hate it when I came out here. She'd stomp around the house, start the vacuum, open and close the door, anything to tell me she was annoyed I was escaping. It's not like she didn't have her little rituals of escape. She'd go out for drinks with her group of girlfriends, or lie in the sun all Saturday afternoon, her body glistening with baby oil while I struggled with the kids — her way of making me parent. Or simply run out the door when I came home, telling me she'd had a bad day and needed shopping therapy. Oddly enough, those shopping trips were the times I didn't resent her alone time as much as I did the others. She'd come home happy and laden with parcels for everyone. She had good taste in clothes. I was proud to take her out; caught a lot of looks from guys, even into her fifties.

I pull *Days of Wine and Roses* by the jazz guitarist, Wes Montgomery, out of its sleeve and place it on the turntable. I set the needle, flip the switch and sit in my chair.

It's been odd without Fiona at The Wheaton this past month, odd walking past her door without dropping in to gather her recycling then share a cup of coffee. I've come to accept the fact she probably had begun drinking again. And even though there was nothing I could have said or done that would have stopped her, I feel guilty for not going to the meeting at Marigold's with her, or simply staying and talking; being the friend she thought I was.

The only way to not be affected when someone dies is to have no friends, no one to love. And how does anyone get through life with not a single person in it? It's impossible unless you're a monk living in a cave in a far-off corner of the world. It's like Marigold said; the cost of living. For a year and a half after Elaine died I tried to be that monk as I slept my way through my grief and my guilt. I figured if I stayed away from people, they would stay away from me.

I didn't realize, until Fiona said she considered me a friend, that perhaps I had reached out to her, had sent out signals that I was lonely. Likewise, it hadn't crossed my mind when Ernestine or Marigold asked me in for drinks, that I was hungry for some companionship; I thought I was doing it as a favour to them. It seems they also saw me as needing a friend.

I doze off then wake up when the record ends. I stand and find my Bunny Berigan album and put it on the turntable. Clem stretches and yawns then settles back down beside me. In the first moments of sleep, her tail softly thumps the floor. I close my eyes and feel the light-headedness of sleep swirling behind my eyes then slip into slumber with the song, *I Can't Get Started*, playing in the background of my dream.

'Dad,' Mark says, 'you just don't understand him. He's not bad, he's lonely'.

'Uh-huh,' I say as Mark's face swims in and out of focus.

'He's adopted,' Mark says. 'His parents abandoned him at a hospital when he was five years old. Left him sitting on a chair and told him they'd come back for him. At the end of the day he was still sitting there. He was placed in different foster care homes year after year. His parents were never found.'

'That's too bad,' I say.

'Thinks no one cares about him. That's why he does the things he does. What should I do, Dad? Should I tell him not to steal? Should I tell a teacher?'

I put the album on the turntable and sit in my chair. 'Later Mark,' I say. 'I'll talk to you later, ok? Had a tough day. Need to relax.'

I wake with a start and think I know who the grim reaper might be.

Chapter twenty-seven

Clem and I stand on the front step waiting for Mark to answer his door, my heart thumping in rhythm to Clem's pants. I can hear him inside telling Rose not to open the door before he gets there, but she does anyhow.

"Grandpa," she says as she jumps into my arms.

"Hey, Pumpkin. You should really let your mommy or daddy answer the door."

"I knew it was you, so I opened it."

"How did you know that?"

She looks shyly at me.

"Rose," Mark says as he comes around the corner, "I thought I told you," he sees me. "Oh, hi, Dad. Didn't know it was you."

"I did, I did!" Rose says. "I knew it was Grandpa so I opened the door."

"Well, next time wait for me, Rosie." He puts his hand on my shoulder and says, "Come in, Dad."

I cross the threshold with Rose in my arms and Clem at my feet. Deanna emerges from the hallway carrying Amanda who's far bigger than I remember. Mark sees me staring.

"She's just about one, Dad. Time goes by fast, hey?"

"Been too long since I've seen her, or you, Deanna."

Deanna gives me a hug. "We know you're working hard at your new job. I'm sure the people there just love you."

"I guess I've been a negligent grandpa."

"What's negligent mean?" Rose asks. Her sweet breath wafts into my face.

"It means not doing what you think you're supposed to be doing," I say.

Deanna glances at me.

"Has Grandpa been negligent?"

"No, he's just been very busy. Your grandpa loves you and your sister."

I hug Rose. "I do, little girl. I do love you. And I promise I won't be negligent anymore, even though your mommy said I wasn't." I say to Mark, "Can I talk to you?"

"Sure, Dad." He looks at Deanna with the baby in her arms then says to me, "Is it ok if Rosie comes with us? She can play on the swing while we talk."

"Of course."

"Would you like a beer or iced tea?"

"Better make it iced tea. Have to go to work from here." I blush when I hear myself making an excuse. "Sorry. Need to get over when I have no other obligations."

"Don't worry about it. We're just as much to blame as you. Life gets in the way sometimes."

I set Rose down and Mark ushers me outside. Clem and Rose bound off the deck and head to the sandbox and swing-set. Mark and I sit facing the yard.

"So, what's up, Dad?"

Clem barks at a cat walking across the top of the fence. "Clem, no barks," I yell. "You're going to think I'm losing my marbles," I say to Mark.

"Something wrong?"

"No. Just thinking about things."

"Daddy," Rose shouts. "Look Daddy, I made a castle."

Clem knocks the sand castle down with her paw and Rosie laughs.

"You're a good father, Mark. You and Deanna are good parents."

"Thanks."

"I wish I could have been as good at it as you are."

Mark pauses, "I remember lots of good times."

I take a gulp of iced tea and press the cold glass to my forehead. "Remember when you got in trouble for shoplifting and I blamed you?"

"I do," he says slowly then looks sideways at me.

"I've come to apologize for not believing you, and for not listening to you the day you tried to talk to be about that boy."

"I forgave you for that a long time ago, Dad."

"I was so caught up in feeling sorry for myself, like I was the only one in the family, I didn't think about anything else. Your mother's death, it's changed me. I should have enjoyed you more."

"You were the best father you knew how to be. I don't hold anything against you."

A hawk chases a chickadee out of the birdfeeder and Rosie yells at it to get out of her yard.

"We all struggle with things," Mark says. "You were raised without a dad. Hell, he left you. I can't imagine how that would have felt." He takes a gulp of his iced tea and swallows hard. "You stuck it out, and believe me some days it's tough. I'm sorry I didn't understand that until I became a dad myself. I know Barbie is having a hard time, but deep down, I'm pretty sure she understands. It'll just take time."

Tears sting my eyes and I can't answer. We sit in silence as we watch Rose swing and Clem dig a hole in the sand.

"And," Mark continues, "you were right, I shouldn't have been hanging out with that kid. If I hadn't had good parents, I'd probably have gone off the tracks too. It was because I didn't want to disappoint you, that I stayed on the straight and narrow. Actually, I heard from an old high-school acquaintance a while back on Facebook. Said Reginald ended up in jail. Died there a few years ago. Was only thirty-eight. I felt bad for him, he had a rough life. But we all have the ability to make something of ourselves. That's what I want to teach my kids."

Clem is sitting to the side of the swing, her eyes glued to Rose as she glides back and forth. A car horn honks, pulling Clem's attention from her prey and she bounds to the gate, knocking Rose from the swing as she passes. Mark and I stand and run, me to pull Clem off the gate, and Mark to comfort Rose as she stands sobbing in the sandbox.

Chapter twenty-eight

Spring has arrived and the backyard of The Wheaton is alive with more than just dandelions and quack grass. Residents, carrying seed packets, plant pots, rakes, and hoes, hurry back and forth across the yard, calling to each other about how to lay out the garden.

"Make sure the radishes are at the edge, Elsie. When you plant them in the middle, everything gets trampled by Earl's big feet when he tries to harvest them," Rachel says. "They're the first to be up in the spring, you know. And don't plant the cucumbers next to the sweet peas. We'll end up with cucumbers hanging from the flower vines up and down the fence like we did last year. Was embarrassed to tell people this was our garden. Looked like some kind of phallic new age art display."

I'm in the far corner of the yard, supervising the planning and the planting when I hear Marigold say my name. I turn, expecting to see her bustling over to me with instructions about something or other, but instead, I see her speaking to Barb and Colin standing on the patio next to the building. Clem jumps from her spot on the edge of the garden and runs to greet them.

"Nice to finally meet. John has said so much about you," Marigold says.

Barb scratches Clem behind the ears while she cranes her neck looking for me.

Ignoring reprimands from the gardeners, I step through freshly furrowed rows to greet my daughter and grandson.

"Grandpa." Colin runs to me, the self-consciousness I've seen in him when he's in front of friends or even his sister, not apparent to-day. I put my arm around his shoulder and he gives me a hug, then we walk up to Barb and I give her a hug. Her body remains stiff.

"What are you doing here?" I ask.

Avoiding my eyes, she says, "Colin kept asking me if you texted yet, but you hadn't. So, I thought we'd drop by. Hope that's ok."

"Of course it's ok. Sorry for not setting anything up. I…."

"No problem, Dad," she says. "Didn't expect you to." She looks around the yard without meeting my eyes. "Can he stay for a couple of hours? Julie's at a play date, and I've got a few errands to do and it's easier without kids tagging along. I'll pick him up around noon."

"Why doesn't he stay for lunch?" Marigold says. "Just let me go and tell the cook I've invited a guest."

"No, no, Marigold. That's ok," Barb says. "Don't go to any trouble."

"Please, Mom," Colin says. "I'd like to stay for lunch."

"It's no trouble," Marigold says. "The residents love it when someone's kid comes for a meal. John's grandson, believe me, this young man will be the centre of attention." Before Barb can object any further, Marigold hurries away, flapping her hands in the air as she goes to talk to Dave.

Barb's shoulders sag. She looks at her watch. "I'd better get going."

"At least let me give you a tour of the place," I say.

"Uh," she glances around her. "Sure. Ok, Dad."

I wave my arm. "Well, as you can see," I say, "this is the backyard. The residents plant a garden every spring. We're just laying it out now."

Barb nods and I know what she's thinking; the only thing I've done with her mother's garden for the past two years is let it go to weeds. I tell Clem to stay and take Barb and Colin in the backdoor.

"I'd really better be going," she says after I've shown her the main floor.

"Sure, sweetie." I touch her hand; she pulls away.

"I'll be back by one, Colin. Wait for me here in the lobby. I don't want to have to try and find you in this," she sweeps her eyes across the lobby, "maze."

As soon as his mother is out of sight Colin asks, "Can we go to the basement now, Grandpa?"

"I have to let Alma know first. And we'll have to make it quick; I have a few things to get done before lunch."

On cue, Alma's door opens and she walks down the hall towards us. "Alma, you just missed my daughter, Barb. This is my grandson, Colin."

"So pleased to meet you, young man. Your grandfather speaks of his grandchildren often."

Alma is nothing if not formal.

"Colin wants to see the basement."

"The basement?"

"Thinks he can find the old entrance I told you about."

She cocks an eyebrow at him. "I suppose that's the kind of thing young lads like. Are you staying for lunch, Colin?"

I answer for him. "Marigold is speaking to Dave right now."

"Ok. We'll see you later," and she swooshes away in her skirt.

Marigold bustles up to us. "It's all set, young man." She looks over her shoulder at Dave, then whispers to Mark, "Dave was a bit miffed, but he'll get over it."

I open the basement door and flip the switch. I finally remembered to put a new bulb in last week and for the first time, I see the staircase walls as I pass; they're cement, covered in peeling white paint and cobwebs. Colin runs down the stairs, dragging his hand across the wall the entire way. I follow at a slower pace.

"Which door is the kitchen, Grandpa?" he asks.

I point, and he opens the door. Just as I remember from last time, dust bunnies begin swirling around the floor the moment the air hits them. My first thought is one would have to be down on their luck to sleep in this chaos, although a vagrant would probably deem himself, or herself lucky to come across such a sweet deal. I suppose if I was homeless, I would as well. We step inside.

Colin begins tapping on the back wall.

"What are you doing?" I ask.

"If there's an outside door, it would probably be on this wall be-hind some panelling or a cupboard. That's where they always are on my video games."

"Oh," I say, unfamiliar with such things. The only video game I've ever played is the one at Christmas.

As Colin taps his way across the back of the kitchen, I walk to the place I found the mattress and picture the last time Marigold and I were down here. They're gone, unless I'm in the wrong spot. I look around. There's the cutting board with it's ancient blood drip-ping down the sides, there's the canisters, bulging with rust, and the pots and pans hanging from the beam in the ceiling tangled with spider webs. I'm sure this is the right spot, but the mattress is gone. Perhaps the homeless person noticed there'd been people down here and he skedaddled, afraid of being found out and arrest-ed. Colin starts to yell.

"Grandpa, Grandpa. I found something! Come here."

I shuffle through the dust swirling at my feet. The freezer door is closed and a door that was hidden behind it is open. Colin is stand-ing at the top of a staircase, the backyard of The Wheaton visible behind him.

Chapter twenty-nine

Colin sits at the table while I push my beverage cart around the room. Marigold was correct in assuming he would be the hit of the lunch hour. Many residents have come up to introduce themselves. Colin barely has time to eat his macaroni and cheese.

Mr. Granger hangs his thumbs from his suspenders. "You're John's grandson, I hear. He's a good man. Grow up to be like him and you'll do yourself proud."

"You're a lucky boy to have such a great grandfather," Rachel says. "My own grandpa didn't want me around. Barely allowed to come into his house and when I was allowed in, I had to be relegated to the kitchen." She wags her finger at him. "Count your blessings, young man."

"Good of John to let you accompany him to work. You look a lot like him." Carl points to Colin's plate. "Make sure you eat those Brussel sprouts. Put hair on your chest."

Marigold whispers in Colin's ear and they have a laugh. Probably something about Carl being bald.

I keep busy while Colin endures all the advice. He doesn't seem to mind them speaking to him, as a matter of fact, he seems to be enjoying being the centre of attention.

The residents finish their lunch and amble out of the dining room, some stopping at the bulletin board to see what's new, some helping themselves to a second cup of coffee before they leave. The outside door opens and Barb enters. She looks uncomfortable amid all the people. I hurry out to greet her.

"Hi Barb," I say. "Did you get your errands done?"

"I did, though it's a miracle. Always too much to do." She has her head bent to her purse as she searches for something. "Groceries today, then buying Julie some new sneakers. At least school will be out soon. I only have two weeks off so I have the kids enrolled in camps the rest of the time, but I need to buy some….." She lifts her head and meets my eyes when she realizes she's having a conversation with me. She quickly looks away then puts her hand on Colin's back. "Thanks for having him here, Dad. I hope he wasn't in the way. Come, Colin. Time to go home."

"Just a sec, Barb," I say. "I'd like to speak to you."

"Speak to me?" she turns Colin to face her. "Did you misbehave?"

"No," I say before Colin can defend himself. "No, of course he didn't misbehave. You've raised a nice young man. You should see him talking to all these people, does a better job than I do. You'd be proud." I smile at Colin. "No, what I'd like to talk to you about is me."

"You?"

For just a moment, as I stare into Barb's confused face, I wish I hadn't said anything and allowed myself to keep our relationship on a superficial level. You can remain oblivious to your faults when you don't delve too deep. Apologizing leaves one vulnerable, open to criticism that you can't defend yourself against. Unless there's a caveat. I was always good at caveats. 'I apologize but the reason I made a mistake is because….'

I take a deep breath, then begin to talk, squeezing in as much as I can before I lose the courage. "I want to apologize for all the times I wasn't a good father when you were growing up. For the times I wasn't there for you, for not listening to you, for thinking I was the most important one in the family, or at least, the only one with problems." I sigh. "Maybe an apology isn't enough, maybe it seems like too little, too late, but it's all I can think of doing. Maybe we could start getting along, at the very least have a normal conversation. I'll try if you will."

Barb stands very still. I can't tell if she's angry with me or happy. What I do know is I feel like a weight has been lifted.

Finally, she begins to talk. "What the hell is this all about? Are you dying? Are you trying to make me absolve you so you can continue with your life without a second thought of how you hurt me? Do you think a simple apology will make everything better?"

"No, Barb. I just…."

"Since when do you care if we talk? This is how you've been with me my entire life." She looks around at some of the residents who have glanced our way. She whispers, "Do you remember one time, Dad, just one time where we had a heart to heart? I can't. Not even on my wedding day. And when Mom died, you hid. You wouldn't even give me a hug the night she died, as if her death only affected you." Again, she puts her hand on Colin's back and begins to push him ahead of her. When they near the door, she turns and says something that gives me hope. "And this is not the place I want to discuss this."

"I'll come by the house then," I say to their backs. "I'll come by and we'll talk then, I promise."

The doorbell chimes inside the house and I dig my toes into her front step to stop myself from running. Her car is in the garage so I know she's home, but I hear no footsteps approaching. I wait a few seconds then ring the bell again. I wish she'd hurry; I have to get to the grocery store then walk Clem yet today. The door swings open. She says nothing, waiting for me to be the first one to speak.

"Hi, Barb, can I come in?"

Her hand remains on the knob, blocking my path and I think she's going to deny me entry, or worse, make me stand on the step to apologize. She removes her arm and I step inside.

It's nine in the morning, but the house is dark under the threat of rain clouds. Barb opens the living room curtains.

I step into unfamiliar surroundings. "You've redecorated," I say.

"Finished over a year ago."

"A year ago?"

"I started about six months after Mom died," she says. "Mom helped me pick out colours and textures while she was sick. It gave her something else to think about besides chemo, throwing up and losing her hair. She had good taste. I wanted to get everything done while it was fresh in my memory as a kind of tribute to Mom." She keeps talking while I follow her down the hall towards the back of the house. "I've asked you over many times to see, but you've always declined."

I have a vague recollection of Elaine talking about redoing Barb's house, but I didn't pay much attention. I thought it was just her hinting that she wanted to redo ours. I was so involved with getting her to the hospital for treatments and feeling sorry for myself I didn't notice how others were coping. "It looks really nice, Barb."

We arrive in the kitchen and she turns. "Is that why you came over, to tell me my house looks good?"

Again, I just about leave. "No, of course not."

She faces the countertop and puts her hand on the coffee canister, then stops. I sit on a chair with my coat on, like a guest who doesn't know if he's staying or not.

"Do you have time for a cup of coffee?" Barb says without turning around.

I glance at my watch. "I don't know – sure."

"How much time have you allotted for me today?"

"Just groceries and dog walking to do," I say, then realize she's being sarcastic. She takes her hand off the coffee. "But groceries can wait," I say. "And so can Clem."

With her back to me, she flips the light switch on over the new island and begins to fill the coffee pot with water. Her phone rings.

"Hello," she says. "Yes, ok, that's fine. Tell Brian's mother I'll pick you up at four. Be safe and have fun. Look after your sister. See you later." She says over her shoulder, "Play date. Mom with the same age kids as Colin and Julie. We trade doing things with them during the summer."

"You're a good Mom," I say. "I've always seen that in you. The way you talk to your kids. You get that from your mom, not me.

Elaine was a great mother."

"She was." She begins to grind the coffee beans. When the grinder stops she says, still with her back to me, "Why are you here, Dad?"

"Pardon me?"

She turns to face me. "What do you want? Why are you here?"

"I think," I say, "I owe you an apology."

"So, you're here to ease your own guilt? You don't really want to know what you did that hurt me, you just want to be forgiven so you can forget about it."

"What?"

"If you apologize and I say that's ok, you'll feel better, won't you?"

"I hope I will."

"So that's why you're here, so you can apologize and have a clear conscience?"

"No," I say. "No, that's not true. You're putting words in my mouth."

"Then tell me."

The coffee starts to gurgle and sputter; it smells like home when Elaine would make me a cup. Even after two years, I'm homesick for what I lost. "I'm here to say I'm sorry. I'm here because I feel bad that you're upset. I only want you to be happy. That's all I want for my kids, that's all your mom and I ever wanted for all of you, just to be happy. I don't want you to cry anymore, I don't want you to be uncomfortable around me. I am not here to make myself feel better, nor am I here to make excuses. I'm only here for you."

She doesn't respond but instead takes two cups from the cupboard. She places them on the table along with the cream and sugar and sits in the chair opposite me. "So why are you so distant with me? If you see me trying to get closer to you, why won't you talk to me?"

"I talk to you."

"Dad, come on. You don't want to get close and you know it."

I rub my face. "I suppose I always thought that wasn't my job. I thought I was doing what was expected of me. And maybe I was afraid of screwing up too."

"You can't screw up if you don't try."

"Exactly."

"But when I was a kid, didn't you see I wanted you to try? Didn't you hear it in my voice, see it in my actions? I wanted you to be there, no matter what you said or did."

"I didn't want to embarrass you."

"What teenager hasn't been embarrassed by her parents? It's just life. No one's perfect. If you embarrassed me that was my problem, not yours." She pours us both a cup. "I don't know why your dad left. I imagine, as a kid, it made you feel responsible. But as an adult, you must realize your dad was responsible for his own actions, it had nothing to do with you. And you're different, Dad, you're not him. You stayed with us, gave us a good life." She passes me the cream. "You can't change the past, you can only move forward."

I'm reminded of a conversation Elaine and I had all those years ago about having a family, about her thinking I married her because she was pregnant.

"How do you think I feel when I see your car in the driveway after you've told me you're busy?" she says.

"You come by and check on me?"

"I come to check on Clem." Clem lifts her head when she hears her name. "But I see the lights on and the car home. How do you think I feel? Since Mom died I thought maybe you'd want to get closer. But nothing's changed. You still don't want to be involved."

"I'm busy."

"I know, and I'm sorry for not respecting your job. I'm glad you found something to fill your days, something you seem to enjoy. But you know more about the people at work than you do about your own grandchildren. I just think there should be some sort of work, family balance, that's all."

"I'm afraid of making a mistake. I always say the wrong thing, just ask your mother."

We both smile.

"She was always correcting me, informing me I said or did the wrong thing. And usually she was right."

"She never said a bad word about you to us, you know. Even when I complained about you when I was a teenager. She always defended you. She loved you, Dad."

"She did." I take a sip of coffee. "This is good. Your mom ground her own beans too. I just buy the cheap stuff; tastes like cardboard. Marigold puts whipping cream and whiskey in hers."

"We can do that. I have whiskey behind the bar."

"You have a bar?"

"Finished the renovations to the family room in time for the first Christmas after Mom died, the one you declined to attend." She places her hand over mine. "Would you like a tour? See everything Mom and I planned?"

Chapter thirty

"Who is he?" Alma asks.

Since the night I figured out who I believe has been sneaking into Ernestine's room, I've stalled in telling Alma, not sure if I I'm right. I hesitate before speaking.

"Just tell me, John."

"Dave."

"Dave? You mean our Dave?"

"Yes."

"Dave, the cook."

"Yes."

"Why in the heaven's name do you think it's him?"

I tick off my fingers. "Well, he resembles Ernestine's husband. He likes jazz as does Ernestine, and he was adopted, at least according to Melanie. And he's angry all the time, just as Ernestine says her husband was. And the first day I met him he complained about me making two salaries. I don't think he has much money. I think it might have been him that was sleeping in the basement."

"But what does that have to do with him sneaking into Ernestine's apartment, and why would he be sneaking into her room just because he looks like Ernestine's husband, and was adopted? I have a nephew who's adopted. That hasn't made him into a stalker. I don't understand what you're trying to tell me," Alma says.

"I think that he thinks Ernestine is his mother."

Alma says nothing.

I try again. "He thinks she's his...."

"I heard you. But Ernestine had no children."

"She didn't raise a child, no. But she did admit to me over tea and cookies that she gave a baby boy up for adoption about sixty years ago."

"And how much amaretto had she had by then?"

"She seemed to want to get it off her chest. Said she'd never told anyone but it didn't matter to her anymore if people found out."

Alma leans forward in her chair. "So, my question is still, why would he be sneaking into her room just because he thinks Ernestine is his mother?"

"I suspect he's looking for proof. I found that picture of Beverly Hawkins in the basement. I'll bet he stole it."

Alma says nothing for a few moments and I wonder if she believes me. She pounds her fist on the desk. "This is what I hate about being in charge. Confrontation is not something I'm comfortable with. But," she sits back and pulls a pencil from the jar, "I suppose I have to ask him. Can't have the staff going into residents' rooms uninvited." She begins tapping the pencil, a nervous habit. "You might be wrong," she says.

"I might be, but I don't think I am."

"Well, if you're right and it is him, I hope he's not looking for money."

"Ernestine's never mentioned anything to me about being robbed."

"I don't mean being robbed." Alma pauses. "Has Ernestine ever told you she's probably one of the wealthier people living here?"

"I know she has money, she told me her husband was a wealthy son of a bitch."

"She does like to swear."

"But I didn't know she had more than the others living here."

"Try billionaire. Her husband made his money in diamond mines. Then after he died Ernestine made some shrewd investments and doubled her money. She's a smart woman. Dave could be looking for proof so he can stake his claim, so to speak."

"I wonder how he knew she was here?"

"Ernestine and Marigold are the owners of this, and a few other converted hotels around the country. But they like to stay in the background, so that's between you and me."

"Marigold and Ernestine own this place?" I'm flabbergasted, though that does explain a lot.

"Twenty-five years ago, the two of them were in the headlines of the local paper when they began converting this building to a seniors' residence. I suppose, if Dave knows his birth mother's name, he could have read about them and figured it out. Though why he waited twenty-five years to do so, I haven't the foggiest." She shrugs, "My guess is he's simply stumbled onto her."

A voice in the lobby makes us stop. It sounds like Melanie.

"What now?" Alma says.

We leave the small office to find Melanie descending the last step then rushing across the lobby floor her boyfriend in close pursuit, yelling something about her being a drama queen and to quit blowing everything out of proportion. Not words, in my opinion that would make Melanie turn around and discuss whatever is causing her to flee.

"What's the problem?" Alma asks.

"Nothing," Melanie says. "Just need to get out of here."

"You were done your shift over half an hour ago," Alma calls as Melanie nears the sensor that activates the door. "I'm surprised you're still here."

"Had some things to do."

The elevator opens and Darlene rides her scooter off. Then Irma, Christine, Ester, Neil, Ivy, and Carl, shoulder each other out of the cramped quarters. They begin pointing fingers and yelling "thief, thief, stop them," as they race across the lobby floor.

"Wait a second, Melanie," Alma says.

Melanie stops and turns. Her face is flushed and her blouse is untucked. Her blue locks are tangled at the back of her neck.

"What's this about?" Alma asks.

Everyone in the group talks at once.

Alma holds up her hand. "One at a time please."

"We caught her stealing." Darlene points at Melanie. We wait for her to elaborate but she says no more.

"I need a bit more information than that, Darlene," Alma says.

"I met Ivy in the hall as we were heading to Ester's for happy hour. She bought a new kind of wine, supposed to be excellent. From Spain. Aged in oak barrels."

"Just the high points," Alma sighs.

"Caught her with this." Darlene holds a paper weight in the air. "It belongs to Christine."

Christine nods.

"You caught Ivy with Christine's paper weight?" Alma asks.

"No, no, of course not. Ivy and I caught Melanie with it."

Alma shifts her gaze to Melanie. "You had Christine's paper-weight?"

"No!" Melanie shouts. "I mean, yes, but I didn't steal it."

"What were you doing with it then?" Darlene asks.

"I found it."

"Found it, my ass. You're the thief and you know it," Darlene says.

"I'm telling you I found the damned thing on the floor in the hall! Picked it up before someone tripped on it."

"Just like Fiona Brighton's watch," Ester stares at Melanie. "Yes, she told me about you trying to steal her watch. She was drunk at the time, but she told me nonetheless."

"If you think I'm the thief than you're off your rocker. I am no more the thief, than," she looks at the group, many of whom have sauntered out of the community room to see what the ruckus is about, "her." She points at Ivy.

"What were you doing upstairs in the first place?" Alma asks. "You're done work for the day."

"I had …. a showing of the show suite."

Darlene says, "And was your boyfriend helping you? Surely you don't take that man with you when you show the suite to a potential resident? What were you doing if not something nefarious? Hiding from us, I imagine, after you robbed Christine."

Melanie hesitates.

"Well, are you going to answer me?"

"We weren't stealing from anyone," she stares at Darlene. "And we sure as hell weren't hiding from you!"

"Did you have a showing this afternoon?" Alma asks. "I don't remember seeing anything on the books. And since when do you stay after your shift to do any kind of work?"

Darlene pipes up before Melanie can open her mouth, "There was no showing," she says. "There was only the two of them in there. They were up to no good, I can tell you that much."

"Well," Alma says. "What were you doing?"

Melanie rolls her eyes. "We weren't stealing from anyone. We were," her voice lowers to a whisper, "on a date."

We all stare.

"A rendezvous, a date," she says a bit louder.

Still we stare.

Melanie looks directly at Darlene. If she could shoot fire from her eyes, Darlene would be up in flames. "We were hitting the sheets, doing the deed, making love, you old bag, or are you too dried up to know what that is?"

"Melanie!" Alma says. "You and that man were using the show suite for your romantic trysts?"

Melanie shrugs. "We both live at home, we have no choice."

"You have no choice? You mean you've done this before? Is that where you disappear to when you're not at the desk?" Her eyes open wide. "Is that where you were when Mrs. Brighton went outside last winter? The day you said you were with Ezra?"

Melanie scuffs her feet like a small child being caught stealing pennies from her mother's purse. "Weren't hurting anyone. And we wouldn't have been caught this time if it wasn't for these old busy-bodies snooping around the hallway like they're neighbour-hood watch or something."

"Apparently that's exactly what we need with people like you sneaking around," Darlene says.

Melanie takes a step towards Darlene, who to her credit, does not roll her scooter back.

"Melanie, go home," Alma says as she holds out her hand. "And give me your key on the way out. I think you are no longer employed here."

"I'm fired?" Melanie says. "Just for that?"

"I suppose I should have added, no tête-à-têtes in the show suite to my list of what's not allowed while employed here." Alma shakes her hand in Melanie's direction. "Give me your key, Melanie."

Melanie stomps towards Alma. She whips the key off her neck and slaps it onto the desk instead of Alma's waiting palm.

Chapter thirty-one

1974

I stumble home in a daze, my legs weak, and my heart beating so hard the veins in my neck are throbbing against my shirt collar. I undo my top button and step into my house. My mother is in the living room watching TV and calls my name. I ignore her as I try to process the news Elaine has just given me.

Pregnant. That's what she said.

The words sounded foreign, as if she was speaking a different language. Although, at that particular moment in the back seat of my '65 Mustang, my desire to comprehend was at a minimum. I was deep in my quest to seduce Elaine with my lips pressed to her ear and one hand massaging her neck. The heater was on and the car was warm as I smiled and nodded without actually listening, encouraging her to remove her blouse by adding an 'uh-hum,' when I thought it appropriate. We'd been making out for two months now, always in the backseat of my car as we both still lived at home with our parents, so taking one's boyfriend or girlfriend to our respective beds was out of the question.

But tonight she didn't succumb to my charms and instead put her hands on my shoulders, pushing me away. I felt my temper flare and forced myself back into the nape of her neck until she cupped my cheeks in her hands, pulling my face just a few inches from hers and said it again.

"I'm pregnant, John."

This time her voice resonated in my brain, the sounds solidifying into syllables then melding into whole words. Believing was another story. Pregnant was something other people talked about, older people, adults. Not us. We were still kids, weren't we? "Pregnant," I repeated? "Is that what you said, you're pregnant?"

She smiled, rather demurely, and said yes, she was pregnant. About six weeks along. She hadn't told anyone yet as she thought she should tell the father of the child before she told her parents.

Naively I said, "The father?"

To which she answered, "Yes, John, the father."

Before I realized what I was doing, I'd slid backwards towards the door like she was contagious. Her eyes flashed with hurt, but I didn't slide back to her side. I knew I should hold her and tell her I love her, two words I'd already said to her in the heat of passion, but now I couldn't bring myself to speak them. Instead, I patted her on the hand and lied, telling her everything would be fine. Unable to think of anything else to do, I climbed out of the car and stood in the parking lot of the abandoned drive-in theatre taking great gulps of the night air as Elaine climbed out after me and gave me a hug. I stood stiffly, my arms by my sides, then patted her on the shoulder like she was my long-lost aunt. I opened the driver's door and she climbed back in, wriggling her body over the console and into the passenger seat. I climbed in behind her. She put her hand on my thigh as we drove back to her house. I kept both hands on the wheel. Again, I told her everything would be fine and I'd call her in the morning and we'd make some decisions.

"I'm not getting an abortion, John," she'd said.

"I know," I agreed, even though I didn't know. I had no idea what people in our situation did. I gave her a smile and a peck on the cheek then reached across her belly, being careful not to touch it, and opened the door. She walked up the path to her house, looking back a couple of times before she reached the front door. I waved goodbye, then, in an effort to not screech my tires, I conservatively pulled away from the curb.

I now stand in the foyer of my own house, my mother calling for me to come and watch *Love Boat* with her, something we do together on Sunday evenings. I climb the stairs, unable to speak, unable to answer her.

Three weeks later I wake to see my new suit hanging from the closet door. A suit that cost me a month's wages at the security company. I acquired the job right out of high-school with the idea I'd save up enough money to travel the world for a few years, then come home and make my fortune. Now, it's become a job I need to support a family since Elaine and I have decided to marry. The suit is hanging there, dark against the white wood, shouting to me that today is the day I become a husband.

I hear my mother downstairs, bustling around the kitchen and speaking to my sister as she makes me breakfast.

I still don't know how Elaine and her mother arranged such an elaborate wedding on such short notice. We're even having a dance; A DANCE! With a live band! I've only ever pretended to dance at the odd high-school function, and a couple of weddings of aunts or uncles my mother dragged me to. I'm not sure if I'm more afraid of the wedding than of the marriage. Already my stomach is in knots.

"John," my mother calls up the stairs. "Breakfast is ready. You'd better get a move on."

I lie quiet so she'll think I'm still sleeping.

"John," she pounds on my bedroom door, "wake up. You've got a lot of things to do today, getting married not the least of them."

I swing my legs over the edge of the bed. "I'm up," I shout. Then more quietly, "I'm up, for God's sake."

I shuffle down the hall to the bathroom and look in the mirror. The bags under my eyes are so puffy and black, I look like I've been in a fist fight. I fell asleep at five in the morning. That's two hours sleep to take me down the aisle, face the relatives, and show everyone I'm ready for this. That I'm mature enough. That I can support a wife in the way in which she and everyone else expects. I know, because of our young ages, there's gossip as to why we're marrying. Of course, how could anyone not think that? We're only nineteen and twenty. But I love her. This is the right thing to do, everything will be fine. I shower and go down to breakfast.

"You look like you've been hit by a truck," Grace says.

"Thanks, Sis. That makes me feel a whole lot better."

"Just teasing." She gives me a little hug. "So, what's first?"

"Breakfast." I stand by my chair not sure I have the stomach to eat. "Then I'm meeting Elaine at the hall to help with the decorations. Then I have to pick up the rings, then the flowers, then…."

"Don't forget, I want your car back here at one so I can put some Kleenex flowers on it."

"Yeah, yeah, I haven't forgot."

"Sit, eat," Mom says.

I sit and gag down the last breakfast my mom will cook for me as a single man.

I've opened my bedroom window for some air. The pancakes I ate six hours ago are still sitting in a lump in my stomach and I wish I could throw up just to be rid of them. I met Elaine at the hall where her mother glared at me, and Elaine laughed and pretended everything was fine. Then I picked up the rings and the flowers, then finally staggered home to the quiet of my bedroom. I now sit on the edge of my bed with my head in my hands wishing this day were over. There's a knock on the door.

"Can I come in?" Mom says.

I sit up straight and put a smile on my face. "Yes, Mom. Come in."

She enters and sits on the bed beside me. I stand to go to the bathroom to shave even though once a day is usually all I need, but she pushes my shoulder and I sit back down.

"So, John, you're getting married today."

"Yup, I am. Getting married today." I rub my eyes with the heels of my hands.

She's quiet and I know she's mulling something over. Just like in high-school when she found that pack of cigarettes in my dresser. She began that talk by telling me she smelled smoke on my shirts. What could I say? I quit that day, didn't like it anyway. Today she begins my lecture by telling me she's noticed I've not been myself lately, saying she's seen me nervous and distracted and she thinks maybe I'm having second thoughts.

"I think every single man on the face of the earth is nervous and distracted before they get married, Mom."

"You know, John, if you don't want to marry this woman,"

"Elaine."

"If you don't want to marry her, there's no law that says you have to just because she's pregnant. She's a strong woman, I'm sure she'll do just fine on her own. Believe me, if I can raise two kids on my own, so can she. And she has her parents to help her," she wrings her hands in her lap.

"I know, Mom."

"I don't want you to make the same mistake your own father did, abandoning your family after they've learned to need you. No one deserves that, not even her. I won't think any less of you if you chose not to get married today. Better to walk away now, than later."

"But I will, Mom. I will think less of me. I want to marry Elaine. Even if she weren't pregnant, we'd still get married. We already discussed this. Maybe not so soon, but we would have married at some point."

The air is cool and crisp this early spring day as I approach the church. The trees are still barren and the last of the snow lies dirty and brown in the gutters. I open the back door of the church and a gust of wind blows me, along with some leaves, into the small annex off the altar. I peek at the assembly. People keep arriving and guests take off their coats and bunch them behind them as the room becomes hot and cloying. I'm sure many from Elaine's side of the family are only here today to see if this person who probably knocked up their niece or cousin, granddaughter or friend, will actually go through with this façade. The minister is standing at the front of the church. He looks at me and taps his watch. I leave the little room to stand by him and we both look expectantly down the aisle. The music begins and the procession of bridesmaids lead the way. Elaine has her arm entwined with her dad's as they walk towards me. I focus my eyes on Elaine, knowing I'm not going to back out, but still unsure if I'm doing the right thing. She's beautiful, she's smart, and she's carrying my child. What else would I do with my life if not this?

I manage to say *I do* without mumbling, get a plate of food for both Elaine and I at the buffet without dropping anything, dance with Elaine and her many cousins and aunts and her mother, without tripping, and finally get to leave the hall, the air stagnant with cigarette smoke and sweat.

Our home is a small rental house Elaine's mother found. She paid for the first three months, apparently their wedding gift to us. Tonight, I enter for the first time and see she's also bought us a couch and a dining room table, a crib for the baby and a bed for us. She's even bought sheets and blankets, dishes to fill the cupboards and food to fill the fridge. I'm grateful for her generosity, but know she's doing this for her daughter, not for me. I know her parents are disappointed in her daughter's choice for a husband, disappointed I'm going to be the father of their grandchild. I vow to be a good husband and father, vow to be a better man than my own father was to me, my sister and Mom.

For the next couple of months, I dutifully get up and go to my job at the security company wondering how I'm going to make ends meet once the baby comes. My salary barely covers the rent and groceries for two of us, let alone buying everything needed to support a baby. Though she doesn't tell me, to my shame I know Elaine is getting money her mother secrets away without her dad finding out. I keep telling myself I'm going to have to put a stop to that, going to have to be the breadwinner for our family, but I can't bring myself to tell her no. I'm too afraid I'm going to fail. This is where my own dad left, when the pressure of supporting a family got too great. I can't be like him, I won't be like him.

My boss calls me into the office and hands me the phone. "Call for you, Davies, don't take too long."

"Hello," I say.

"Mr. Davies. Your wife is here, at University Hospital."

"She's in the hospital? But it's only three months." My first thoughts are *Maybe she's lost the baby* and I'm ashamed of myself.

"She's asking for you."

"I'll be there as soon as I can."

I drive to the hospital, worried for Elaine, but since I've never in all my life held a baby in my arms, it's surreal to worry about a baby I've never seen. I think if she's had a miscarriage, then we can begin our life together like other young marrieds; no responsibility other than ourselves.

I arrive at the emergency ward to find Elaine hooked up to an IV. Her face is as pale as the sheets she's lying on and her cheeks are stained with tears. She tells me she's miscarried, and falls into my arms. Her swollen breasts press into my body with every wracking breath she takes. She says it was a boy. I try to console her but because deep down I feel more relief than grief, it's shallow and disingenuous. The doctor comes in to Elaine's curtained off cubical and stands at the edge of her bed. He judges us because we're so young, his mouth a thin straight line cut into his face painted with superiority. His pale hands rest calmly on the blanket as he talks, while I sit on the plastic chair, my own weather-worn fingers gripping the sides. He uses words like *uterus* and *fallopian tubes*, *tearing* and *bleeding*. He advises us that with time these things heal and most women are able to get pregnant again, but it's something that can't be predicted and there is a chance Elaine won't ever be able to conceive. As I squirm on my chair, uncomfortable in the presence of the doctor, all I hear are the words Elaine won't get pregnant again, and relief for the fact I won't have to struggle the rest of my life counting dimes and nickels as I feed one mouth after another, washes over me.

Elaine stays in the hospital overnight and I take the next day off without pay to take her home. She spends a month recovering both physically and, she tells me, mentally, before going back to work at her job as a cashier in a grocery store. I go back to work the next day.

***

Elaine grieved for over a year. I resented her for this. I didn't understand how she could feel bad for something she had never seen or held in her arms. I felt she was being overly dramatic and doing it to make a point that the miscarriage didn't seem to bother me as much as it did her. I tried to grieve, to feel bad for this life lost that the two of us had made, but no matter how hard I tried, I felt relief, not sorrow.

We stopped using birth control and for the next three years I made love to my wife free of worry. I assumed, because she didn't say anything, Elaine thought as I did, that she wouldn't be able to get pregnant again. So when she announced we were going to have a child, my anger surfaced.

Chapter thirty-two

"Tell me about your son, Ernestine," Alma says.

"My son?"

"John mentioned you had a son."

She frowns at me standing by the office door. "I said to John it made no never mind to me if he told someone but I didn't think he'd blab his mouth off so soon."

"Of course. You don't have to say anything."

"I don't mind," she tears her eyes off me. "Was a long time ago."

"Did your sister adopt him?" Alma asks.

"Raised him as her own."

"You visited him as he grew up?" I ask.

"Never saw him a day in my life. Told my sister to take him away as soon as he was born. She was married to a missionary. Thought I was a heathen with my drinking and my cussing. He agreed to take my son if he was allowed to convert him." She shrugs. "I figured life with him as his father would be better than life with Mr. Hawkins, so I agreed. My sister was a loving, kind woman. She'd be good to him, I knew that. They moved to a third world country to do their good works and I never heard from them again. Why are you asking me about him?"

"Do you think your sister would have told him who he was, who you are?"

"Perhaps. We were close when we were girls. Told each other everything. When she married that fanatic we certainly drifted apart." She asks again, "Why are you asking me questions about my son?"

"Because John thinks he's here."

The room becomes quiet except for Ernestine's breathing. Finally, she says, "I had a feeling, just never pursued it."

"You know?" Alma says.

"Well, Dave does bear a striking resemblance to Beverly; difficult not to notice that. Maybe a mother always recognizes her offspring."

Alma and I are speechless.

"Look," Ernestine says. "I haven't been totally honest with the two of you. Didn't really see why I should have to be, it's my business. But since John seems to have figured it out, I suppose it won't hurt anything to tell you." She wags her finger first at Alma then at me. "But it's to go no further than this room, you hear me? Don't need to be judged, not at my age." She takes a deep breath. "It's not just because of Mr. Hawkins I didn't keep my son." She closes her eyes. "Some women are born not wanting a family, it's just a fact of life. Not every woman is cut out to be a mother." She looks at Alma. "But it seems to be a sin to have those feelings, at least when I was young that's how other women thought. They'd criticize, judge and most times either didn't believe you or thought you were sick in the head. It's true Mr. Hawkins would have made a terrible father, no question about that. Even if I'd wanted to keep my son I'd have had second thoughts because of Mr. Hawkins. But the truth is, I didn't want to be a mother. I was raised in a loving family, good parents, but having a brood of kids around me all day long like my own mother was not something that interested me. Couldn't imagine wiping snotty noses or changing diapers. Not something women are supposed to admit to, at least not sixty years ago. I mean, even now after all these years, look at the two of you, judging me for my ideas."

"Sorry, Ernestine. We don't mean to make it sound like we're criticizing you."

"Angers me that people pigeon-hole women. We have to keep the house spotless, bake cookies, raise a brood of brats. Even now, in the twenty-first century, women are expected to have a family as well as a career, supposed to be able to do it all. Never wanted to be stereotyped." She looks up at us, her brown eyes, moist. "How did you figure it out?"

"Mostly, like you said, Dave's appearance," I say. "And he told Melanie he was adopted. Said he learned to cook as a boy in the church."

"You were in the news all those years ago when you and Marigold renovated this place." Alma says. "Dave could have seen you or read about you, if he knew who you were. Maybe he knows you're wealthy."

"But that was years ago. Why would he wait so long to find me?"

"My guess is, he got a job here and stumbled on to you."

"Do you think he's the one I've been seeing in my room? He's looking for proof so he can claim some inheritance?"

"That thought did cross our minds," I say. "That's why we thought we'd better mention it to you. Or maybe he just wants to find some family."

"If it's money he wants, I'm more than happy to oblige. Family," she sits back in her chair, "don't think I'm ready for that."

Chapter thirty-three

I've often thought Alma should have been in live theatre. I could easily see her as Mary Poppins, or Tinker Bell, flying through the air in her long skirts, charming the audience with her clear and perfectly enunciated English.

Just as when she spoke to Melanie about leaving the front desk unattended, Alma's now in her office speaking to Dave about sneaking into Ernestine's suite. Her voice booms down the hall and I shuffle a few papers behind the reception desk, trying to catch as much of the conversation as I'm able.

"I told you, I don't know what you're talking about," Dave says. "I didn't go into anyone's suite."

"We found your mattress in the basement. I wish you'd come to me and said you were having financial troubles. I could have seen what I could do to help."

"Like you'd give me a raise! All these rich people living here and you pay the staff next to nothing."

"Why did you take employment here?" Alma asks.

The elevator door opens. "John, could you call me a cab, please?" Ernestine says as she taps her cane across the floor.

I swivel my head back to the voices, hoping that Dave doesn't pick this moment to leave Alma's office.

"Needed a job, had no choice."

Ernestine's face registers recognition of the voice and she stops walking.

"You didn't come here because you knew Ernestine Hawkins

lived here? Because you think she might be your mother?"

He says nothing.

"You can't be going into apartments, no matter the reason. I'm afraid I'm going to have to let you go."

The legs of a chair scrape across the floor and Dave's voice becomes louder as the door opens further. "Good luck finding another cook. All the cooks know that this place is a pain in the ass to work in. Too many people who are difficult to please. Too many kitchen staff who don't know what they're doing."

"Was it you who John chased out of here that night? What were you doing in my office? Trying to find information on Ernestine?"

"I don't have to put up with this shit."

"You look like your dad," Alma says.

For a moment, there is no talking. I peek down the hall, the office door is ajar and I can see Dave's fingers wrapped around the frame. At last he speaks.

"Why the hell would a mother give up their child? Never even so much as a birthday gift. And she's rich! My parents gave everything they made to the church while we went hungry. God almighty."

"Why did you wait so long to find her?"

"Wasn't trying to find her. Didn't know she lived here until I heard her name. My dad told me that all my real mom loved was money. After I got outta that godforsaken church, I had no desire to find someone who didn't want me."

"How did you get into her suite so many times without her knowing?"

"Door was always unlocked. She's deaf as a doornail. Found that picture so I took it. Wasn't there more than three, maybe four times, tops. After I found the picture, I stopped going in. All I wanted was the proof. Don't need a mother at this stage in my life."

"How do you account for all the times she saw someone in her room?"

"She's crazy, everybody knows that."

Dave's footsteps begin down the hall and, in panic, Ernestine darts her eyes around, looking for a place to hide. Dave emerges into the lobby and when he sees Ernestine, I think this is going to be it, he's finally going to approach her and ask if she's his mom, settle this once and for all. He stares at the woman he believes to be his mother, the woman who gave him up sixty years ago, his face full of anger. Ernestine lifts her chin and looks him in the eye, her face filled with fear. Dave and Ernestine stay locked in this stand-off for what seems like forever, but is probably less than ten seconds.

Ernestine takes one small step towards Dave. "If you need money...."

Dave turns and leaves the building.

Chapter thirty-four

1974

"Just one dance with your sister," Grace says to me.

I shake my head.

"C'mon. It's a wedding. Everyone's had too much to drink to pay any attention to your dancing skills, or lack thereof. And anyhow, it's the bride everyone watches. The groom is only the schmuck she's married. Besides, I'm a great dancer, just follow what I do."

"And how did you, at the ripe old age of fifteen, become such a great dancer?" I ask.

She does a little jig in front of me, ending it with a twirl. "Sleepovers. My girlfriends and I stay up all night and practice our moves so at our own weddings we won't make fools of ourselves on the dance floor."

Grace has always had a plethora of friends. Always been the popular one, always had places to go and people to go with. She's outgoing and gregarious; a social butterfly. We are opposites, my sister and I, as my mother has pointed out to me on more than one occasion.

I protest one minute longer, then allow Grace to pull me onto the dance floor when the song, *Blue Moon*, by Carmen McRae, begins to play. I asked Elaine, while her mother listened in surprise that I wanted any involvement in my own wedding, for some jazz music to be played at the dance. But Patricia objected, saying no one would know how to dance to that kind of music. In private Elaine said she'd ask the DJ to include some jazz, and that her mom, not knowing anything about music, wouldn't know a pop song from a jazz song if it bit her on the ass.

As I look up and down from my sister's feet to her smiling face, I spot Elaine across the room talking to someone I don't know. What else is new? I don't know ninety-nine percent of the people here tonight. The man she's talking to appears to be in his mid-forties, my height, is lean, has short brown hair and is wearing wire-rimmed glasses. Something about him is familiar, but I can't place him. The two of them look around the dance floor searching for someone.

"John," Grace says. "Your mind is elsewhere."

"Sorry. Just thought that guy with Elaine looked familiar."

Grace, being tall, looks over the heads of the crowd. "Oh, him. He danced with me. Seemed a bit creepy. Kept staring. Never introduced himself. Thought he must be from Elaine's side of the family."

I watch him for a few moments longer, then look back at my feet and try to concentrate on my dancing. But just moments later, worrying that he's someone I'm supposed to know, I'm watching him again. Maybe he's one of my long-lost uncles that came for the free food and drink and Elaine is doing her best to be diplomatic. Or maybe he's a wedding crasher. I've heard of such people, though I can't for the life of me figure out why someone would willingly attend such an affair.

Elaine pulls the stranger onto the dance floor under the silver ball we hung from the light this morning and begins to weave between the dancers. She peers from face to face until her eyes stop on Grace and I. She waves. I wave back. She motions for me to come to her but I keep dancing, pretending I don't see her beckoning me.

"Your wife wants something," Grace says.

"My what?" I say.

"Funny boy. Better get used to hearing that. Only sixty some years to go, give or take. Your wife and that man who I was dancing with. They seem to be calling for you to come over."

Grace leaves me alone on the floor to sit with Mom who's at a table with some cousin of mine I haven't seen in fifteen years. Mom stands and gives Grace a hug then looks at me as I snake between dancers, making my way towards Elaine and the stranger. As I near, the man keeps his eyes on me, and the feeling I know him from somewhere becomes stronger. When I get about ten feet away, I stop, allowing the dancers to surge around me. He bends to Elaine and says something in her ear, then turns and leaves without introducing himself to me. I glance at Mom; she's turned her back to us.

I push my way between bodies, finally stopping in front of Elaine. "What the hell was that all about?"

Elaine doesn't answer right away, as though she's trying to come up with a reasonable explanation. She lifts her face to the ceiling. "Just someone who thought he knew you."

"And he didn't?"

"I guess not." She looks towards the door the man fled through. "Guess as you neared, he decided he'd made a mistake."

***

I am frozen to the lobby floor. The look on my father's face at my wedding dance was the same as the look on Ernestine's face as she stood in front of the son she'd given up. Fear of rejection. And for a fleeting moment I see clearly how my own father felt. I understand why he didn't come back into my life and I feel sorry for him for all the years he missed with his family.

Chapter thirty-five

It's a hot morning in July, with the forecast for temperatures to be in the high twenties by three in the afternoon. The residents hurry through their breakfasts so they can get out to the garden to weed and pick some produce before the heat really takes hold.

There's been no burglaries since Melanie was fired, which leaves a sour taste in some of the resident's mouths as they still insist she must be the thief. They feel she got off too easily by only being fired and should have charges laid against her. Even the ones who didn't think it was her have been swayed, as have I.

This morning I look around the dining-room and notice Ivy isn't here. It's not unusual for a resident to sleep-in; staying up to all hours of the night seems commonplace, as if they don't want to waste a minute of life. But in the nine months I've worked at The Wheaton, I've never known Ivy to stay in bed past six. She's always one of the first ones up, taking her seat in the lobby before the morning shift begins. When I arrived this morning and she wasn't there, I assumed it was because she was outside, sitting on a bench in the garden, enjoying the cool air before the heat set in. Now that she's not here I'm slightly concerned, but I'm sure she's just catching a few more winks because I know she had some people to her suite last night for a cribbage tournament and she does like to have a couple glasses when she has people over.

"Have you seen Ivy yet today?" I ask Marigold as I hand her a cup of black coffee.

"I haven't. Mind you we did have a bit too much of the grape last night. Battled it out for the winner until two in the morning. Perhaps she's sleeping in for a change."

"That's what I figured," I say.

"I'll go and check on her if you like."

"No, no, you finish your coffee. I'll go up."

With a lump in my throat and butterflies in my stomach, I push the button for the elevator. It's not like I've never checked on residents before; I do it quite often actually. Darlene is one I check on at least once a week, but she's usually simply fainted, or on the phone telling someone something or other and lost track of time. Ezra is another, sometimes having forgotten it was meal time, though not as often as he was a few months ago. But because I'm confident why they haven't come downstairs, I've never been too concerned. This morning feels different. Ivy is one of the residents that has not seemed to age, or shown any signs of dementia, so I shouldn't be apprehensive. I'm sure she'll open her door in her housecoat and slippers, her hair a mess and embarrassed at me seeing her without lipstick on, or her hair sprayed into the coif that never moves, sheepishly telling me she slept in because she had one glass too many. The elevator whooshes me upstairs and I stay inside a while, my finger on the door open button, preventing it from closing and taking me back down. Something has got me worried, some kind of intuition, though Elaine would scoff at that. In her mind, my capabilities for perceiving anything that wasn't already fact, were about the same as a weather man who makes his predictions after he looks out the window. I exit the elevator. The hallway is deserted. There's no music or laughter coming from anyone's suite, but of course, everyone is down at breakfast, already in the garden, or sitting on a shady bench with their morning coffee. I arrive at Ivy's apartment and rattle the knob; it's locked. At least I know she locked it after everyone left last night.

I knock. "Ivy, you there? It's breakfast time."

I hear nothing.

I knock again. "Ivy, time to wake up."

Still nothing. I take out my master key and unlock the door, gently pushing it open. "Ivy, it's me, John," I call into the apartment. "You okay? Thought I'd better come and check on you. You're not usually a late sleeper."

I walk down her hall. The carpet is plush, unlike the thin carpet that was in Fiona's suite, or the polished hardwood that's in Marigold's and Ernestine's. This is thick pile, very soft and spongy underfoot and I'm conscious of leaving footprints in my wake. It's dark in here, none of blinds have been raised or the curtains drawn. A clock ticks somewhere in the apartment and a tap drips its rhythm in the kitchen sink. I make a mental note to bring up some pliers and fix the drip. Her bedroom door is closed but I walk past towards her living room to open the blinds and curtains to bring life to the apartment. I'm hopeful she'll hear me and exit her bedroom, dressed and ready to go downstairs to breakfast.

I stand facing west, looking out the window. Rachel is in the garden, leaning on her walker as she pulls out weeds and thins the carrots. I laugh as I watch her adjust the tomato cages and push the row markers further into the ground.

I really should have done something with Elaine's garden this year but I waited too long and now it's too late. Between going to work, doing all the errands, and walking Clem, I don't know when I'd find the time, even though Elaine always did. I wish Barb didn't make me feel so guilty. At least we had a bit of a talk the other day. Some of the stress between us has eased up. There were times during our talk I felt like I shouldn't have to apologize any longer. Don't all parents make mistakes? How can you raise a child perfectly? One is bound to mess up at some point or other. But we hashed out some of our differences and I tried my best not to sound pompous or take anything too personally, to just let it roll off my back. If she can forgive me, I thought, then I can also move on and try to be closer to her.

After stalling for another minute, I turn around and walk back to Ivy's closed bedroom door. I knock. "Ivy, it's John. Can I come in?"

No answer. I turn the knob and enter.

Except for light spilling into the bedroom from the night light in the half-bathroom, the room is dark. For a moment I see nothing, not even the bed and I stay put so as not to trip. I find my courage and reach back, sliding my hand along the wall, searching for the switch. I flip it up. Ivy is lying on her bed beside a curio cabinet, her hands folded in her lap over a statue of some sort. From this distance, I can't tell if she's breathing, but instinct tells me she's not. Perhaps it's the stillness about her, or the resemblance to Elaine when she died. There is an unmistakable look to a dead person, as opposed to the living. I step forward and touch her wrist — her skin is cool. I find no pulse.

I pull the phone out of my pocket and dial 911.

"What's your phone number and the nature of your emergency?" an operator asks.

I give her the information and she connects me with a paramedic who asks me if Ivy has a pulse.

"Not that I can feel," I say. "What do I do?"

"Do CPR until the paramedics arrive. I want you to lift the patient onto the floor."

I do as I'm told. Then under her supervision, I begin CPR. Compression, five times, she tells me, then feel her neck as you watch for her chest to rise and fall. I put the phone on speaker and set it on the floor. The EMS worker counts. "One, two, three, four, five," she says. Then I place my fingers on her neck and watch her chest.

"No pulse," I say. "And she's not breathing."

"Keep going," she says to me. "You're doing great."

She counts again, "One, two, three, four, five." Again, I put my hand on Ivy's neck. Still no pulse.

I don't know how long I stay kneeling by Ivy's side doing compressions, or how long the woman on the phone is counting. I don't notice the pain in my knees or the throbbing in my back. I don't think about the residents getting grumpy waiting for their coffee, or Clem by the desk perhaps having to pee. Or Dave and Melanie being fired, or Ernestine not wanting to be a mother. I don't worry about Fiona dying, or my children coping with the death of their mother. The whole world becomes counting my compressions and checking for a pulse as I try to breathe life back into Ivy. When the paramedics and police, led by Alma, rush through the door, I stand and step back. Alma retrieves the DNR stuck to Ivy's fridge and takes it to the paramedics. They attach it to their clipboard, then lift Ivy onto the gurney and carry her away. The last I see of her is her running shoes, just as she saw Ed Brown's brown shoes all those months ago. I walk to the kitchen and slump into a chair. Alma sits across from me.

"You ok?" she asks.

"I've been better."

"Come, we should leave this place, get you some air."

Weak from kneeling for so long, I walk on stiff legs to the elevator. Marigold meets us at the bottom and the two of us follow Alma into her office. Alma opens a drawer in the desk.

I pat my pocket. "Damn it. I left the phone on the floor in Ivy's bedroom."

Alma stands. "I'll go, John."

"No, no. You sit. I'll be right back."

Her bedroom door is open and the phone is still on the floor beside her bed. I step inside. The statue that Ivy had in her hands when I lifted her to the floor has fallen and I pick it up, meaning to put it back in the curio cabinet. It's a small figurine of Saint Francis. I only know this because Rachel had an ornament of him she had had stolen from her apartment. She showed me a picture of her at a shop outside St. Peter's Square, holding it in her hand after she purchased it, to let me know if I ever came across it in someone's suite, that it belonged to her. I scoffed and said I doubted one of the residents would have taken her statue, but she pulled her glasses down her nose and looked me in the face with that same look she gave me on my first day, and I knew better than to argue any further. What is Ivy doing with Rachel's statue? Perhaps she found it and was going to return it? I turn my attention to the glass doors of the curio cabinet; its shelves are brimming with items. There's the prayer flags and Ganesh Darlene purchased in Tibet. And the candy dish Jack

Belgrade lost that belonged to his mother. And the cufflinks and the bracelet and the glass Ogopogo and the crystal vase. There's Fiona's emerald ring. I step back. My surprise at discovering that Ivy may have been the thief is no less than my surprise at having found her passed on. As a matter of fact, finding her the thief may even surpass finding her dead.

"Ivy, what have you done?" I say.

As I'm leaving I pass the bathroom. The night-light that I saw before I discovered Ivy dead in bed, begins to dim, then blinks out, turning the bathroom black. I flip the wall switch then exit the suite faster than I entered to go downstairs and inform Alma of the stolen goods. She and Marigold are in the office, each with a glass of scotch in front of them.

"Wasn't even doctoring, as far as I know," Marigold is saying when I pull open the office door. "But I suppose that's how I want to go," she continues. "No fanfare, no lengthy hospital stays. Just one minute, here, and the next, gone. Like going to bed on one side and getting up on the other."

"I remember Ivy saying something about that at Christmas. Blink out, she said. Just blink out like a light and be gone." Alma takes a sip of her scotch then sets her glass down and pours me a finger as well. "I've found at least a dozen residents passed on in the last twenty years. Most times it's the housekeeping staff that finds them. Still in their beds, looking like they've slept in. Gives you quite a start. Not something you get used to, but something you have to accept as part of this job."

I take a drink then clear my throat.

"What is it, John. You're looking like you have something you don't want to say."

"I found some things in Ivy's suite."

"Some things?" Alma picks up her glass.

"Yes. Some things. Some, um, missing things."

"What do you mean?" she takes a sip.

I toss back my glass of scotch in one gulp. "Many of the items that people have told me have been taken from their suites, they're in Ivy's suite. In a curio cabinet in her bedroom. When I found her, she had a statue in her lap that I believe belongs to Rachel Johnston."

My throat is still dry and I hold out my glass. Alma pours us all another finger with a shaking hand.

"But she let us think Melanie…."

"She did."

We sit quiet for a few minutes trying to think of what to do.

"I don't want her name sullied," Alma says. "She was a good woman who befriended a lot of people in here."

"Me neither."

"Can we remove the items somehow?" Marigold asks.

"But what do we do what with them?" I say. "We don't want anyone else to get blamed for something she did. And I certainly wouldn't feel right throwing people's possessions in the garbage."

"That's true." Alma taps her pencil on her desk.

It's Marigold who finally speaks. "What about if I make a shadow box? Put the stolen items inside. Then tell everyone we found it in Ivy's suite."

Alma drops her pencil into the jar. "That's not a bad idea Marigold. She'll still be the one who stole the items but for the purpose of remembering people. Honouring them in a way."

"And you don't think anyone will be mad about this?" I ask.

"Are you kidding?" Alma says. "The ones who haven't had anything taken will wonder why she didn't take something from them too." She refills our glasses.

I finish my third drink in half an hour then wobble out of the office behind Marigold and Alma. We begin moving items and in less than half an hour, have them stacked on Marigold's dining room table.

Chapter thirty-six

2014

I stop on the sidewalk, unsure whether this is the house. It looks far more run-down than I remember, but that was fifteen years ago. I doubt the place has had any renovations done to it; not in this neighbourhood. Even if I do have the right house, the same people probably aren't living here anymore. I decide this is a big mistake and turn to leave. The door opens a crack.

"Hey, Man, what do you want?" a voice thick with phlegm shouts.

"Uh, wrong house," I say. "Sorry. Was looking for someone else."

He opens the door wider. "Say, I know you. Aren't you the mailman that used to deliver here?" He walks out onto the crumbling front step. "Helped my kid get home from school one day when he was being bullied. I remember you now."

I hold my hands above my eyes, squinting into the sun as I pretend I've stumbled onto his house. "Isn't this a coincidence? Don't know how I managed to end up here."

He waves his thin arm at me, motioning me inside. "Come on in. Have a cup of coffee."

"Sure, sure," I leave the busy street and enter the porch, then step into the living room.

The house is semi-dark, with ragged curtains on the front window that throw shafts of daylight across a sagging couch on the far wall. He leads me to a tiny kitchen and we sit at an ancient chrome table. Not wanting to touch anything, I keep my hands in my lap.

One rusty pot sags on a burner on the stove, and a coffee pot is pushed into a corner of the counter. The tap is running in a steady dribble but he doesn't seem to notice or care. He does not make me a cup of coffee, for which I'm grateful.

"You haven't changed," he says. "'Cept for no postie uniform. You must be retired by now. Watcha' doin' in the hood? Don't mailmen have some kind of awesome pension?"

His voice is throaty and thick until he clears it, which he does after every other word. His hands flutter in front of his face as he speaks and he constantly wiggles his body around in his chair.

"What I wouldn't have done for a job like yours. Mighta bin able to pull myself outta this hellhole if I'd had the same chances as you. But I guess you live the life you're given." His hands drop to his lap where they lie still for the first time since we sat down. His face becomes slack and he stops talking. He seems to go into an almost comatose state. I'm just about to stand and leave when his face brightens and he lifts his head. "So, watcha' doin' here?"

I take a deep breath. "Was, uh, well, actually, to tell you the truth, I didn't come here by accident."

"Yeah. Already figured that. People like you don't just wander into our neighbourhood. Lessen ya looking for a fight, or drugs." He clears his throat.

"I was wondering if, uh, if you have anything I could buy from you, some…."

"Drugs you mean? You're askin' me for drugs?" He moves his head in small quick nods.

"Well, yeah. fentanyl, I'd like some fentanyl, if you can get me some."

He laughs, showing teeth yellowed from years of smoke. "Big man comin' to the hood to ask me for drugs. What's the world coming to?"

"Not for me, you understand."

"No, of course not."

"Really, not for me. For my wife."

"For your wife?"

"She's sick. She's dying."

"Hey, I'm sorry, Man."

"Thanks."

"She needs drugs though? Thought people who was dyin' got all kinds of drugs handed to them on a silver platter."

"She keeps asking me," I paw the sweat off my face. "She keeps asking me to give her more. Doctors' will only give her enough to take away the pain. She wants enough to —" I stand. "— This was a bad idea."

He grins his brown toothed smile, then places his filthy hand on my knee. "Not a bad idea. Not a bad idea at all. You want drugs, you got them. Least I can do for you rescuin' my boy that day. He'd a bin beat to a pulp if you hadn't come along. Was always a small lad, couldn't swing a punch even if it was a girl swinging at him. Turned out good. He's a lawyer in some other city. Takes a lot of cases involving bullying. Sends me a Christmas card once a year. Doesn't talk to me anymore, but that's ok. At least he got out of here."

She thrashes her head on the pillow. Her hair is sweaty and sticks to her face.

"Did you get it, John?"

"Yes." I touch the pocket of my jacket.

"I need you to help me. I'm too weak to do it alone."

"I can't do it, Elaine. I just can't. I don't want to lose you any faster than I'm going to."

"You won't be losing me. I'll always be with you." Her voice is cracked and I put the glass of water to her lips but she lets it run from her mouth as she pushes it away. "Please, John, do it for me. I don't have the strength."

She's been asking me this same question for the past week. I've not had the courage to follow through. Tonight, her pleas are more insistent. I pull the small envelope out of my pocket and take out two small pills. I press them to my palm. She puts her hand on mine and gently pries my fingers open. She puts the pills to her dry lips. Then with strength I didn't know she had left in her, she takes the water from her nightstand and puts it to her mouth. This time she manages to swallow.

I pull the car into the garage with no clue as to how I got here. I hear Clem barking and drag myself inside. She meets me at the door but I walk past her.

"Leave me alone, Clem. You don't know what's happened." I sit on the edge of the couch and she sits directly in front of me. I feel her wet nose on my fingers. "What is it, Clem? What do you want?"

She paws my knee. "She's gone, Clem," I say and push her away. She brings me a toy and paws my knee again. "I told you, she's gone. We aren't playing ball, not tonight." I hold her head in my hands, "Don't you understand? She's gone. We're all alone now." Clem runs upstairs and lies beside Elaine's side of the bed waiting for her to come home, just as she's done for the past two months. I lie on the couch, wondering how I'll be able to live the rest of my life without her, and how I'll be able to live the rest of my life knowing what I've done.

Chapter thirty-seven

Fall 2016

I finished my shift a couple of hours ago and now Clem and I are sitting in the backyard of The Wheaton watching the residents harvest the last of the garden then toss the produce into boxes Marigold and I stacked on the lawn. At my feet are two empty bottles of wine I brought to share with those who wanted to partake. Also at my feet is a recently purchased CD player and a few of my favourite jazz CD's. The song playing is Duke Ellington's, *Loveless Love*. It doesn't sound too bad, though I'll never truly convert to this medium.

The shadow box was a huge success. Everyone exclaimed what a brilliant idea it was and I watched Marigold puff up once or twice, but to her credit, she never uttered a word. Ivy was buried a hero, someone who wanted to remember her friends, who cherished her friends.

Dave never returned to talk to Ernestine. I asked her if she was going to try and find him and reconcile, but she said she wouldn't speak of it again. Perhaps some things are best left unresolved. Since Dave's departure, Ernestine has stopped seeing the grim reaper.

Before I began working at The Wheaton I'd been to exactly three funerals in my entire life. One was a postie friend of mine who'd carried mail for thirty-four years and helped me acclimate to the new job. He died shortly after he retired. One was my mother's, the other was Elaine's.

In the past year alone, I've gone to three funerals. Fiona's, Ivy's, and then shortly after Ivy passed on, so did Jack Belgrade. He had a second heart attack and this time they couldn't revive him. I sincerely hope his mother and brother met him on the other side.

It's warm in the sun and I look up to watch the clouds as they sail by. The wind is blowing the leaves from the trees, and with my eyes closed I can hear them scraping against the windows as they're lashed about. My mind begins to wander and I remember doing this same thing when Elaine would harvest her garden. I'd sit in my lounge chair on the patio — we had matching lounge chairs in those days, though I seldom saw Elaine use hers — and lift my face to the sun, listening to her hum as she dug potatoes and tossed them into a box. I never did tell her how reassuring that made me feel. How comforted I was by the normalcy of her task.

"You're a good man," a voice says.

I open my eyes. No one is here but Clem, and she cocks her head at me as if she's heard something as well.

"Did you hear that, Clem?" I ask. "I thought I heard someone speak." I pat her head. "Never mind. Go back to sleep, girl. Must be the wind."

Clem lies back down and again I close my eyes.

"Look around you, John. What more could a man want?"

"Okay, who's playing tricks on me?" Clem is now standing and looking right at me. Her tail is up and a smile is on her face.

"Did you say something, John?" Marigold shouts from the garden.

"No, er, uh, yes. Did you call me?"

"I did not."

"Thought I heard someone talk to me."

"Not me," she says and goes back to pulling corn off the stocks, though I see her glance at me a couple of times.

"I think we're going crazy, Clem. You heard that too, didn't you?" she wags her tail.

Again, the voice speaks. "You did the right thing."

"Elaine?" I say. I sit up straight. "Elaine, is that you?" Clem puts her paws in my lap and whines. We both wait, hoping we hear something else but the voice has gone quiet. "I love you," I whisper. "We love you, Elaine."

I see Marigold watching me but she doesn't ask any questions. Her attention turns towards the side gate of The Wheaton. "Glad you could make it," she says as Barb, Janet, Mark and my grandkids come around the corner, an empty box in each of their hands, ready to help harvest.

The End

Acknowledgments

I would like to acknowledge the following people for their invaluable support and encouragement.

Alice Kuipers for ALWAYS believing in me.

Ann Ireland for her honesty in editing. I could not have completed this book without her input.

Thanks to my daughter, Maureen, and son-in-law, Aaron, for all their computer help. And thanks to my son, Scott, and daughter-in-law, Mary, for building me a website and having the patience to explain it to me.

To readers: Kathy Seamer, Beverly Binfet, Kathy Jump, Frieda Salikin, Heather MacDonald.

Thank you Tom, my husband of forty-five years, for his support and encouragement throughout the writing of this book.